SAM POLAKOFF

ESCAPING MERCY

ESCAPING MERCY
Published by Komodo Dragon, LLC
Forest Hill, Maryland

Book design by GKS Creative
Cover image used under license from Shutterstock

Author photo by Alan Pototsky

ISBN (print): 978-1-7338898-1-0
ISBN (e-book): 978-1-7338898-3-4

Library of Congress Control Number: 2021905724

FIRST EDITION
Printed in the United States of America

www.sampolakoff.com

This book is dedicated to my family,
for whom I am eternally grateful.

Toward the end of the twenty-second century, world leaders, desperate to preserve the planet and its dwindling resources, agreed to reduce the population through extraordinary means. The solution they chose was called "Mercy."

PART I

CHAPTER 1

São Paulo, Brazil, 2151

Purple Dust. His Portuguese was passable and the voices faint, but Erik deBaak was sure of the words. It was unmistakable, even from the far corner of his cell. The prison guards could have meant nothing other than the worst. Sitting on the damp stone floor in his weakened condition, he turned his head toward the door and tried to make out the conversation.

"We deployed Purple Dust over Rotterdam last week."

"The enemy has already responded. Their bombing raids have destroyed key Southern Hemisphere cities. São Paulo could be next."

A chill ran down deBaak's spine. If Southern Hemisphere armed forces dropped the horrific chemical agent over his home in Rotterdam, his parents and little sister were in grave danger. His opa, or grandpa, told him stories of Purple Dust being deployed sixty-eight years ago during World War III. deBaak would never forget the tear gently falling from Opa's eye as he recalled the aftermath. Once-proud leaders of their respected nations and their citizens had their minds reduced to intellectual rubble. The famed Washington, DC Treaty ending the third world war outlawed this horrific form of warfare.

As a POW in the Brazilian camp, Erik deBaak had little knowledge of the war or outside events. Through the malaise of each passing hour, not knowing whether it was day or night, the sounds of war beckoned in the distance. São Paulo would be a primary target for the Northern Hemisphere forces.

He coughed, trying to release the ever-present phlegm from his raspy throat. The stone-walled cell was his solitary confinement. deBaak guessed it had been more than a year since his capture. Apart from a metal bucket with which to relieve himself, the cell was barren. Emaciated and weak, he moved a bony finger up to his matted hair and scratched. The culprit was a mite of some sort. He crushed it between his fingers and rubbed the remnants on the damp stone floor. deBaak longed for a proper bed, a hot shower, and a shave. Being dehumanized was how they broke you. He would never let that happen. He rested his head against the rigid wall and stretched his legs. He was nodding off when the creaky old metal door alerted him to visitors.

"Get up, spy!"

deBaak stirred. Before he could protest, two prison guards were on him, literally dragging his body by the arms. Thank heaven he had some old rags to wear, or his already raw skin would have been scraped to the bone. The guards moved deBaak around the corner and threw him onto a metal table where he was strapped down and gagged. He moaned, the only sound he could manage in his current state.

The guards left, and a tall, powerfully built man entered. He was wearing the gray uniform of the Argentine Army. "I am Colonel Paz, your new best friend."

deBaak shook his head, left to right and back again. Paz removed the rag from his mouth. deBaak gagged, cleared his throat and almost yelled, "Your goons have tortured me every way imaginable and I have told them nothing. Go fuck yourself!"

Paz responded with a smirk. "What you've been through so far has been a mere annoyance." Paz approached and placed a thin nylon cap over his head. Through the material, deBaak could feel light filament wire pressing firmly against his scalp.

"This mindwave technology will literally pull the information from your brain. There is no way to resist."

deBaak squirmed on the table, struggling to get free.

Paz stood over him and said with condescension, "Do not struggle, spy. It will be over soon."

Paz walked over to a control board and turned a dial clockwise. Immediately, the filaments in the lightweight cap heated and then vibrated violently. His skull was on fire. In a matter of two minutes, his brain might burst.

"Your memories are being extracted. When the process completes, I may do you the favor of placing a bullet in your head."

deBaak writhed in agony. He screamed. The pressure in his head was beyond anything he ever experienced. Praying for death, he tried to place his mind elsewhere to ignore the searing pain. He closed his eyes, waiting for the end. His chest was heavy, as if something dropped on top of him. *Was he experiencing a heart attack?* deBaak opened his eyes and tried to process the scene. *Was his battered mind playing tricks?*

The bloodied, bullet-ridden body of Colonel Paz lay across his chest, and a US Army sergeant was shutting down the mindwave torture chamber.

Erik deBaak blinked his eyes, trying to focus. His mind was in a fog, but he would never forget the words called out by the US soldier.

"Sir, the war is over. We have liberated this camp. You are going home."

CHAPTER 2

Rotterdam, 2175, twenty-four years later

Erik deBaak stood on the mezzanine of his corporate office, along with his chief operating officer, Hennie Van de Berg, who was tall, nearly approaching his own accentuated height. The morning sun from the picture window on the front of the Rotterdam building shone brightly over his shoulder and reflected against the metal sign mounted high on the wall, bearing the name of his worldwide conglomerate, Crematie.

deBaak's mind was elsewhere. His company's latest innovation was on full display. Two staffers placed a recently deceased human body in the chamber, and an operator did nothing more than press a button. Within ten seconds, the chamber lit up and the body simply vanished. No ashes, just complete obliteration. His engineers harnessed the instantaneous incineration process by using a Tanzig ray, named after Fritz Tanzig, the infamous early twenty-second-century scientist who created it. The combination of intense heat and powerful suction from the wall-encased units removed any debris and readied the chamber for the next body.

"Erik, the Tanzig will change the world. Profits will be immense," exclaimed Van de Berg.

deBaak only sighed in reply. He was already one of the wealthiest people on the planet. Unlike most, his extreme holdings enabled him to live a life of luxury, far removed from the misery of the overcrowded world. He rubbed his right hand across the stubble on his shaved head and replied, "Yes, this is a fine development. Our engineers have done well. Keep me apprised of the testing progress. I want a full report before we convert crematoriums across global markets."

She nodded her assent, along with the longing in her eyes. She cared for him, but his focus was on the business. She would be nothing more than an occasional booty call.

He had to go. It was almost time for his meeting with Aloysius Travanche, the Director-General of the World Health Organization. Driving through the streets of a city like Rotterdam was near impossible. He recalled stories from Opa about how cars were once commonplace throughout the world. Not anymore. There were too many people flooding the streets and roadways, even in the suburbs of major cities. Homelessness was rampant, as was the spread of disease. World leaders were clueless how to solve the problem. Had he not created Mercy and enlisted the aid of Travanche to push it through, the world would be in much worse shape. No, air travel was the only option beyond the high-speed maglev trains constructed for public and cargo transport. The luxury cars he owned could just as well remain in the garage. His private air transport was an AirStadt, routinely referred to as a pod. The AirStadt comfortably seated six and could make the journey to Switzerland in only fifteen minutes. deBaak smiled to himself. In Opa's day, the flight would have taken an hour and a half by commercial airline.

He met the pilot at the landing pad on the roof of the Crematie building and waited for the lift to carry him to the cabin at the top of the pod. The pilot activated a remote control, and a high resin plastic dome elevated, permitting the tall, lithe frame of Erik deBaak to board. He sat comfortably while a safety restraint automatically came down from the top of the plush leather seat and fastened itself. The pilot closed the clear case dome and began liftoff.

deBaak was exhausted. Pushing fifty, he found he no longer had the energy he once possessed.

The pod's thrusters engaged from the bottom of the craft, lifting the vessel into the air. The journey to Switzerland would be short. The meeting with Travanche was pivotal. The WHO leader would be an essential element of his plan to introduce a new phase of Mercy—all of course, he thought sarcastically, for the betterment of the planet and its ability to survive.

CHAPTER 3

The mind, once stretched by a new idea, never returned to its original dimension. Dex Holzman couldn't recall whether it was Ralph Waldo Emerson or Oliver Wendell Holmes who first uttered those prescient words. The photos sent from Australia were unbelievable. The image of the green sea turtle altered his mind forever. Belly up, the luminescence of the bright orange shell matched the brilliance of the setting sun over Golden Vines, the Napa Valley town he called home. The green sea turtle's normally yellow-colored underbelly shell, known as the plastron, contained bright orange particles. A few patches of the shell's natural color tried to break through, but the unidentified substance ruled the surface. If that weren't odd enough, the orange particles caused the turtle's head, legs, and tail to transform from the normal yellow, gray, and light brown variants to a murky dark mustard. It was not uncommon for dead sea life to wash ashore with everything imaginable attached from barnacles to algae, but the discoloration of this turtle piqued his curiosity. Somehow, maybe this episode held some sort of clue to ending the ominous dilemma the planet faced.

Dex was incredibly humble, even though he was the most respected marine biologist on the planet. The press referred to him as a modern-day Jacques Cousteau. He was sure that's why Jules Maybin, the local authority in Queensland, Australia, contacted him. After Maybin sent him the photos and they had a brief conversation, Dex was on a plane. He previously studied the prophecy of doom for the green sea turtle.

In the twenty-first century, extinction threatened these noble stewards of the earth's oceans. In the early 2000s, dedicated US marine biologists from the National Oceanic and Atmospheric Administration (NOAA) worked hand in hand with their counterparts across the globe to protect this treasured species and enable its return to natural habitats. Dex wrote his college thesis on the subject. Coupled with his affinity for sea turtles and his attraction to the lure of the unknown, the opportunity to help was simply too powerful.

Maybin was arranging for the dead reptile's transport to his small laboratory an hour south in the town of Lockhart. The turtle's carapace, or outer shell, measured over 1.5 meters and weighed 340 kilos, an outlier for green sea turtles. Dex hadn't seen one this big, only the larger leatherback species. Given the remote location of the find and the size of the carcass, Dex figured it would take Maybin at least a day to arrange for proper transport. That gave him time to make the sixteen-hour flight from San Francisco to Brisbane, the regional flight to Northern Peninsula Airport, and the two-hour commute by SUV to his ultimate destination, Scrimshaw Beach. Many of the world's more advanced forms of air travel were not available in the few low density population areas. So, he figured, the dead animal would have been lying on the beach for at least two days before he could examine it. Maybin estimated the giant carcass had been resident on the beach less than twelve hours.

Dex met Maybin on the outskirts of the sandy access road, and they made their way to the site, roped off by wooden stakes and caution tape to ward off errant tourists and passersby.

"Do I call you Jules?"

The other man smiled. His British accent and toothy grin against the dark skin accentuated his charisma. "You could—that's the name my mother gave me—but everyone just calls me Maybin."

"Sounds good," Dex replied.

Before the turtle was in eyeshot, Dex's nose revealed they were close. The smell was pungent, a sort of musky scent that proved annoying but palatable. Probably the turtle swelled under the weight of the sunshine and moisture. In just the few days since the discovery, every orifice would have closed, leaving no way for building gas to escape. Couple that with maggots attempting to feed off the decomposition, and you had one hell of a sight.

The pictures were startling but paled compared to seeing the beached reptile in-person. Clearly, time and nature conspired to change the physical appearance of the turtle in a short period. Dex and Maybin circled the enormous carcass, effectively trying to take it all in.

"Have you been able to examine a sample of the orange substance?" Dex inquired.

"Yes, my lab rats are working on it, but so far, nothing," Maybin replied in his British accent. Dex worked with ocean exploration professionals across the globe but still chuckled when confronted with the expressions common to specific regions. Was the reference to "lab rats" one such remark?

"Nothing? Really?"

"According to my senior-most researcher, the orange particles resemble nothing known to mankind."

Dex shook his head in disbelief. *That's why I'm here*, he reminded himself. Three motor vehicles caused his mind to detour.

Maybin smiled. "That would be the transport to my lab in Lockhart."

"Have you completed photographing the specimen?" Dex asked.

"Just before you arrived. I also have a completed intake form."

Two flatbeds and four men in an SUV pulled along the sandy beach road. One flatbed held a beach crane to lift the turtle and move it to the companion vehicle.

Dex was familiar with this procedure, having seen it many times before on beaches across the world. His prior experience was mostly with whales of varying types and a few sharks, one a whale shark measuring over eighteen meters. The oddest beached sea creature he ever encountered was a colossal squid on an Enderby Beach along the frigid Southern Ocean in Antarctica. Thinking about that experience caused a slight chill to run down his spine. It was easily the coldest expedition of which he'd ever been a part.

As the transport crew readied for the move, Maybin strapped a gas mask to his head and picked up a battery-powered drill. Maybin was going to release the build-up of gas to make the carcass more amenable to transport. He walked to the turtle's posterior, kneeled, and turned on the drill to penetrate the swollen cloaca. The release knocked Maybin's slight frame backward, where the softness of Scrimshaw Beach tempered his landing.

"Hey, man, are you okay?" Dex yelled as he ran toward his fallen colleague.

Maybin sat up then stood, lifted the mask from his face, and brushed himself off.

"They don't teach that maneuver at university, now do they?" mused Maybin.

Dex smiled and held his hand over his nose. Maybin needed a change of clothes and a shower from the powerful blast of odorous wind.

Dex stood back from Maybin to avoid the odor as the six workmen, all gagging from the stench, wrapped the giant turtle with straps. Maybin instructed them to be careful around the orange particles since no one knew what effect they might have on human contact. All the workmen wore leather gloves. The crew secured the straps. They inserted a hook at the top of the harness, creating the leverage required to lift the carcass from the beach. It wasn't every day that these men lifted and transported a green sea turtle.

Dex reacted immediately when the turtle shifted inside the loose straps. With the turtle just a meter off the ground, Dex yelled to the crane operator, "Put him back down. We need to tighten the straps."

The foreman came to the crew's defense, pointing at Maybin. "That bloke said to keep the straps loose, mate. Said he didn't want the orange crap comin' off."

Seeing Maybin getting frustrated, Dex tried to intercede. "Yes, that's right. However, we can't have the turtle sliding out of the harness and crashing to the beach. It would make an already challenging necropsy much more difficult."

"Necropsy?" replied the foreman. "What in bloody hell are you talking about?"

Dex should have known the foreman wouldn't understand the language of the marine biologist. He replied politely, "Sorry, it's what we call an autopsy."

Reluctantly, with both arms raised skyward, the foreman signaled with one hand turning in a counterclockwise motion for the crane operator to lower the reptile. The workmen tightened the straps. Once satisfied, Maybin gave a thumbs-up to the crane operator, who drove slowly down the beach to the access road and the waiting flatbed truck.

Maybin stroked his razor-thin goatee and flashed a toothy smile. "We did it."

"You did it. I was here to watch. Tell me about your facility. Do you have everything we will need?"

Maybin raised both arms and, with locked fingers, placed his hands on top of his slicked-back wavy hair; a clear sign the answer was negative. Finally, he uttered, "I've got a small team waiting at the lab in Lockhart to supervise the unloading. We have a modest facility with limited resources and a budget that's almost laughable. I'm afraid we have no one who has ever performed a necropsy on a creature this large. That's why I reached out to you."

"Do you have a room big enough to perform the necropsy?"

"Yup," replied Maybin. "Unfortunately, it's our outdoor patio. We will have to lower the turtle onto the patio and erect a canvas awning over it."

"Is there room for the crane to get through to the patio?"

Maybin's facial muscles visibly clenched, "Umm, it'll be tight, but it should work." He smiled humbly. "My team will have a bed of ice chips spread on the patio and will erect the awning as soon as the turtle arrives. From the looks of it, we are already outside the desired twenty-four-hour window for a productive necropsy."

"Let's plan on performing the necropsy later today as soon as is practical. We don't have the luxury of time if we want any useful data from the procedure."

Maybin looked relieved. Before agreeing to make the journey, Dex had quickly done his homework on Maybin and the Lockhart facility. Maybin's employer, Nexterus Marine, was a UK-based company that purchased the lab and sent Maybin down with a three-person team and a shoestring budget. Their mission was to research the Coral Sea, hoping to find anything that might make money for the company while solving the rampant problems of illness and world hunger.

With the workmen having completed the loading of the turtle onto the flatbed vehicle, Dex and Maybin had a few minutes to themselves. As the waves softly made their way onto the shore of Scrimshaw Beach, Maybin expressed his gratitude. "Thanks for your help. On our own, we'd be over our heads."

"My pleasure," Dex replied. "What brought you down here in the first place?"

Maybin flinched and then said, "Been here three years now. It was an excellent opportunity to have my own post, so to speak. The real reason is the remote nature of this place."

Dex didn't have to guess what that meant. The overcrowding of the earth was out of control. The UK was among the most difficult places in the world to survive. People flooded the streets, food and clean water were in short supply, and everyone was always sick. On most of the planet, having a plot of land to call your own required a substantial amount of wealth or a job no one else wanted. Dex was one of the lucky ones. His little haven in Golden Vines was a sanctuary he never took for granted. Living there alone with so much poverty across the world made him feel guilty. He took comfort in dedicating his life to the betterment of mankind through the exploration of the planet's waters.

"So, no guess where the orange particles originate?" Dex asked.

"Best guess?"

"It's as good a place as any to start."

"Over the past three years, I've done a good bit of diving along the coast, including right here at Scrimshaw Beach. I don't need to tell you this region has some of the most abundant and magnificent marine life on the planet. It's a gift from God himself. And given what the rest of the world is suffering through, this place is paradise."

Dex listened patiently, waiting for Maybin to answer his question.

"But I digress. The locals here believe this area was once home to a civilization that sank to the bottom of the Coral Sea. Legend has it that this lost city was called *Aeternum*, and that their citizens created a magical healing extract."

Being a world explorer, Dex was all too familiar with local legends, almost all of which amounted to nothing more than a good campfire story. Still, he played the straight and narrow with Maybin. "Do you place any credence in the story? What would this have to do with today's discovery?"

Maybin paused and said, "I've learned to never say never."

Dex shook his head, wanting to dismiss the story but trying to give it the benefit of the doubt. "When did Aeternum presumably sink?"

Maybin shrugged and said, "No one really knows, but locals trace it back two or three thousand years."

"And you think a lost civilization sitting on the bottom of the Coral Sea might have something to do with orange particles on a dead sea turtle?"

Maybin just smiled. "Can't rule anything out at this point." After a momentary pause, he said, "I am heading back to Lockhart. Do you want to follow me?"

"Thanks, but I think I'll hang here for a bit."

Dex Holzman took off his shoes and sat barefoot on the beach near where the enormous green sea turtle had been discovered. He ran his hand through his sandy blond hair and soaked in the relaxing beauty of the Coral Sea. *If so much of the earth's sea bottoms remain unexplored, who was he to rule out local legend?* Intellectually, he found zero credence in the story. In his gut, though, there was something to it. Deep beneath the surface of the Coral Sea is where the answer would be found. He was sure of it. He just couldn't explain why—at least not yet.

CHAPTER 4

"My husband is dead because of this asinine Mercy program," exclaimed Cam Atkinson. "The world is in such sad shape. When will the madness end?" Cam receded angrily into the depleted cushion of her ancient chair at the meager offices of Baugh and Atkinson in downtown Los Angeles. At thirty-four, she was a named partner in the struggling five-year-old firm dedicated to the civil rights of an overcrowded and unhealthy population.

"Your husband was very ill. Leukemia, was it?" asked her boss and the founding partner, Thurman Baugh. He was doing his best to be sympathetic, but Cam's angry streak was in full bloom.

"Yes, and I know it was an uphill battle, but goddammit, the fucked-up legal system never gave him a chance. What kind of government forces a sick man into a euthanasia program, leaving his wife and small child to survive on their own?"

"Unfortunately, that's the world," Baugh remarked.

His kind spirit was offering comfort, but Cam's skin was turning red. That was her trigger, the reminder that she needed to step away, breathe, and use her skills and passion as a civil rights attorney to fight the system for those who could not fight for themselves. She leaned back in her chair, closed her eyes, and drew a deep breath. She thought of Tom, her best friend and one true love. Eighteen grueling months since his own government murdered him. Every moment of those eighteen months ravaged her soul. He was taken too early. If they had allowed him to seek treatment and fight for his own life, she might have accepted his premature loss a little better. Somehow, the world had gone sideways.

The government's rationale? To reduce overcrowding, food shortages, depleted medical resources? Leukemia was on the government's list of "terminal diseases." At least the US hadn't lost all of its senses. There was still a hint of compassion and humanity. Ten years earlier, the US implemented a limited version of Mercy. Under this system, they made only those people deemed terminal enter the program. In almost every other country in the world, the Mercy program meant certain entry for any illness that *might* cause death. *If it cost money to heal someone, the government deemed them expendable,* she thought with disgust.

Cam worked with Tom to plan their escape. Because most every civilized nation in the world had already adopted the full Mercy program, there was essentially nowhere to run. Remote corners of the world could offer a haven from the madness, but only if you were healthy. Mercy wrote the story's end once they diagnosed Tom with leukemia. Accepting it, however, was a completely different matter. Cam's instinct to fight whoever and whatever took flight. The US proved to be the best of the bad choices, and so she had done all she could, including court challenges, enlisting the help of her congressional representative, and even writing to the governor. Her request to Governor Samson was like a death row plea for clemency. *Wasn't that really what it was?*

Tom would have wanted her to throw herself into her work, to change the system by whatever means possible. Save for her work, her life revolved around their ten-year-old son, Corey. It was just the two of them now. The thought of Corey's smile and that mop of curly blond hair made the tension subside in her neck and shoulders.

She gazed at her boss and mentor and snapped back into the reality of the day. His large brown eyes looked at her sympathetically, seeming to droop with the excess of his jowls. He was a large man but spoke with a gentle nature. "Cam, maybe you are too close to the Barker case."

She sighed and stared him down in a competitive but respectful manner. "Look, Thurm, I understand why you think that, but I'm Ken Barker's best shot at a Mercy exemption. He needs a heart transplant but can likely live without one for six to eight months. Medicines and restricted activities are keeping him stable. He is a minimal drag on the healthcare system."

"For now," he replied sullenly.

"We both know that I've won Mercy exemptions for people worse off than Ken Barker. Have a little faith."

"You haven't heard?"

"Heard what?"

"The US is going full bore with Mercy. It aligns Governor Samson with the president. She is saying there is simply no way to avoid what the rest of the world has been doing for years."

Something this big couldn't be kept under wraps. Thurman Baugh had a pipeline to Sacramento. The governor's chief of staff once worked with Thurm at LA's biggest civil rights firm.

Cam sighed. She couldn't believe the news. It was like a dagger through the heart. With difficulty, she suppressed the lump forming in her throat. "When?" was all she could say.

"There is a press conference scheduled for tomorrow morning at the White House. President Sofer is going to announce the adoption of the full Mercy program effective next week."

"Oh my God!" she exclaimed. "That's a death sentence for millions of sick people."

"That's why this firm exists. We will do all we can to fight the injustice."

It nauseated Cam. It was as if the world were crashing down on her. "I've got the Barker hearing in an hour. I need to get Barker a Mercy exemption before this new round of insanity takes effect."

Cam began gathering her laptop and associated files into a leather carry bag. The courthouse was only two blocks from their office, but navigating through the throng of people on the streets would make the going extremely slow.

"Let me know how you make out in court," said Baugh. He was like a father to her, always sympathetic while reining her in with a firm but gentle hand if she went off the rails.

"I will," she replied as her portable combox buzzed. The caller ID read "Otter Park Elementary School." Her stomach muscles tightened. Corey's school never called her at work.

"Hello," she said tentatively.

"Mrs. Atkinson?"

"Yes."

"This is Nurse Albright at Otter Park Elementary. I'm afraid Corey isn't feeling well. He is very pale and running a high fever of 40 degrees Celsius. Our protocol, as you know, is to send sick children directly to the Mercy Evaluation Center."

Cam's blood boiled. "Don't you dare! You care for him at the school. I'll be there as quick as I can."

CHAPTER 5

Dex drove south to Maybin's lab in Lockhart with the windows down. Being a man of the seas, he preferred to breathe nonconditioned air. The tepid Queensland breeze had a muggy feel. While a light sweat broke out on his lower back, the drive was otherwise pleasant. The rental he drove displayed a photo of the building on his screen as his arrival became imminent. He shouldn't have been surprised at the unremarkable one-story building, but he was. On plain sight, Dex estimated the facility to be just under nineteen hundred square meters. The yellow-colored structure stood mundanely. The concrete walls contained a stucco finish. A small, white aluminum sign along the asphalt driveway read "Nexterus Marine Research."

He pulled the SUV into an open space next to the building and walked to the front door. Giving the locked brass handle a tug, he retreated to the back of the building. As he rounded the corner, past some dense foliage, Maybin approached from underneath a sprawling burgundy canvas propped up by eight steel poles. On the cement patio, the giant sea turtle lay on its carapace in a thin blue plastic liner that Dex quickly surmised to be about thirty centimeters deep. As Maybin prescribed, they filled it with ice chips to preserve any further degradation and make at least some part of the necropsy viable. Maybin smiled and extended his right hand, freshly extracted from a rubber glove. "Welcome to Lockhart!"

Dex shook hands with the shorter man and gagged in a way he was sure he hadn't hidden very well.

Maybin understood. "Sorry, no time to shower. We don't know how long the turtle was on the beach before we got there. Simply no time to lose."

Dex said nothing but retracted his hand and smiled an awkward smile. He had been in Maybin's shoes. Any marine biologist's penchant for accurate data would prevail above all else.

Maybin politely stepped back a few steps. "I don't know what you packed, but we have a coverall suit for you along with latex gloves and boots and a face shield."

"Great. I assume you have the standard array of necropsy materials for a procedure of this type?"

"I believe so. We stock fileting knives, scalpel blades, saws and shears, calipers of varying size, all the standard preservation and diagnostic solutions, and the smaller equipment for excising and examining specimens drawn from the necropsy."

"Excellent," Dex replied. "Do you have the latest digital imaging technology?"

Dex once again got his answer from the pained expression on Maybin's face. Dex would work with what was available, but the robotic digital imagery from twenty-second-century equipment was his preference.

"I'm afraid all we have is an old-fashioned SLR camera," he replied hesitantly.

It had been many years since Dex used an SLR camera. The single-lens reflex device had an obsolete mirroring system enabling a fair-quality image. The problem was it required a lab tech to remain free of the hard work of the necropsy to move around and continuously capture still-life images of each phase of the procedure. Dex preferred the superior robotics from the present-day aerial device. "No worries, I brought a hummingbird. All we need is a decent-sized monitor."

Maybin was astonished. "A hummingbird, you say? I've seen them on internet videos, but I've yet to work with one. This will be a treat. How many headsets did you bring?"

"I have three. That should do. Me, you, and one more for a member of your team. Your other two techs can catalog and handle biopsy samples if we can get them."

"Smashing," responded the overjoyed Briton. "Can't wait to get started."

Dex followed Maybin into the rear entrance of the building, where they found a small anteroom and one of Maybin's team suiting up for the necropsy.

"Dex, meet Amelia Brown," Maybin offered.

Dex shook hands with the small woman he guessed to be late twenties. He was of average height but towered over her athletically built miniscule frame.

"Pleased to meet you, Amelia," Dex said warmly.

Maybin chimed in. "Amelia is a late bloomer in the marine biology world. She's been with us just over a year now."

Amelia blushed slightly. "That is, in fact, true," she replied. "While my colleagues were attending university, I was working on perfecting the balance beam."

"You are a gymnast?" Dex inquired.

"Was," she replied sheepishly. "It sounds silly to say for a twenty-nine-year-old, but I am retired."

Maybin laughed. "She's being modest. Amelia was in the last two Olympics. She's a celebrity Down Under."

Amelia blushed once more. "That's all in the past—just wonderful memories at this point." She turned to Dex and offered, "I have a pair of coveralls and rubber boots for you, as well as rubber gloves. Since we learned you were coming and you are somewhat well-known yourself, it was quite easy to order the correct sizes."

He reached down to take the articles from her. The intensity of her crystal blue eyes was stunning. "Okay to suit up right here?"

She nodded and said, "Yes, this is our 'mudroom.'"

"Mudroom?" Dex asked, somewhat amused.

"Yes, you know. When you were just an ankle biter, your mum had you take off your muddy boots in a small room before entering her clean house . . . a mudroom."

Dex contemplated her comment as he stroked his right index finger through the cleft in his chin, liking her perkiness. "Yes, when I was an ankle biter, as you call it, my mom had a mudroom."

Amelia smiled somewhat meekly but continued, "Men's showers are around the corner to the right for afterward. The other members of the team should be in momentarily. They just finished preparing the specimen on the patio and laying out all the equipment on portable tables and carts. We should be ready in about fifteen minutes."

"Sounds good. I'll be ready," he replied, liking her. She was confident yet shy for someone who competed often in front of international audiences.

Just then, the door opened and the remaining members of Maybin's team walked through. Maybin smiled and stated, "Boys, meet the world-famous Dex Holzman."

The smaller of the two men was a redhead with a fair complexion but a solid build for a guy only 177 centimeters tall. The second man was enormous, clearly a bodybuilder in his spare time.

Dex extended his hand, first to the smaller man, and said, "Great to meet you. How are you?"

The redhead replied sarcastically in true Aussie humor, "Not bad for a bloke who smells like turtle slime. Noah Williams is the name. Pleased to meet you, sir!"

Dex looked up at the large man and said, "And you will come in handy today. We will need all that strength to dissect the decaying turtle."

The opportunity pleased the large man. "Thanks, Dr. Holzman. I'll do my best."

"You're American," Dex proclaimed. "And all of you, please call me Dex."

"I'm Jack—Jack Brightman, born and raised in Brooklyn, New York."

"What brought you out here?"

Jack shrugged. "My dad and his dad were in the navy. I loved the sea, but I didn't have the discipline for life in the military. So, I studied marine biology at the University of Miami and after an internship or two, found my way to Maybin's company. Besides, it beats the hell out of the crowds in New York."

Dex looked over Maybin's team. They looked like a good bunch. Dex estimated what they lacked in experience they would make up in enthusiasm.

"Let's see if we can figure out what killed that turtle."

Ten minutes later, the group assembled at the makeshift necropsy lab, and Dex issued instructions. "Maybin, you, me, and Noah will don the headsets for the hummingbird. Jack, you will be up top, working to remove the plastron, and Amelia, you will receive any samples we can extract for analysis. Face shields are mandatory."

Dex paused for questions and, not hearing any, continued. "I am guessing none of you have worked with a hummingbird before, so just follow my lead and everything will go smoothly."

From a small metal container, Dex extracted a robotic bird that resembled a real hummingbird. He handed headsets to Maybin and Noah and switched on the bird. The bird's eyes glowed green to signify power, and then it rose straight in the air on fluttering wings and circled the reptile.

"The hummingbird will produce continuous ultra-high-definition hyperspectral video from every angle." Dex explained.

Everyone stood back as the small robotic bird flapped its mechanical wings. The group watched in amazement as the eyes of the hummingbird pulsated continuously.

"The hummingbird will capture hyperspectral video with 1000x zoom in just under two minutes. It will record the orange substance and all lesions close up."

Two minutes passed and, true to the bird for which it was named, the device flew in place, high above the turtle. The three men with headsets then heard a female voice speak from the hummingbird.

"This specimen is a green sea turtle. I estimate the weight of the specimen to be 341 kilograms. The carapace measures 152 centimeters in length and 142 centimeters in width. The plastron measures 132 centimeters in length and 107 centimeters in width. This specimen is female." The bird hovered in place over the turtle and then spoke again. "The estimated time elapsed since the death of this specimen is approximately 34 hours and 16 minutes."

Dex smiled at the astonished faces of Maybin and Noah. Jack and Amelia couldn't hear the hummingbird's voice but could see the data and voice translation displayed on the large flat-screen. Dex looked up at the hummingbird and said, "Thank you, Denise."

"You are most welcome," replied the robotic bird.

Maybin gawked, still in a state of marvel at seeing the hummingbird in action. "You named her Denise?"

"My mother's name. You can name them anything you want when you set them up."

The technology stunned Maybin's team.

Dex again addressed the device. "Denise, please provide the initial exterior findings."

The mechanical bird flew down and around the carcass then pointed its long beak in the air and spoke. "Multiple lesions detected requiring biopsy. I cannot identify the foreign substance on the outer surface of the specimen."

Maybin looked over to Dex. "What do you make of the information?"

"Two thoughts. The turtle has been dead long enough that getting an accurate, complete blood count will be difficult if not impossible, and rigor mortis will make the entire necropsy questionable."

Noah chirped in, asking, "Do you think the orange discoloration on the exterior is from postmortem degradation?"

Dex shook his head. "Doubt it very much. Postmortem degradation can certainly cause discoloration but not in the manner presented here."

Dex motioned to Jack. "Okay, big guy. Now it's time to remove the plastron. Face masks down for everyone. Once that underbelly shell comes off, expect a biblical trove of maggots. Jack, once the plastron is off, step back and let the hummingbird back in."

With a sharp knife in hand, Jack nodded and gradually progressed alongside the turtle. He started at the trachea and moved clockwise. Once Jack arrived at his starting point, he used the same knife to go back and cut through any remaining muscle attachments, preventing the view to the turtle's insides. Dex waited with the other members of the team as Jack lifted the plastron from the body. As Jack cast the carapace free, Dex's prophecy of a biblical trove of maggots came to pass. Dex was feeling fortunate they were outdoors.

The hummingbird, within seconds, emitted a wide, pale yellow cone of light, immediately disintegrating the intruders and any remaining larvae in the turtle's cavity. A fine mist that rapidly neutralized the acrid odor emanating from the decaying carcass quickly followed this amazing feat. The flat-screen displayed a round of new interior video.

Once the hummingbird completed this process, Dex moved in with a scalpel to excise the first of the lesions. The lesion he chose was glowing bright orange. It was a raised and rubber-like growth marked by three notched ridges meeting in the center with an elevated dot. Dex narrated his findings, and the hummingbird system captured the data from his spoken words. While Dex worked meticulously on the biopsy sample, Maybin took a syringe to extract a blood sample from the heart and then called to Amelia, who would take the sample and combine it with an anticoagulant.

"Oh, buggers!" exclaimed Maybin. "The blood in the heart congealed. I can't draw it."

Dex sighed. This was an expected occurrence with a sea turtle that died over twenty-four hours ago. "Maybin, don't worry about it. We will need to abandon the notion of a full necropsy. The turtle is too far gone. Let's biopsy what we can and remove the vital organs. Every tissue sample, including the skin, may hold a clue, even in its current state."

"Agreed," said Maybin. "I want to get the liver for further examination. It looks inflamed."

"Good call. The tissue doesn't look normal. Some type of contaminant could have caused it."

"What are you thinking?"

"Tough to say . . . could be many things."

Two hours later, the team had accomplished all that was possible. Dex called off the procedure and recommended a quick break for showers, a bite to eat, and then a review of their initial findings.

Maybin concurred. "I am just in awe of that hummingbird device," he remarked.

Dex was used to first-timers' reaction to the hummingbird. It was an ingenious device that held an extraordinary database on all known marine life and powerful artificial intelligence. As smart as the device was, though, it wouldn't provide the answers they sought.

CHAPTER 6

deBaak looked at Aloysius Travanche with disdain. *How could such a slovenly man become the leader of the World Health Organization?* Travanche was perhaps seventy years of age, bald with a gray outer rim of wispy hair. His sagging jowls barely stayed above his collar while his protruding stomach barreled over his belt. The bags under his dark brown eyes were in sync with the rest of his face which, deBaak thought sarcastically, was losing its fight with gravity. As Travanche moved across the parquet floor to greet him, deBaak extended his right hand but did not remove his ever-present black gloves. In this world of pestilence, deBaak would not succumb to the errant spread of bacteria.

deBaak smiled, displaying his slightly crooked front teeth, and said with a warmth he did not feel, "Aloysius, you are looking well, my friend."

"It is because of the supplements I take and staying off the streets," replied Travanche.

deBaak smiled and deftly transitioned to the purpose of his visit. He wanted to spend as little time as possible with this old bag of wind. "I am hoping to persuade you to recommend a more stringent form of Mercy to world leaders."

Travanche looked mortified. "More stringent? My God, Erik. How could we in good conscience do more?"

"Look out your own window. Homeless people flood the streets. They spread disease amongst themselves and become carriers, causing illness to proliferate across the globe. How could we afford not to implement more stringent measures?"

Travanche cringed, clearly uncomfortable with the conversation. "The homeless problem is worldwide. Countries all over the world have run out of land to house these people. Even ancient cemeteries have been excavated and built upon."

"As they should be. The ancient practice of human burial is a wasteful use of precious land resources. What solution do you see?" he asked, knowing full well that Travanche would have nothing to offer.

"Well . . ." Travanche cleared his throat, hesitating. "There is always colonization of other planets."

deBaak could barely keep himself from laughing out loud. "Come now. You and I have been around and around on that topic. No other planet in our solar system is habitable by human beings, and besides, the logistics of getting hundreds of millions of people into space presents an insurmountably difficult problem for which we have no solution."

"Couldn't we work on populating the outer regions of our own planet?" asked the older man.

"The same logistics issues remain. Besides, what government has the resources to make jungles and polar caps habitable for millions of people? Not even the United States can do that."

Travanche just shrugged. To deBaak, the conversation felt old, like the WHO leader. He took the time to meet with Travanche only because of how easy he was to manipulate. And for some reason, world leaders paid attention to him. He was simply a means to an end.

"Speaking of the US, I understand they just agreed to implement the current level of Mercy," proclaimed deBaak proudly.

Travanche nodded. "The president had no choice. Dwindling resources, illness, and the lack of a functioning economy outweighed his desire to be a humanitarian."

"That is why I am here today. I am glad the United States has agreed to join the current Mercy standard, but I strongly believe the world must ramp it up another level."

Travanche looked shocked. "Recommending anything more might further the growing sense of anarchy already present in the world's most crowded countries. Do you refer people to Mercy when they get the common cold? Where does it end?"

deBaak crossed the chasm with Travanche. Every time, it was the same. He waded into the murky waters of Mercy, with its extended benefits and a recommended rollout plan. Then Travanche gently protested but ultimately gave in, knowing full well there was no better answer.

deBaak, keeping his composure, as always, merely replied in a collegial manner, "Aloysius, I again ask, what choice do we have?"

Travanche sighed. His fleshy face was ashen as he answered with a sense of despair, "What have you got in mind?"

deBaak reached into the inner breast pocket of his jacket and pulled out a small pen-shaped device. Three small legs formed a tripod stand that he set on the rectangular conference table between them. He depressed the button on one end, and a hologram appeared.

deBaak inhaled deeply as his own image danced before him, ready to make the presentation aiding the next part of his plan. The hologram displayed deBaak in miniature in a tan suit with a white shirt open at the collar. His image reminded him how pale he looked. His shaved head and inverted cheeks made him look unhealthy. The black gloves that rarely came off punctuated his fear of germs. He watched with Travanche as the holographic image of himself spoke.

"Friends and world leaders, my name is Erik deBaak, founder and CEO of Crematie. As you know, our planet faces unprecedented peril from overcrowding, the spread of disease, and sunken economies. We live in a world in which only the super-wealthy can assume a life approaching anything one might call normal."

deBaak looked over at Travanche, who watched with interest. His presentation paused momentarily to display scenes of sick people living in misery on the streets of countries around the world. A saddened violin melody accompanied the horrid scenes to convey a sense of hopelessness.

"Farmers can no longer grow needed crops, water supplies have dwindled, and we overwork our medical facilities. We have less hope with each approaching day."

Even Travanche, who was intimately familiar with global conditions, could not look away from the compelling holographic message.

"The current level of Mercy has been effective but has not made the required progress for the world's survival. I encourage all world leaders to immediately implement a Level 3 emergency state of Mercy covering all illnesses, excluding the common cold, considered lethal contagions. We must stop the problem in its tracks and reclaim the earth for future generations."

deBaak could read the expression on the face of Aloysius Travanche. The old man looked horrified. deBaak hit pause on the presentation. Travanche appeared ashen.

"Erik, have you gone mad? What you propose goes well beyond the current Mercy program, which many already feel is barbaric. Besides, people will claim your motivation is profit-based. You own eighty percent of the world's crematoriums with long-term contracts from all major governments."

deBaak smiled coolly and replied, "Keep watching, Aloysious."

"Recognizing that Crematie stands to generate billions of dollars in additional revenue should you adopt this proposal, I am prepared to file paperwork with the Dutch government, where we are based, to create a nonprofit entity. One hundred percent of Crematie profits will be allocated to the renewal of the earth. The nonprofit will hire the world's foremost experts in the restoration of the land and seas to return our planet to its former glory."

Travanche's mouth was open. No one of immense wealth would ever make such a tremendous philanthropic gesture.

deBaak studied his colleague's face as the hologram shifted to scenery of the earth in all its past splendor, with energetic music to bring the scene alive.

"Erik, I am at a loss for words. You are a true gentleman and a fine steward of our great planet."

deBaak smiled faintly without opening his lips. He hated revealing his crooked teeth. He pointed Travanche's attention back to the hologram for the grand finale.

"To aid this effort, I am seeding the nonprofit with one hundred billion euros from my personal fortune. We will call our new entity 'Earth Reborn.'"

Travanche applauded. "Tell me what you need from me."

deBaak took a solitary moment to revel in his triumph. He now had the influential WHO leader right where he wanted him. "Get me a meeting with Gathee."

"But . . . but, she . . ."

"Detests me? Yes, I am aware. She believes me to be nothing more than a snobbish bore and a profiteer, even though we have never met. I've heard her public comments. The hologram will help convince her otherwise. Forward it to her with your endorsement."

Travanche nodded in agreement.

There had not been a time over the past decade when deBaak had failed to get Travanche to bend to his will. Fortunately, the man was very pliable. Now, a meeting with Leader Akeyo Gathee of Earth, the successor to the old United Nations, would be the key to getting a seat at the table to implement the full depth of his plan.

CHAPTER 7

Driving the four kilometers from her office to Otter Park Elementary School should have been easy. Cam honked her horn continuously to encourage the homeless masses to clear a path from the streets where cars were intruders. Three-quarters of an hour elapsed since the disturbing call from the school nurse. At the current pace, it might take hours to reach her ten-year-old son. Cam pushed a call button on her steering wheel to activate the portable combox.

"Call Darcy," she commanded of the system.

Two rings, then three . . . finally, her administrative assistant picked up.

"Darcy, I need you to file an immediate electronic continuance for Ken Barker. The judge won't be happy about it, but you can explain the emergency. Also, give the Barkers a call. Tell them we will let them know when we have a new date. They weren't planning to attend the hearing, so you can probably find them at home."

Now idling, her car's ventilation system couldn't mask the smell of despair in Los Angeles. The smog, pollution, and sweat combined with human urine and feces was ramping up her anxiety. Moving so slowly was agonizing. Cam's heart ached thinking of Corey waiting for her to show up in the nurse's office. Her car's audio system was playing, but it failed to drown out the sounds of the street: people moaning and public address systems telling people not to congregate. Although not permitted by law, a beggar approached her vehicle clamoring for food or water. Cam wanted to help all of them, but rolling down her window to help a single person would invite a riot. That was a chance she couldn't take. The welfare of her son came above all else. She smiled faintly at the beggar and waved him away.

Once she broke free of the downtown area, the going became easier. Still, the entire four-kilometer trek took over two hours. Cam parked the car and raced into the main entrance of her son's school. She popped her head into the office, introduced herself, and sought directions to the nurse's station.

"Around the corner and to the right," she was told.

Cam hurried down the linoleum corridor lined with lockers and made a beeline for the wooden door that said "NURSE."

Once through the door, she encountered a woman, fiftyish, with graying hair secured in a tight bun.

"Hi, I'm Cam Atkinson, Corey's mother. How is he?"

The nurse shook her head. "Mrs. Atkinson, I tried to comply with your request, but when you didn't show up or call for two hours, I had no choice but to send Corey to the local MEC."

"MEC? You sent my son to the Mercy Evaluation Center? Are you that insensitive? If anything happens to my boy, I'll be suing this school and LA County faster than you can blink an eye." The rage from Tom's death returned. Her skin was hot to the touch. Her head throbbed. She added, as a final thought for Nurse Albright, "Remain confident you will be named personally." And she stormed out, slamming the door behind her.

Cam sat down in her car and exhaled. The MEC that held her son was the same facility where she had gone to retrieve Tom after he was forced to go by his employer. Once a hospital before Mercy, the building wasn't far from the elementary school. She had to get Corey, and nothing else mattered, but the anxiety of entering that place again made her queasy.

When she arrived, she found the familiar three-meter chain-link fence surrounding the parking lot of what was once a quaint and respected community hospital. The Mercy Enforcement Police, or MEP, were standing guard at the entrance. Their aim was to keep sick people inside and prevent those from entering who might have designs on helping the ill escape. Both MEPs were armed and wore the latest in oxygenated filtration masks. Their voices were hollow and machine-like.

"State your business," demanded the uniformed MEP officer.

"My son was brought here from his elementary school."

"Name?"

"Mine or his?"

"His."

"Corey Atkinson. He is ten years old."

"I need to validate your ID, ma'am."

"Certainly," she replied. Cam sat still while the MEP officer held his rectangular scanner up to her face.

The device spoke in a monotonic female voice. "Camille Atkinson, thirty-four years of age, 170 centimeters tall, lives at 437 E. Cherrybrook Road in Los Angeles, California."

Satisfied, the MEP officer waved her through, and she parked in the first visitor spot she could find. Cam found the sign that said "Mercy Evaluation Center" and proceeded forward. Having lived in this area most of her life, she recognized the old emergency room entrance.

Before she could enter through the automated glass doors, a young female MEC employee handed her an oxygenated filtration mask. "You must place this over your nose and mouth before entering."

She had been through it all before with Tom. They would allow no visitor or staff to risk contracting an illness from those being referred to the MEC. She placed the mask over her face, turned on the flow of oxygen from the miniature vial on each side, and went directly to the registration area.

"I'm looking for my son, Corey Atkinson." The sound of her voice was tinny. She hated these damn masks, but it was for her own protection.

The lady at the registration desk said nothing in reply. She merely pointed to a triage area. Cam raced over and frantically began looking for her son. The crowd in the triage area was standing room only. They camped people with masks and their ill friends and relatives on every chair, table, and open area of floor space. Cam's eyes desperately scanned the room in search of her son's mop of curly blonde hair, but Corey was nowhere to be found. Cam found no one willing to help, so with scant options, she began opening and closing every exam room curtain in the narrow corridor while calling her son's name through the tinny sound of the oxygenated filtration mask.

She ripped open a curtain, calling, "Corey." She retreated apologetically as an older woman with enormous red welts across her body was being examined by an MEC physician. Her heart lifted when she heard his voice from across the corridor.

"Mom, Mom . . . I'm in here."

Cam whirled around and threw the curtain to the side, thrilled at the sight of her son, who she loved more than life itself. She wrapped her arms around him and held him tightly, never wanting to let go. When the embrace ended, Cam placed her hand on her son's forehead. It was warm. "How are you feeling, sweetheart?"

"Not that bad," he replied. "Is this where they brought Daddy when he got sick?"

A chill ran down Cam's spine. She never wanted to lie to her son. She chose her words carefully. "Yes, it is. But remember, Daddy had a blood cancer. You just have a minor illness like all children get from time to time."

He looked at her with the innocence of youth, his blue eyes seeming curious in appearance and said, "Are the Mercy people going to end my life like they did to Daddy?"

Cam's heart was breaking. It was a travesty that her son should have to grow up in a world where a ten-year-old boy worries about such things. She placed her right hand by her eye to wipe away a forming tear and tried to remain composed. "No, honey. What Daddy had to go through will not happen to you. We will see a doctor and then I am taking you home."

"Okay, Mom."

Not five minutes later, a young woman in a white smock walked in and introduced herself as Dr. Holly Longfellow. She couldn't be more than twenty-five or twenty-six. Her dark brown hair had blonde highlights and hung shoulder length. She also wore a mask.

"Corey has a mild fever and has tested negative for all known medical conditions. I am recommending a booster shot and bedrest until he recovers."

The diagnosis relieved Cam. She had prepared for a fight to get her son released. "What's in the booster shot?" she inquired.

"It's a cocktail of antibiotics, herbs, and vitamins. Just a precaution, really," stated Dr. Longfellow.

"Okay," Cam said. "Let's do it. Then we can go home?"

Dr. Longfellow smiled in return to Cam's question, patted Corey on the head, and said, "Then you can go home."

Corey sat still as Dr. Longfellow pulled open a metal drawer and withdrew the device that would administer the booster shot. The device was silver and had a round head. The doctor applied it to Corey's upper arm.

"Ready, Corey? Here we go. One, two, three . . ." Dr. Longfellow depressed the button on the device, and Corey flinched but showed no overt pain. When she pulled the device away, a silver disc remained on Corey's arm.

"What's that?" Cam asked.

Dr. Longfellow smiled and said pleasantly, "It's a sensor that follows the injection of the booster. It's now required by law. The sensor will continuously monitor Corey's medical condition for two weeks and send the data back to us at MEC. If his condition worsens or he fails to get better, the sensor will blink a copper color. If that happens, it will require you to return immediately."

Cam shrugged, thinking the whole thing ridiculous. A day or two of rest and some chicken noodle soup, and Corey would be as good as new. She was contemplating what she could use to pry the sensor from her son's arm when Dr. Longfellow interrupted her train of thought.

"Corey," she said, looking right at the little boy, "Don't pick at the sensor. It will fall off in two weeks. If you try to pull it off before that, an alarm will trigger, and the Mercy Enforcement Police will show up at your door."

Corey, naïve and oblivious to the ramification of the perverse Mercy program, just nodded.

Cam was sick. Memories of Mercy and the demise of her husband flooded her brain.

CHAPTER 8

Showered, changed, and slightly refreshed, Dex sat in the largest of the Nexterus Marine conference rooms with Maybin's team and three large pizzas freshly delivered from a local restaurant. Dex took a bite from his first slice and made a face, illustrating his surprise at the unusual taste.

"Not quite what you expected?" asked Amelia.

"It's different from American pizza. What's in it?"

She chuckled at his lack of experience with Aussie tastes. "Instead of marinara sauce, we use barbeque sauce. That's the main difference, apart from the fact we like thin and crispy as opposed to deep-dish."

"And you top the creation off with bacon and egg. Also unusual from my perspective."

She laughed gently in reply. "At least the mozzarella is the same."

"I'm with you, Dex. Give me an old-fashioned deep-dish any day," replied his fellow countryman, Jack Brightman.

"Touché, Jack," Dex replied.

"Well, I side with Amelia," proclaimed Noah. "The food Down Under is better than anywhere else."

"I think all of you have forgotten that England, the country that discovered half the world, still sets the standard for culinary excellence," offered Maybin.

Dex held his can of Foster's midair and in his best Aussie accent replied, "Bloody hell, mate."

They all laughed at the good-natured fun. Amelia, done after one slice, began the upload of the necropsy results to the computerized board commonly known by its most prominent brand name, the Palette. The floor-to-ceiling board on the north end of the room would receive and display all the data. Its touch screen capability enabled a multitude of analytics features and could also receive voice commands to help answer the scientists' questions. Dex valued the instantaneous lab results.

Amelia touched the Palette power button, and the data came to life. Dex observed the left side of the screen populate automatically with the hyperspectral videos taken by the hummingbird, all organized by exterior and interior and labeled appropriately. In the middle of the Palette, the executive summary of necropsy findings displayed, and on the right, there was a blank section labeled "Questions."

As the Palette populated itself with images and data, Maybin stated the obvious by reading the major headline from the Palette's center section. "Cause of death: organ failure from the presence of crude oil." Underneath, in smaller type, the Palette displayed the words, "Oil was detected in the mouth and throughout the gastrointestinal tract. Liver damage from oil was also present."

"Crude oil?" remarked Amelia. "Was there a recorded spill from a cargo ship?"

"Not recently—and then, not in this part of the world," replied Dex.

"There was a minor incident a year ago in the Pacific Ocean off Mexico's west coast," stated Maybin.

Jack chirped in. "Could this turtle have migrated that far and back?"

"Unlikely," replied Dex. "Green sea turtles migrate long distances. But from the Coral Sea to the Pacific along Mexico's west coast—that would be unusual."

"Could this turtle be the exception?" inquired Noah.

Dex shook his head. "I doubt it very much. The distance is at least five times greater than the normal migration for a green sea turtle found in this region."

Maybin placed his index finger on the right side of his face in a state of deep contemplation. "Could the presence of crude oil in the turtle's system have something to do with the strange orange color?"

The Australian-accented male voice recognition system of the Palette heard Maybin's question and answered. "Diagnostics reveal no correlation between the presence of crude oil and the orange color on the specimen's interior and exterior."

Dex placed his beer on an old veneer table Maybin likely purchased from a local secondhand store and walked over to the Palette. He wanted a close-up view of the videos. He chose one of the full lesions, similar to the one he removed for biopsy. Holding his right index finger against the photo caused the Palette to offer results of the biopsy.

Again, the Palette spoke. "The biopsy of this lesion indicates cause by a foreign substance permeating the specimen's skin and internal organs. My database reveals no match for the foreign substance."

Perplexed, Maybin spoke to the Palette. "Place this issue in the Question queue."

Immediately, on the right side of the Palette, the words "Orange substance origin" appeared.

Dex scratched his head and addressed the others. "So, we have a dead sea turtle with the cause of death coming from ingestion of crude oil, which is separate and apart from the orange substance and lesions appearing on the skin. I can't say I've ever encountered a mystery quite like this one."

Amelia spoke first. "I'll do some research to see whether there have been any new oil discoveries in waters in this part of the world."

"Good," said Dex. "That will help us understand how the turtle died and, depending on the location, may also help us figure out where the orange substance originated."

Maybin again had the Palette place this issue in the Questions column.

Dex had an additional thought. He looked up at the Palette's middle section under the heading "Stomach Analysis." The only result was a mostly digested scyphozoa, the scientific name for jellyfish. Dex scratched his head, silently admitting it puzzled him. Jellyfish were common prey for leatherback sea turtles, but the green sea species were herbivores. They ate seagrass.

It broke his chain of thought when a horn blared in the parking lot.

"That would be the transport crew. The same guys are going to take the carcass south to Brisbane, where there is a marine life crematorium. Jack and Noah, go lend them a hand and then break down the outside lab," Maybin stated.

Jack and Noah nodded and left the room.

Amelia looked up at Dex. "You still look unsettled."

He nodded in agreement. "We have no clue where this orange substance came from. Even though it's not the cause of death, we need to figure out what it is. It could be harmful to the sea and/or its marine life inhabitants."

"I don't believe we can ignore its presence in the equation. Where do we begin?" Amelia pondered aloud.

Maybin just smirked. "I know what I would do, but you might not like it," he said to Dex.

Dex peered at him stoically. "What's that, Maybin?"

"Earlier today, when we met on Scrimshaw Beach, I told you about the local legend."

"The sunken civilization at the bottom of the Coral Sea? That legend?" he asked incredulously.

"That's the one. Natives today still tell the story of the magical healing extract."

"Have we reached the point of desperation already?" asked Dex.

"We've already tapped the world's most powerful databases and have come up empty. I told you I have dived off Scrimshaw Beach. I've seen times where the water has produced a mild orange sheen but chalked it off to seasonal algae blooms. Now, I'm not so sure."

Suddenly, a wave of exhaustion overwhelmed Dex. The travel from California to Australia and the busy day since arriving was now taking its toll. He cupped his face in both hands and contemplated the madness of an unthinkable journey to the bottom of the Coral Sea in search of a sunken civilization called Aeternum.

CHAPTER 9

Akeyo Gathee looked older and smaller than he imagined. Her long, braided hair was nearly all gray, not uncommon for a woman in her early seventies. She wore generous heels and still appeared short. Before traveling to Manhattan, deBaak had his administrative assistant produce a complete dossier on the Earth leader. He had waited far too long for this meeting. deBaak prepared with diligence.

Gathee was born and raised in Kenya. She made her name leading a land renewal effort with emphasis on saving endangered species that once proudly roamed the African plains. Today, lions, giraffes, and elephants lived only in small numbers on tiny wildlife preserves across the great continent. The planet's dilemma reduced the rich lands of Africa to scorched and barren wastelands. Millions of homeless people starved out in the open. Gathee led efforts to recreate the natural habitat of the people and animals of Africa by developing biosphere communities. deBaak's file pointed to the history of these domed areas dating back to the late 1900s. Gathee had more success than most in developing these communities across Africa, but they ultimately succumbed to the two problems that crushed every good idea for the Earth's survival: money and space. Funds for projects like these were as scarce as the land on which to build. There were simply too many people with nowhere to go. Understanding Gathee's passion coupled with his own enormous wealth were the keys to gaining control of the woman who was the world's de facto leader among leaders.

Unlike its predecessor organization, the United Nations, Earth had a charter signed by every country on the planet appointing a leader to make decisions for the common good of all. The leader served at the pleasure of the Ruling Council, comprising the heads of state for the nine largest economies at any one time. Leaders were most often selected from apolitical backgrounds. They were humanitarians, philanthropists, or those that cared more for the lands and its people than power and greed. Service was for a ten-year term, renewable by the Ruling Council for as long as they chose. Gathee was nearing the end of her third term with no clear successor in sight.

deBaak sat in a conference room large enough to hold fifty people. They dubbed the room the Observatory because the view from the top of the round, one-hundred-floor building offered an astounding view of both the Hudson and East Rivers. deBaak hadn't been in New York in quite some time. He thought it sad that landing pads on top of every building marred such a magnificent view. All a necessary evil with the inability to get anywhere on the ground, he lamented.

Akeyo Gathee gazed up at him with her brown eyes. For such a small woman, she certainly packed quite an intimidating death stare. He could feel her disdain for him before he even said hello.

"What is it I can do for you, Mr. deBaak?" Gathee spoke with a distinct Kenyan accent. Her gold-framed glasses gave her face an added sense of wisdom.

deBaak did his best to smile, lips only, not wishing to reveal his crooked front teeth. "Please, call me Erik. It is my pleasure to make your acquaintance," he said, trying to engender a feel of respect and collegiality.

Gathee said nothing and just stared at him, appearing to wait for him to play his first card. deBaak appreciated she would want to take the measure of a man before saying anything that didn't aid her point of view.

He resumed his attempt to forge a bond, avoiding the temptation to dive right in. "I have been reading up on your career, Leader Gathee. I have great respect for your efforts to renew our planet. Your work bore fruit long before the Ruling Council selected you for this much-deserved post."

Gathee smiled faintly. Apparently, she was not one to be buttered up. "I saw your hologram video," she replied monotonically. "I must be frank. I'm not sure I believe your philanthropic gesture is genuine. Yet out of respect for my friend, Travanche, I agreed to hear you out. You have ten minutes. Then this meeting is over."

deBaak's blood boiled. How dare this obstinate woman scoff in the face of his effort to support her life's work? How many others had the financial wherewithal to offer what he was offering? Was it possible she saw right through his shallow exterior? No, he was not yet willing to concede that point.

"Today is Monday. By Wednesday, I shall have the nonprofit, Earth Reborn, legally formed in Rotterdam. By Thursday, I shall capitalize the venture, as stated in the hologram, with one hundred billion euros of my money. I will send you documentation proving this and the plan to have all profits from Crematie donated to Earth Reborn."

Gathee's expression appeared to soften. She paused for a moment and sighed outwardly.

deBaak was pleased. He believed he penetrated Gathee's preconceived notions and outward hate for who he was and what she thought he stood for. He waited patiently for her to break the growing silence.

"As intriguing as this sounds, it all rides on an increased level of Mercy forcing millions of sick people to die. I cannot abide by such an action."

deBaak prepared for this stance. "Leader Gathee, no one is trying to appear unsympathetic to your view, but certainly you can appreciate that even if a magical cure for all known illnesses descended upon us from the heavens, the planet no longer has the space and resources to support a global population approaching one trillion souls."

Again, she paused. Her eyes roamed the ceiling as if waiting for some form of divine intervention before responding.

He had her. Shrinking the population was the only thing that made sense. World leaders inherently knew this, but political correctness prevented them from saying it out loud.

Again, she sighed and said in a somewhat dejected voice, "Who do you have in mind to run your new entity?"

deBaak was waiting for that exact question. He clasped his hands together in a steeple and said, "Why, there is only one person ideally suited for the role of leading Earth Reborn."

"And who might that be?" she asked curiously.

"You."

The shocked look on Gathee's face would have measured 10 on the Richter scale. "Me?" she said, stunned. "I am an old woman nearing the end of my career. Surely, you have someone much younger in mind who shares my vision."

deBaak was now enjoying his designed manipulation of the Earth leader. "There is only you. What a phenomenal way to end your illustrious career. Having hundreds of billions at your disposal to hire the world's best minds to renew the planet for generations to come. Free yourself from the strain of global politics and rededicate yourself to what you truly believe."

He was breaking through her stone-cold exterior. She was thinking about it.

"What about you? What role would you play in the new entity?"

"Although I believe in time, you and I will forge a powerful bond, I pledge that my only role will be silent financier. You will have complete autonomy to run the organization as you see fit—subject, of course, to the oversight of a board of directors that you will choose."

Her left eyebrow arched as if she had him in a gotcha moment. "And I presume you will be the chairman of this board?"

"Only if you ask me to assume such a role. Otherwise, I remain completely in the background to offer advice if, and only if, you desire it."

Her inhibitions melted away. Gathee was burning out after nearly thirty years of leading Earth. It was well-documented that she had no obvious successor.

"So, let me get this straight. You are creating a nonprofit entity to help renew the planet for future generations. You are donating one hundred billion euros of your own money and all the profits from Crematie but only after world leaders sanction an increased level of Mercy . . . and you want me to leave my post here and run the nonprofit."

"Yes, that is correct."

"What do you get out of this?"

A warming sensation flowed through deBaak's body. His sense of satisfaction was clear as he laid his ultimate card on the table. It was the trump card for which Gathee would have no comeback. "I get to be you."

"I don't follow."

"It is quite simple," he said confidently as he crossed his long legs under the table and stared at her intently. "Earth typically has chosen its leaders from esteemed humanitarians and philanthropists. After I announce news of Earth Reborn, the world will hold me in the highest regard. You get the opportunity of a lifetime to make a real difference for the planet, and I get your current job."

Gathee looked defeated. "So, essentially you are telling me that the position you just offered wholly depends on you taking over for me here at Earth?"

"That's correct."

Gathee's fighting spirit appeared to rebound. "Are you blackmailing me, Mr. deBaak?"

"Blackmail is such an ugly term. I prefer to say that I am offering you the opportunity of a lifetime."

"But once your hologram gets out, you will look foolish if you renege on your promise to create the nonprofit and fund it in the manner you described."

"True enough. But as we speak, every world media outlet has received a reworked version of the hologram. It shows both you and me jointly announcing your retirement from Earth to go lead the new entity and my expression of gratitude for you recommending me to the Ruling Council as your replacement."

Gathee's face contorted in horror. "You really are the monster everyone thinks you are. I'll simply deny the authenticity of the hologram."

deBaak looked at her with his cold, steely eyes and removed a folded piece of paper from his inner breast pocket. He slid the document across the table.

"What's this?" she asked.

"Open it," he commanded.

A look of horror overwhelmed Gathee.

"I have already submitted your electronic letter of resignation to the Ruling Council and transferred a signing bonus of fifty million dollars for joining Earth Reborn to your personal bank account. So, you hold proof that the wheels are already in motion."

"All the money in the world wouldn't let me work for you," she protested. "Nothing you have done here isn't reversible. My credibility is far greater than yours, I assure you." She took on a look of satisfaction, as if she had won.

deBaak reached back into his jacket pocket and pulled out a photograph that he tossed at her. The photo hit her in the chest and bounced onto the table, landing upside down. "Look," he chided.

She turned over the photo, and her eyes widened like saucers.

"You were hoping no one found out, weren't you?"

She nodded as the tears started gently rolling down her cheeks. She reached into a pocket for a tissue and dabbed her eyes. "How did you . . . ?" Overwrought with emotion, Gathee couldn't finish the question.

deBaak didn't answer. Instead, he scowled and simply stated, "The husband you told the world was dead is very much alive, isn't he? Battling cancer, I hear."

She nodded through the tears.

He continued. "You violated the law by helping him evade Mercy and arranging for him to be treated in a secret mountain retreat in Vermont."

She looked at him, her eyes pleading for sympathy.

"Tell me, what will your credibility be worth when news of this scandal breaks?"

CHAPTER 10

Cam hated her appearances before the Los Angeles City Medical Court. Homeless people lined the sidewalks and the two dozen cement steps leading up to the entrance. Cam related to these people with nowhere else to go. Nearly all of them were starving. Her heart broke each time she took to the streets. She was doing what she could, yet it never was quite enough.

Although it was a typical hot weather day in Los Angeles, Cam broke out into a cold, clammy sweat as she climbed the cement steps leading to the entrance of the medical court. The sensation was not an indicator that she was getting sick but rather a stark reminder of her own childhood growing up in LA. Her father's long-standing career as a police officer came to an abrupt halt when the authorities asked him to work on the early medical round-up teams. The LAPD fired him after he steadfastly refused. The inept FOP lawyer went through the motions, but the lawyer's heart was not in his work. This left Cam, her parents, and two older brothers out on the street, homeless for two months, living in different shelters and scrounging for their next meal. Her father's suicide still haunted her, as did one catalyst, the FOP lawyer. It's what inspired her to pursue a law career and fight for those whose way of life depended on someone who truly cared. Today, Cam would take that suppressed anger and let it pour out constructively to prolong the life of her client, Ken Barker. She was thankful that Darcy scheduled a continuance.

Cam reached the main entrance and pulled a handkerchief from her leather bag, holding her legal files and belongings. She mopped her forehead, pushing to one side the swaying black hair. She took out a small makeup mirror and held it up to her face. She looked pale. Her brown eyes were haggard and for a woman approaching thirty-five, she looked more like forty. Cam snapped the compact case shut and went through the glass doors. Today, she would argue for Ken Barker's Mercy exemption in Courtroom B, which was the down the hall and to her left. She walked up to the three-meter-high set of double wooden doors and read the electronic sign to the right: "Courtroom B – Medical Hearings – Judge Alastair P. Jackson presiding." Judge Jackson would not have been her pick for the uphill battle she faced in helping Ken Barker. An albino, Judge Jackson possessed a nasty disposition and on his best day failed to hide it. Governor Samson's predecessor, a staunch Mercy advocate, had appointed him. Cam had her work cut out.

She entered the crowded courtroom and took a seat in the last row of the high-back wooden pews. As expected, the lights in Judge Jackson's courtroom were off. As an albino, his eyes, devoid of iris color, were sensitive to the light. Everyone worked off the natural lighting of the picturesque Roman windows high on the front wall behind Judge Jackson. When Jackson's court was in session, attorneys could use small flashlights if needed, but most documents were on tablets. God help the attorney whose flashlight accidentally tilted upward toward Jackson's face. This happened on more than one occasion. Those cases went down faster than a house on fire.

While she waited for the Barker case to be called, a young lawyer stood before Judge Jackson and was pleading for a Mercy exemption on behalf of a middle-aged woman recovering from her second bout with hepatitis C.

Judge Jackson's fiery-white eyes drilled into the young lawyer. "Mr. Franklin, your client has tested the limits of our medical system. The MEC has referred her for final processing. With this country's resources so stretched, why on earth should we tax them even farther for your client?"

Jackson's disdain for human life and people as individuals made her sick. *How do assholes like this get appointed to the bench?* The thought struck her again that Jackson took out his personal misfortunes on the very people he presided over. *What a misguided way to adjudicate the law.*

The young lawyer confidently stated, "Your Honor, my client has entered an experimental treatment program that involves a drug discovered from a rare herb found only in the Amazon. The results have been remarkable in other parts of the world, but the study is just beginning here in the US."

Jackson's face crunched up in contemplation. He looked pained because the lawyer presented something unexpected. "Do you have data on this study, Mr. Franklin? From the US or other parts of the world, as you say?" Jackson's voice dripped in cynicism.

"Yes, Your Honor. I have transmitted the data for your review."

With that, Jackson growled, "Ninety days! This will give the court time to consider the data and to see if the experimental treatment yields results. But I warn you, Mr. Franklin, if your client is still sick in ninety days, all the data and fancy treatments in the world won't save her." He slammed the gavel down hard and yelled, "Next case. Barker."

Cam collected her leather carry bag and stood up as Franklin, the young attorney, strode out of the courtroom. He made eye contact with her and muttered under his breath with a sense of frustration, "Have fun."

Cam drew breath deep into her lungs, reminding herself to keep her temper in check. With a judge like Alastair P. Jackson, it wouldn't be easy.

She walked down the aisle and approached the front of the courtroom. After laying her bag on the table reserved for attorneys, she stated for the record, "Camille Atkinson representing Kenneth Barker, Your Honor."

Jackson stared down at her from the bench. "I see Mr. Barker needs a heart transplant and has been on a waiting list for six months."

"That is accurate, Your Honor. However, we urge the Court to consider that Mr. Barker is now third on the national waiting list for a transplant and sending him for final Mercy processing would be a needless act of inhumane barbarism when a short-term exemption could save his life."

As the words flowed out of her mouth, Cam instantly regretted them. She inadvertently let her true feelings about the Mercy system invade her thoughts. This became clear when Jackson stood up, revealing the unfit frame of a man who led a sedentary lifestyle, and bellowed, "Barbarism? Who the hell do you think you are? My job, in fact, the job of this court is to oversee the system to ensure the needs of the healthy."

Cam had screwed up. The blood drained from her face as Jackson sat back down. She could sense he was still seething, and she needed to mollify him the best she could for Ken Barker's sake. "Your Honor, I meant no disrespect. It's just that Mr. Barker has a wife and family. His grandchildren adore him, and I am trying desperately to fight for his life. With so many people in final Mercy processing, those in need of organ donations are waiting less time than ever."

Jackson's facial muscles looked tense. His pale lips descended downward, and when he finally spoke, it wasn't with words of sympathy for her or her client. "Ms. Atkinson, had you been here for your original court date, before the US enacted the new level of Mercy, I might have been able to grant your motion for a Mercy exemption. However, with the new guidelines, your client could be in line for his new heart tomorrow and I couldn't help him. This court rules that Mr. Barker be turned over to the Mercy Enforcement Police for final disposition. The order shall be carried out within seventy-two hours."

With that, Judge Jackson let his gavel crash downward on Cam's spirit and her hope of saving Ken Barker.

CHAPTER 11

Crude oil. Its presence completely befuddled Dex. He just couldn't reconcile the turtle's cause of death with the mysterious orange particles. There were no oil refineries anywhere near their current location. The jellyfish found in the turtle's stomach was a possibility. Jellyfish could migrate long distances, but it was so improbable. He interlocked his hands, cracking his knuckles, a nervous habit he'd yet to shake, and grabbed a cup of coffee from the break room in Maybin's facility. There had to be a logical explanation. He just couldn't put his finger on the reason. He plopped down on the secondhand sofa and closed his eyes.

"Hey sailor, wake up," prodded Amelia.

Dex shook his head to clear the cobwebs. "Sorry, I didn't intend to nod off. You know how it is. The travel, the excitement of the necropsy, and then when the action stops, your body tells you how overworked it is."

"Yes," she giggled. "I understand. Were you having some sort of dream?"

"Dream? I don't recall any dream. Why? Was I talking in my sleep?"

"You mumbled something about oil."

"Oh, that. I was thinking about the turtle's cause of death. I can't say for sure, but the only logical explanation is the jellyfish. Only jellyfish don't travel from here to oil refineries, and green sea turtles don't normally consume jellyfish. So, I'm stuck."

She laughed out loud. "The great Dex Holzman can't make the connection? You must be tired."

He smiled, trying to decide if she was flirting or taunting. "Help me out then."

"Well, if you don't mind a theory coming from the team's rookie . . ."

"Lay it on me."

"Okay. Consider that the jellyfish may have hitched a ride on an oil tanker en route to the Australian coast."

Dex considered her idea and with a furrowed brow replied, "Not a bad thought, rookie. But even if that were true, how would oil from the inside of a tanker permeate the hull in sufficient quantity to invade the jellyfish and kill the turtle?"

"Well," she blushed, "I don't have all the answers." She stood near the break room refrigerator and leaned against it. Dex could see she was in deep thought. Her expression revealed the intensity he imagined she once applied to competitive gymnastics. Finally, she spoke. "My dad used to work in an oil refinery down the coast off Bulwer Island. He used to show me pictures of the oil tankers when I was a little girl."

Dex wasn't sure her childhood memories were going to offer anything constructive, but he enjoyed the way her small button nose crinkled up when she was in serious contemplation.

An idea burst upon her like fireworks, illuminating a dark sky. "Could the jellyfish have attached itself to one of the oil tank openings?"

He pondered this for a moment and said doubtfully, "I imagine it's possible."

"Sorry to barge into your conversation, but barging in might just hold the key to what you are discussing," Maybin said with a grin.

Amelia looked up at him with a sense of curiosity. Dex turned his attention to Maybin, who was stroking his finely trimmed goatee.

Maybin smiled as if he were the detective who just wrapped the mystery no one else could solve. "As Amelia mentioned in the recollection about her dad, there are oil refineries up and down the Australian coastline. It's not always practical to have the supertankers transporting crude oil from each refinery, some of which are small, so—"

Dex cut him off. "They use a barge!"

"Exactly," declared Maybin.

"And barge spills, which are far more common, are often unreported in the national registries."

"But the spills are certainly enough to kill a green sea turtle via a jellyfish," Amelia concluded.

"Yes," said Dex. "That is absolutely true."

Maybin added, "The green sea turtle is an herbivore, but maybe she ate the jellyfish hanging around seagrass."

"None of which explains the mystery of the orange particles," offered Amelia.

"True," replied Dex, "but I can't help but wonder if the jellyfish somehow connects to the orange particles."

"I don't see how," replied Amelia.

Once again, Maybin smiled. "Are you thinking about Aeternum?"

Dex hated to concede his years of experience to a local legend but bit his lower lip and said, "Maybe." He wasn't quite ready to give in to the myth of Aeternum so soon. All the normal routes of real scientific theory exhausted themselves far too quickly. With nowhere else to turn, he reasoned out loud, "We know jellyfish can swim near the sea floor. If Aeternum existed and the orange particles were part of this lost civilization, then I suppose a jellyfish could have brought the particles toward the surface."

"Where it was consumed by the turtle that turned orange," Amelia proclaimed.

Maybin beamed. He was proud of his young protégé but also of himself for helping to unravel the mystery.

"It's a working theory, that's all," Dex said firmly.

"I have a bathymetric survey of the entire area off Scrimshaw Beach," Maybin said.

Dex was grateful for this news. A study of the water depth and a map of the sea floor were just what he would have asked to see next. "Let's have a look."

They retreated to the conference room where the necropsy results were reviewed earlier that day. Maybin popped the bathymetric survey on the Palette. The Palette, divided into three sections, produced a display of the Coral Sea from the northeast coast of Australia, an analysis of the data, and a third panel for questions.

The three of them studied the left panel, which contained the hydrograph. Colors of the map changed from red on the outer rim to yellow, green, and blue on the inner core. Almost immediately, the analysis panel of the Palette began populating with data depicting the water depth associated with each color. On one end of the spectrum, red showed shallow water, and on the opposite end, blue signified the deepest part of the sea.

Along with the others, Dex listened as the baritone, Aussie-accented voice of the Palette recited the basics.

Coverage area: Unknown. Stretches across the Queensland Plateau. Sea depth: Variable, deepest 5,422 meters.

Dex quickly reviewed the basics and looked over at Maybin. "Switch the view over to the sea floor."

Maybin swiped his hand across the left panel, and the view changed instantly.

"I see nothing unusual on the sea floor," Amelia stated.

"Nor do I," said Maybin.

"Where do you think Aeternum might have sunk?" Dex asked.

"It's only legend, but I've been told closer to shore," Maybin said as he pointed to the area near Scrimshaw Beach.

"I expected to see a sea trench or something that might give us a clue," Dex said. "Nothing on this survey makes me believe there is any credence to the legend of Aeternum."

Undismayed, Maybin scratched the back of his head. "What if I sent an AUV here?" Maybin pointed northeast of the Queensland Plateau to the Coral Basin.

Dex considered the value of an autonomous underwater vehicle. "What's your rationale for that?"

"Look here." Maybin zeroed in on the outer edge of the survey.

Dex saw nothing at first but then picked up what caught Maybin's attention. It was a small blob of orange, a speck really, and almost undetectable. "I could have easily missed that."

"No worries. I have studied this survey dozens of times. This infinitesimal speck has always piqued my interest. Until now, I never had a reason to send an AUV to check it out."

Dex glanced at Amelia, who was taking in the conversation with great interest. He flashed her a smile, turned his attention to Maybin, and replied, "Now you do."

CHAPTER 12

The world was mourning the loss of Akeyo Gathee. Erik deBaak was not amongst the bereaved. Gathee's sudden heart attack stunned the world. Trying to calm her during their conference room meeting, deBaak simply placed his arm around Gathee's shoulders and pinpricked her neck. She was so distraught at the blackmail attempt, she never saw it coming. deBaak recalled the hollow apology proffered after the edge of his cufflink brushed against her skin. The cufflink was filled with an untraceable, time-released toxin. She died that evening in her sleep. With nowhere else to turn, the Ruling Council accepted Gathee's "endorsement" and named him the new leader of Earth, all before he left town.

He walked into his new office in Lower Manhattan and admired the view from the large floor-to-ceiling windows. *This office needs some serious redecorating.* Just as quickly, he dismissed the notion. He would serve as leader of Earth from his office in Rotterdam, coming to New York only when truly necessary.

Erik deBaak stared out the enormous picture window overlooking Manhattan. His right cheek leaned against the cold glass and gave him a chill. As he peered out over Lower Manhattan and its extensive poverty, his mind wandered back to the worst days of his life. The POW camp in São Paulo during World War IV, what they called The War of the Hemispheres. The global conflict ended twenty-four years ago, but for deBaak, it was always fresh in his mind. He vividly recalled returning home to Rotterdam to find his parents and his younger sister all reduced to intellectual rubble like millions of others. The horrors of Purple Dust, the banned chemical agent used by the Southern Hemisphere army, caused deBaak's misfortunes. Purple Dust was their misguided idea of humanely taming the enemy.

A knock on the door interrupted the worst of his memories. A young man stuck his head through the doorway as if he were timid about entering. "Excuse me, Leader deBaak. We haven't met. I am Jonah Currituck, your executive assistant."

Jonah was young, maybe twenty-five, and kept the classic look of a middleweight boxer. He was clean-cut and at first blush, very responsible. But he was Gathee's assistant. Time would tell whether he could be trusted.

deBaak managed a tight-lipped smile and approached the younger man. He extended his hand. "Excuse the gloves—one cannot be too careful. I am sorry for your loss. I assume you and Leader Gathee were close?"

"As close as we could be for only working together eight months."

It relieved deBaak. Jonah probably admired Gathee, but there was no long-term relationship. deBaak made a mental note to monitor him carefully.

"Is there anything you need at the moment?"

"Yes, for starters, I need someone to establish a user/login for me with full security privileges. And I need to review Leader Gathee's calendar with you. We will have to address which appointments to honor."

"Yes sir," replied Jonah. "I will get with IT immediately and be back shortly to review the calendar. Is there anything else?"

"Yes," deBaak nearly snarled, catching himself at the last moment. "Box up all of Leader Gathee's belongings in this office."

"What should I do after I box them? I understand she has no living relatives."

deBaak pondered his reply. He had the confidential information. Gathee's husband hid in a mountain retreat in Vermont . . . *at least until I can get him quietly transferred into Mercy.* "For now, place the items in storage. We will inquire amongst relevant museums to see who might like them."

"Yes, sir." With that, Jonah left the massive private office and deBaak returned to the picture window.

As it did constantly, his mind filled with the image of the grotesque Southern Hemisphere colonel torturing him with mindwave technology. To this day, he could still feel the electric current searing through his brain. Their vain attempts to procure information failed miserably. His will to prevail was stronger than their modern interrogation methods. In the end, he gave up nothing, even though the pain in his head was insidious. *How much longer could I have held on?* The Americans liberated the camp in the nick of time.

The doctors told him the headaches from that session would never go away. They served as a constant reminder of his anger's purpose. Throughout the entire war, the ineffectiveness of Akeyo Gathee always infuriated deBaak. Her weak leadership could not prevent the war's outbreak and did little to conclude it.

With Gathee dead, he now had the freedom to reimagine the planet as he saw fit. There would be no need to appoint someone to run Earth Reborn who was not truly loyal to him. From high atop the Manhattan skyscraper, Erik deBaak dreamed of a world devoid of overcrowding and illness. Food and shelter, the basic needs of mankind, should never be in short supply. To move the planet in the right direction before it was too late, he had to act. There was no one in his way. The real trick would be making everyone believe he was on their side.

CHAPTER 13

Nothing required her to be with Ken and Cecily Barker and their family, but Cam's heart ached for these good people. Had she kept her temper in check, Judge Jackson might have granted the exemption she sought, and this moment would have been avoided. Now, she sat in the sterile-looking room, cold and unfeeling with its scant furniture and bare walls. Her stomach was in knots, and she held Cecily Barker, trying to offer comfort while fighting back her own tears. This is all my fault, she lamented. She pulled away gently from the embrace and placed her hands on Cecily's shoulders, looked into her sad eyes, and said, "I'm so sorry." Then, she gave a nod to Ken Barker's two daughters and their husbands and approached the hospital bed where Ken Barker waited for what the Mercy bastards called "final disposition."

She sat down in the chair beside the bed and took in her client. Ken Barker looked pale and drawn. Photos from his recent past were in his legal file. The deterioration before her was evident. The hard plastic mask from the ever-present oxygen tank revealed a red rim around his nose and mouth. It relieved Cam when Barker looked at peace with what was happening. She thought of Tom. Again, she fought back the tears. She could never walk into any Mercy facility without feeling the pain from unfairly losing the love of her life. Tom never stopped fighting. Ken Barker was ready to meet his maker.

Cam gently squeezed his hand, bent over for a hug, and kissed him on the forehead. "Go with God," she heard herself say. These words of comfort would help Ken Barker, a religious man, but to her, they were hollow. She lost her faith a long time ago when the world's injustice caused her father to take his own life.

She retreated to the far corner of the room. Barker's two adult daughters approached the bed from opposite sides. The expressions of love made her well up. She reached for a tissue to blot her eyes. Memories of her own father flooded her brain. She never got to say goodbye.

With Cecily and her two daughters surrounding their loved one, a high-pitched tone pierced the solemn family moment. A red light above the bed flashed. Cam had watched this scene play out more times than she cared to remember. The five-minute warning!

Cam was all too familiar with this cold, vicious process. Ken Barker's family was not. They looked up at her with faces contorted in horror as the youngest daughter asked, almost in hysterics, "Cam, what's happening?"

Cam walked over, took her hand, and said as gently as she could, "It means you should say your final goodbyes." She resumed her position against the back wall and waited for the inevitable.

Time elapsed and two women in white medical garb walked into the room. One of them, clearly the Mercy medical officer, looked at the family and said in a cold, monotonic voice, "It's time. You can remain in the room, but you must go to the back, behind the observation panel."

Cecily and her daughters and sons-in-law each kissed Ken one last time and joined her at the back wall. The Mercy medical officer pushed a button on the wall and a large plexiglass screen lowered from the ceiling. From this vantage point, the Barker family could observe but remain unharmed from the process that would end Ken Barker's life.

Cam again fought back a tear as Ken said in his feeble, scratchy voice, "I love you," to his family.

Cecily and her daughters held each other tightly as the Mercy medical officer and her resident joined them behind the observation shield.

With a simple remote control, the Mercy medical officer depressed a red button activating eight round spheres of blue light from the ceiling that beamed down on Ken Barker. The concentrated zeyon rays would painlessly end Ken Barker's life in under thirty seconds. The flatlined heart monitor and its associated tone confirmed the obvious. The tone broke through the room like a flaming arrow penetrating a paper house. Instantly, the youngest daughter burst into tears. Cecily held her two daughters while their husbands stayed close and glumly looked on.

Cam couldn't breathe. Out of guilt, she maintained an obligation to be here, to offer comfort to the family. Her sympathy for the Barkers was rapidly turning to anger at a system that repeatedly failed good people. Her upper lip throbbed, the telltale signal that her anger was getting out of control.

The resident helped the medical officer cover the body. Cam involuntarily clenched her right fist. They wheeled the body out of the room, and Cam walked out right behind. Ken Barker's remains rode along the east corridor, following signs for the Crematie facility attached to the Mercy Disposition building. *Crematie!* The worldwide monopoly owned by the new Earth leader, Erik deBaak, a man whose reputation for greed proceeded his ascension to the world's top post. To her, deBaak was a symbol of everything that was wrong in the world. *And now he was running the planet? If he were here now, I'd spit right in his face.*

CHAPTER 14

The AUV they employed was named the J-Cous 5000 after the famed twentieth-century explorer for whom Dex was often compared. In Cousteau's day, there was nothing like this modern autonomous underwater vehicle. Back then, a limited-function AUV deployment required a large ship and a crew of several dozen. Today, Dex, Maybin and his team, a group totaling five, would handle the task from Scrimshaw Beach with a relatively small craft. While the J-Cous 5000 could run on its own power for months at a time, constantly sending data back to Maybin's office, this mission would be a day trip.

The trek from Lockhart was being accomplished with two vehicles. Dex and Amelia rode in his rented SUV with the boat in tow while Maybin, Noah, and Jack took the lead in a second SUV that hauled a flatbed trailer containing the J-Cous 5000. Maybin rented the AUV from a supplier in Brisbane. Maybin's employer, Nexterus Marine, covered the rental cost, although Dex offered to take care of the bill.

"Do you really think the AUV will find a sunken city from thousands of years ago?" asked Amelia.

Dex grinned. He was fighting it, but he had to admit he was taken with her. He couldn't help but imagine her in a formfitting wetsuit. Keeping his eyes on the road and Maybin's vehicle in front of him, he took his left index finger, pushed his shades up the bridge of his nose, and sighed. "I guess we can't rule anything out, but if you ask me, the chances of discovering such a thing are remote."

She shifted her petite body so it was angled toward him. The prior evening, he watched one of her Olympic performances and was very impressed. She still tied her hair in the same short, tight ponytail used when competing. They had a long drive, and he wanted to get to know her better. "I watched your gold medal performance at the 2166 games in Tokyo. Very impressive."

Amelia blushed and replied through a halted expression, "That was almost ten years ago." She paused, as if she mentally traveled to the competition from so long ago. "Sometimes I think it was just a dream rather than something I actually did."

"Don't lose sight of your accomplishments. The world has a tendency to forget."

"I'll try," she replied humbly. "I think one day, you know, for when I have kids."

Dex was always uncomfortable with that type of comment. Did she say that in casual conversation, or was she fishing to see if he wanted a family? He always found himself on the shy side with women. It was his modus operandi to be a gentleman and let nature take its course. He found that strategy helped his relationships with the opposite sex, few as they were, to develop naturally and on equal footing. Suddenly and without warning, a kangaroo appeared on the highway, causing Maybin to slam on the brakes. Dex did the same and had a moment of acute anxiety when the AUV trailer in front of him looked like it might come unhooked. In a flash, the kangaroo hopped safely off the road, and Maybin and his trailer straightened out.

"Did you see that?" he exclaimed with sweat now forming on his clammy forehead.

"The kangaroo?" she replied laughing. "For a tall poppy, you really are a bit of a lovable drongo."

Dex used a napkin left over from a drive-through meal to wipe the perspiration from his face. "You know, it sounded like English, but I have no idea what you just said."

Amelia laughed out loud, bit her bottom lip, and then blurted out, "A tall poppy is a successful person and a drongo is an idiot. I meant no offense, but your excitement at seeing a kangaroo made you sound like a wayward tourist."

"No offense taken. I may just need to teach you how to speak English properly," he joked.

"I'd say I already do!"

Dex admired the flirtatious banter and how, as a somewhat shy person, she had no trouble putting him in his place.

Amelia pointed to a highway sign up ahead indicating they were almost to Scrimshaw Beach.

"Is this your first time working with an AUV?"

"Yes, I admit it. I'm a virgin."

Now there was no doubt. Amelia Brown was definitely interested. Not wanting to jump into a precarious situation distracting him from his work, he arched one eyebrow and commented, "I'm sure this will be an excellent learning experience for you."

Dex could sense the disappointment in Amelia as he failed to engage. Fortunately, he was saved by the bell as he followed Maybin onto the access road for Scrimshaw Beach.

ooooo

An hour later, the AUV and the boat were in the water about nine hundred meters from shore. Maybin, driving the boat, declared, "We are nearing the point where we saw the orange speck in the bathymetric survey."

"Time to release the AUV," Dex responded.

Maybin instructed Noah and Jack to unharness the five-meter-long AUV and begin lowering it into the Coral Sea using the hydraulic lift-gate mounted to the boat.

As the men worked, Maybin glanced at Amelia, his least experienced crewmember, and said, "This J-Cous 5000 is a scientific marvel. It will, of course, take several measurements, such as water temperature, pH, and chlorophylls. In addition, the J-Cous 5000 will send us high-definition images and holograms in real-time via an underwater wireless optical transmission or what we call Li-Fi."

"Li-Fi?" asked a perplexed Amelia.

"It's short for light fidelity. It uses light to transmit the data," offered Maybin.

"Fascinating! We studied AUVs at university, but I've not worked one before," she replied.

Dex badly wanted to make a wisecrack about her being a virgin but held his tongue. It wasn't the time or place. "This AUV can also move pretty fast, up to twelve knots."

"That's correct," Maybin added. "It can also dig and retain samples for later examination."

"Yes, but this particular model offers some instant analysis, much like the hummingbird," Dex explained.

"Well, I am to learn quite a bit with two experienced marine biologists by my side, aren't I?" Maybin was clearly in instructive mode for his youngest team member. "It's downright amazing. The J-Cous 5000 has deployable miniature versions of itself that will leave the unit, explore small places, and re-dock, all in a matter of minutes."

"And," Dex picked up where Maybin left off, "the primary unit has a silt prevention system to keep the sea bottom calm while it procures data."

"You mean to keep the silt from getting stirred up and interfering with the mission?" Amelia inquired.

"Yes," answered Dex. "That's exactly what it does."

"Why, that's ingenious. How is that accomplished?" Amelia said curiously.

Maybin laughed, pulled his navy blue Nexterus Marine ball cap down from the bill, and said, "Don't know, don't need to know. I just need it to work as advertised."

With that, Jack yelled over that the AUV was ready to go.

Dex glanced Amelia's way. She was looking over the back of the boat, getting the full view of the AUV being lowered into the water. Dex appreciated the precision engineering of the J-Cous-5000. To Dex, it resembled a giant sturgeon, lithe and athletic but without annoying appendages that impeded data collection. They designed earlier models with great white sharks in mind, but the fins proved too cumbersome. The sturgeon design, coupled with the deployable miniatures for exploring tight spots, solved the problem. Older systems relied heavily on sonar for deep-sea depth measurement and discovery. Now, real-time video analyzed with artificial intelligence supplemented sonar. Short of being at the sea bottom himself, Dex couldn't have asked for better results.

The AUV's first mission would be to sweep the sea bottom in a preprogrammed route to create a new bathymetric survey in far greater detail than the basic one they viewed at Maybin's facility. Once that work was complete, data on the orange speck, as they referred to it, would be precise in terms of latitude and longitude. At that point, they would zero in on the coordinates and let the advanced features of the AUV take hold.

Below deck, Amelia had prepared the diagnostic equipment. A small bank of computers, flat-screens, and a table-based computer with a holographic portal were also present. In the small boat, there was barely enough room for four people to work with the equipment. They would leave Jack up top to captain the craft while the others analyzed the data.

While they waited for data to appear on the displays from the AUV, Noah rolled up his sleeve to show off his first tattoo.

"What is it?" asked Amelia.

Maybin joked, "It looks like a monster made of brown vomit."

Dex closed in on Noah's freckled right arm and said, "Don't listen to his crap. What made you choose a frilled shark?"

Dex scored points with Noah. The look on his face told the story. "Even though they are extinct, I love the legend of these sea bottom dwellers."

"From what I've read, man rarely saw them. They were quite unusual. Their bodies were eel-like, and their gill distribution gathered across the throat. If you've ever seen a picture of one, it would remind you of a creature from a horror movie."

"Sounds absolutely dreadful," Amelia exclaimed.

Noah playfully smirked, enjoying the controversy the image drummed up.

A split second later, a loud boom sounded, and the boat rocked perilously from side to side. Dex's senses immediately went on high alert. It was a beautiful sunny day; no storms were in play. *What the hell could have caused that?*

Dex fell back into a wall but was otherwise unharmed. Noah fell on the floor where Maybin, unscathed, was helping him back up. *Where was Amelia?*

Dex grabbed hold of the display table's edge and walked to where Amelia had been standing. She was on the floor, wedged between the table and the wall, holding her head where a bruise the size of an egg was already forming. He placed his arm around her and drew her to his chest. "Are you okay?"

She gazed up at him with sleepy blue eyes, clearly enjoying the closeness, and mumbled, "I think so."

"You have a knot forming on your forehead. Maybin, any ice on board?"

Maybin nodded in the affirmative and made his way to a modest refrigerator. Dex heard him call up to Jack to make sure he was okay.

"We need to watch you for concussion," Dex stated firmly.

Amelia stood up, ice pack affixed to her head, and said, "Thank you, doctor."

"Earthquake?" Dex offered as the boat settled.

"Battle debris, I'm afraid," reasoned Maybin.

Dex hadn't considered the possibility. "You mean the AUV hit a mine?"

"During World War IV, the northerners planted underwater mines in the Coral Sea to prevent the opposition from bringing aircraft carriers through the South Pacific with planeloads of Purple Dust," Maybin explained. "They manufactured the Purple Dust south of here in Tasmania."

"I was just a young girl when all that was going on. Purple Dust? Wasn't that some sort of chemical warfare?" Amelia questioned.

Dex shook his head, looking down, and said, "Yeah, I was in high school when the so-called War of the Hemispheres took place. Just missed being called up for the draft."

"I'm glad you weren't called up. But what did the Southern Hemisphere army use Purple Dust for?" she asked.

Dex shook his head in despair, as if not wanting to relive one of humanity's worst times. "You hit the nail on the head. Purple Dust is a chemical agent that doesn't kill but permanently reduces a person's intellectual capacity to that of an infant. It was the Southern Hemisphere's 'humane' form of warfare. They reasoned that this was better than killing people."

"Oh, how awful," she said sadly. "It makes me ashamed of being from a Southern Hemisphere country."

Maybin added, "Don't be. Both sides have plenty to feel guilty about. For a world war that lasted only eighteen months, the idiots in charge of the North and South nearly destroyed the entire planet."

"Over ideology?" she asked. "We studied the war in school while it was taking place, but I admit I had little taste for the subject."

Dex chimed in. "The North won the war after eighteen months but not before much of the landscape of both hemispheres crumbled. The North wanted and achieved population control, not in the desired manner but through bombing and electromagnetic storms causing radiation poisoning.

The North ultimately won because the South didn't have the desire to use as much deadly force."

Maybin added, "After the South deployed the first Purple Dust attacks in western Europe, the northern coalition leaders put an end to the conflict with deadly force, as Dex put it."

Amelia's face held a pained expression. It was interesting how insulated a young girl in Australia could be from a world war.

The history lesson was interrupted when the flat-screens and table display came alive with data. To everyone's relief, the AUV was intact and functioning. The new bathymetric survey lit up the room. The table display provided a 3-D holographic view of the sea bottom. Unfortunately, the best silt-prevention technology in the world couldn't stop the dustup caused by the mine encounter. It would be hours before the water's disturbance might settle. Considering Amelia's head injury, the planned search for the lost city of Aeternum would now have to wait.

CHAPTER 15

The Ruling Council convened at Earth headquarters for its first meeting under its new leader. Erik deBaak, dressed in a trademark tan suit with a white-collared shirt open at the neck, assumed his position at the head of the table in the room called the Sphere of Humanity. A rich and lustrous green leather chair adorned with gold edging was reserved for the leader. The other members of the Ruling Council sat in plush dark blue leather chairs around the large, round glass table held up by an impressive clear and shaded crystal globe of the planet.

As deBaak took his first look around the room where many of the world's most important decisions were made, he found himself in awe. It was still hard to comprehend his current position and how it materialized much more quickly than he could have imagined. Before convening the meeting, he glanced around the circular room and took in images of people from around the world intermixed with flags representing every country. Focused, he stood up and spoke to the assembled council of leaders from the world's nine largest economies. They were his to command.

"I would like to begin by thanking you for your confidence in me. I will work hard to preserve and promote the ideals of this great body and uphold those principles dedicated to the preservation of our planet."

deBaak looked around the table and welcomed the smiles and contained applause from the nine participants. A demonstrative speaker, deBaak raised one black-gloved hand in the air and emphatically stated, "Our first order of business is to recognize the extraordinary accomplishments of my predecessor, Leader Akeyo Gathee. It is vital that her legacy be acknowledged, preserved, and celebrated."

Again, the applause came from the small group, this time with more energy. Gathee was a beloved figure. He had no choice but to take this stance. "I have asked my staff to develop a detailed celebration of Leader Gathee's life and work. I hope to have a final recommendation to share within two weeks' time."

He glanced around the table, wondering who supported his ascension to Earth Leader and who might have opposed him. US President Morton Sofer was very amiable. Even now, deBaak was exchanging a warm smile with the athletically built man in his late fifties. His wavy brown hair was just turning gray at the temples. deBaak wasn't much of a baseball fan but was intrigued that Sofer was once an all-star first baseman for the Los Angeles Dodgers. He presumed, at least for now, that Sofer was an ally.

The old man of the group was British Prime Minister Winston Nottingham III. He was a portly man whose protruding stomach kept him from sitting too close to the table. He gave deBaak a friendly nod. *That's two in my camp.* Never having met any of these world leaders, he was unsure what to make of them, but deBaak valued trust highly. He would need to make it his business to determine who he could count on.

Before continuing the meeting, he detected contempt from the two Southern Hemisphere leaders, Karabo Radebe of South Africa and Willow Martin of Australia. These ladies were throwing him daggers. Leftover sentiment from having lost the war, he considered. Gustavo Souza, the president of Brazil, was tough to read. He was a big-boned man with huge hands, a bald head, and a stoic expression to match. Brazil was domiciled in both the Northern and Southern Hemispheres, but the country generally sided with the south. The other Northern Hemisphere leaders were

Zhang Jinhai from China, Yuuto Takahashi of Japan, Gabriele Fischer of Germany, and Selvi Kumar of India.

deBaak took a sip of water from the glass in front of him and considered his position. Under his command, he had nine world leaders. Six of them represented Northern Hemisphere countries, and five were men. Female leaders represented two of the three Southern Hemisphere countries. deBaak viewed that as a negative. He never thought much of women in power. *Too soft when the going gets tough.* He cleared his throat and asked for everyone's attention.

"We have a challenging agenda. This morning, I was handed data proclaiming thirty-five percent of the global population is now homeless. With just under one trillion people, that means three hundred fifty billion people are without homes and other basic needs."

Morton Sofer, the US president, was the first to respond. "As horrifying as that number is, we have made significant progress. Just ten years ago, the homeless population totaled forty-two percent."

"Yes, President Sofer, the progress is commendable, but there is much more that can be done."

Before he could continue, the Australian prime minister, Willow Martin, interrupted him.

"Your barbaric Mercy program is what we have to thank for that progress, as you call it."

deBaak controlled his disdain for her sarcasm. This small woman with the shiny, red shoulder-length hair was once an international movie star. That would explain her flair for the dramatic.

"Thank you for your input, Prime Minister. I don't think there is any doubt that Mercy, whether you consider it barbaric or in the best interests of the planet, has helped achieve our big picture goal."

Willow Martin stared at him with contempt, which, for the moment, he ignored. *No need engaging in a gunfight with someone holding a pocketknife.* Australia recently entered a major recession. It was entirely possible that their economy would drop out of the top nine and she would have to give up her seat on the Ruling Council. Perhaps he would see if he could hasten her demise by throwing a wrench into the Aussie gear works.

Winston Nottingham, the British prime minister, broke in. "With so many people living on the streets and out in the open, could we consider additional allocations of the Kenya Tabs?"

Selvi Kumar, the petite and youthful-looking Indian prime minister, spoke up. "I agree with Prime Minister Nottingham. My country is amongst the most overcrowded, and we clamor for more Kenya Tabs."

Kenya Tabs were the supercharged vitamin pills that dissolved in people's mouths. Named in honor of Gathee's place of birth and because it was her idea, the tablets were thought to have kept the homeless reasonably healthy despite their living conditions and extreme malnutrition. Pods routinely dropped cases with parachutes of these tablets on throngs of people all over the world. The results were mixed and the subject controversial.

Before deBaak could respond to Nottingham's suggestion, Yuuto Takahashi of Japan spoke up. "There is no data to justify the cost—only the belief that the Kenya Tabs are helping."

The South African president, Karabo Radebe, one of the oldest members of the council, was not shy about speaking her mind. "Esteemed colleagues, please understand that we must do everything possible to support the people who are without homes and living out in the open. These are human beings we speak of, not animals roaming the once fruitful plains."

deBaak sighed. He was just beginning to see the uphill battle in leading a group of powerful and opinionated people. Fortunately, there were provisions for him to enforce his will if the Ruling Council could not reach consensus.

The German chancellor, Gabriele Fischer, wanted the floor. deBaak noted the gigantic mole on her right cheek and the face chiseled from stone resting under an unattractive blonde mop. "If we cannot agree on Kenya Tab distribution, might we consider further appropriation of PSCs?"

This suggestion intrigued deBaak as a short-term measure. He once thought of buying the primary manufacturer of the personal sanitation chamber, or PSC, as they were commonly known. They erected these portable houses in places where people lived out in the open. A typical structure contained a misted disinfectant to "clean" a person and toilets to mitigate people's urinating and defecating in public. These PSC units were integral in the fight against pandemics. PSCs used minimal amounts of water and with the help of the Tanzig ray technology used in his newer crematoriums, waste disposal was not an issue.

Gustavo Souza, the menacing Brazilian president, growled, "Some overflowing areas of the world have no PSCs and infrequent drops of Kenya Tabs. We must consider these areas as ticking bombs for the eruption of a pandemic that could wipe out vast swaths of the population."

Not a bad outcome. deBaak could not possibly show his genuine feelings on the matter.

"And of food and water shortages?" asked Sofer. "We have to address these needs."

The group momentarily exhausted the search for answers, and the room fell quiet.

Then, with a roar, the one member of the Ruling Council who had yet to utter a single, solitary word, President Zhang Jinhai from China, broke the silence. "May I end this nonsensical and ill-fated conversation with the only sensible solution we have yet to discuss?"

deBaak didn't disagree with the Chinese leader's well-known position. He knew what was coming and let it play out. It would make his follow-up commentary seem welcome by comparison.

President Zhang continued, "If we cannot consider population control by limiting births, no amount of money and effort will preserve the earth for future generations."

Willow Martin of Australia was the first to respond. "It is just as horrifying an idea as Mercy."

deBaak cringed. This woman made him sick. She was nothing more than an impediment to progress. She always had a criticism but never an idea. "How do we feel about population control by placing limits on family births?" deBaak asked of the group. "Let's take a quick roll call vote to see if the idea is worth discussing further." One by one, deBaak called out the country of a Ruling Council member to have their vote recorded.

"South Africa?"

"I am against," replied Karabo Redebe, her aging face revealing the strain from the issue.

"United Kingdom?"

"Wholeheartedly no, my good man," came the response from Winston Nottingham III.

"United States?"

Morton Sofer paused and finally said, "I recognize the logic behind the idea, but morally, I cannot abide by the notion and vote no."

deBaak then looked over to President Zhang and said, "Being the sponsor of the idea, I take it you vote yes."

President Zhang nodded in the affirmative.

"Japan?"

Prime Minister Yuuto Takahashi looked at his colleagues with a pained expression. "This is a hard call amongst unprecedented times. I reluctantly vote in favor."

"Germany?"

Chancellor Fischer placed a finger on the oversized mole on her cheek and glumly replied, "No, absolutely not."

"India?"

Fidgeting in the chair that was too large for her small body, Selvi Kumar, surprising everyone at the table, stoically said, "I think we should discuss the idea."

"Australia?

This vote would be no mystery. The only question is how much drama the former actress might pour into her answer.

As if in character, she let her jaw drop in feigned indignation and stammered out, "Absolutely not."

"Brazil?"

The president of Brazil was built like a wrestler and had the attitude to match. Always ready for a fight, he took on the majority and proclaimed, "I stand with those favoring more discussion."

deBaak looked down at his informal tally. "Those against total five, creating a majority. I shall table the topic."

He immediately glanced at the Chinese leader. The look of disgust was evident. Clearly, President Zhang was wasting his time.

deBaak now took the reins. "With hundreds of billions living without basic human needs such as shelter and food, the constant threat of pandemics, and dwindling natural resources on the planet, something drastic must take place. If we are unwilling to consider limiting the birth rate, we must consider the only other reasonable alternative."

Again, Willow Martin was the first to speak. "You propose ramping up Mercy, I presume. What a shock."

deBaak tired of her antics. She lived in a bubble while people like him inhabited the real world and dealt with actual problems. He took her head on.

"Tell me, Prime Minister Martin, how long has the Ruling Council been discussing these same issues? I will bet these problems predate most of your memberships. In fact, haven't we already substantiated the progress brought on only from Mercy?"

Nottingham answered for him. "The question on the Mercy program is how far we go with it."

"Unless someone has a suggestion to create more room on earth, transport people to another planet, or magically restore depleted natural resources, I don't see we have a choice," deBaak declared. "President Sofer, what is your position?"

Sofer looked despondent but sure of himself as he answered. "As you all know, we were the last country in the Ruling Council to adopt the full Mercy program. We have explored every reasonable alternative, but without the ability to provide more healthcare facilities, doctors, nurses, medicines, and equipment, there simply was no other choice. I am afraid Leader deBaak is correct in his assertion that we must make the hard choice between preservation of the planet for future generations and our moral underpinnings."

deBaak grinned, acknowledging the influential opinion of the US president.

Selvi Kumar, the Indian prime minister, asked, "Do you have details on how an advanced level of Mercy would work?"

"Yes, I am preparing the final report now. It will detail all illnesses that are subject to Mercy and will place new limitations on Mercy exemptions granted by the medical court system. The new Crematie technology using the Tanzig ray will significantly reduce costs for disposing of remains."

"The whole thing makes me sick," declared Willow Martin.

"I understand, Prime Minister Martin. However, the alternatives are even more grim."

"I thought I was the only actor in the room," she said, almost yelling. "How do you sit there pretending to be the humanitarian when adopting this program at an advanced level will create massive profits for Crematie?"

deBaak held it in check and calmly replied, "It is true that adopting Mercy on an advanced level will require dozens of new Mercy Evaluation and Disposition Centers, as well as new crematorium facilities. I submit that this action alone will create thousands of needed new jobs to get people off government welfare."

He took the pulse of the room. Most everyone appreciated his point of view except, of course, Willow Martin, and to a lesser extent, Karabo Radebe of South Africa.

"Further, I recommend vendors other than Crematie receive a bid for future contracts. To the extent this is not possible, I remind you that Crematie can expand capacity as needed and will donate one hundred percent of all profits to the nonprofit organization I recently created, Earth Reborn."

Sofer came in to support the idea. "Earth Reborn. I read an interview you gave. Astounding and admirable. When will you have the details on the advanced Mercy program?"

"Soon," replied deBaak. "Once you have had adequate time to evaluate with your teams, I will arrange a video conference to see if we can reach consensus."

"Excellent!" said Nottingham. "Tell me, who do you have in mind to run Earth Reborn?"

deBaak expected this question. "Leader Gathee was to assume the mantle. But on her untimely death, I am afraid I had no clear second choice."

Morton Sofer spoke up. "I have a name for you. He is on the younger side, but I can't think of a more wholesome person dedicated to the idea of preserving the planet."

deBaak hated curveballs, and this was one. "Who might that be?"

"An American marine biologist named Dex Holzman."

CHAPTER 16

"It was absolutely horrible," Cam recounted to her best friend, the emotion pouring out of her with each sip of chardonnay, a beverage she rarely touched. Corey was asleep, so Gracie Harper, her best friend from the next block, with her own kids tucked in and her husband in charge, was sitting with Cam in the confines of her modest home on a balmy Friday evening. Cam appreciated her friend's sympathetic ear as she told the story of Ken Barker's last moments.

"The pain his wife and daughters were going through . . ." She gathered herself and continued. "It cut through my heart like a hot knife in butter."

Gracie sipped her wine, saying nothing. She was Cam's rock, the one who was there during and after her marriage to Tom. Gracie always understood and knew when to listen and how to help Cam regain control.

"It was like being with Tom all over again. The agony of trying to be brave. Trying to say goodbye . . ." Cam let go. The tears started rolling down her cheek. Gracie moved over, gently took the wineglass, and set it down on the wooden coffee table. She wrapped her arms around Cam and held on tight, not saying a word until Cam's strength returned.

"I'm not even sure I said goodbye to Ken Barker's family. I was suffocating and couldn't wait to leave. What they must think of me . . ." She began crying again. The second wave.

Finally, the embrace ended, and Gracie looked into her eyes and said, "Listen to me. After what you've endured with Tom, and Corey's episode at the MEC, you have every right to fall apart. That's why I'm here." She smiled and held up the bottle of chardonnay, still mostly full, and said, "And we still have this."

Cam took a tissue from a box on the coffee table and wiped her eyes, blew her nose, and cleared her throat. "Thanks, Gracie. I don't know what I'd do without you."

"Whenever you need me, you know that," Gracie replied.

Suddenly, Cam's stomach turned sour. Her eyes welled up once more. "And having to go to the MEC to get Corey." She sniffled and then let go. She sobbed, her chest heaving and nose stuffing up. "He's all I have left," she proclaimed through the falling tears.

"Corey's fine. My Patrick had a fever last week and bounced back in no time. You know how resilient kids are."

Gracie's arms embraced her once more. Cam held onto Gracie, trying to absorb her resolve to take things in stride.

"You're right. You held Patrick from school and nursed him back to health. Corey got sent to the MEC by that coldhearted bitch of a school nurse." Cam's emotions transitioned over the evening from raw, unadulterated anger to meltdown and were now coming back full circle. Letting go of Gracie, she again took a tissue to her aggrieved face. Another sip of wine and she actually laughed out loud. "I was so mad. I actually threatened to sue the county school system and name the nurse personally."

"You didn't."

Cam nodded and laughed again. "I don't think I'll get any PTA nominations for Parent of the Year."

"Don't worry about that bitch of a nurse. She's just a peon on a power play. Tomorrow is Saturday. You have the weekend to relax and take care of Corey."

"He seems better already. The booster they gave him at the MEC probably helped. He'll want to go out and play with his friends. I'll be the bad guy who keeps him inside and pushes the chicken soup."

"Mom knows best."

Gracie had done it again. She helped Cam regain her ability to deal with reality.

Then Cam's mind turned back to work. "I think I will fill my weekend reviewing every client file I have for patients needing a Mercy exemption. Every one of those cases just became infinitely more difficult with the new US Mercy standards."

Gracie shrugged. "I don't envy you. The world has become a different place from when we were kids."

"And it's going to get worse—and soon."

"Worse? That's hard to imagine."

"Count on it. With deBaak taking over as Earth Leader, he is going to up the ante."

"You really think so?"

"What sank Ken Barker's exemption was the US catching up to the rest of the world's Mercy standard. deBaak is on record saying he doesn't think that's effective any longer."

"Jeez, I don't want to think about it getting any worse."

"Me either. Try being on the front lines fighting for sick people victimized by this sadistic system . . ." Cam paused. Her protective sense overtook her train of thought. "Do you hear that?"

"I don't hear anything," Gracie replied.

"Wait—shhh." Cam sprung to her feet. "It's coming from Corey's room. A high-tone alarm. Never heard that sound before in this house." She hurried toward her son's room and opened the door.

Corey was sitting up, stirred out of sleep from the blinking sensor attached to his right arm.

Cam sat down on the edge of the bed and placed her hand on his forehead. "No fever. I wonder what's causing this thing to go off."

The next sound they heard was a loud, repetitive rap on the front door.

"Stay here," she instructed her son. Cam, with Gracie in tow, walked toward the front door where the incessant knocking continued.

It was nearly eleven o'clock on a Friday night. Who was banging on her door?

As she got closer, the deep voice called to her through the door. "Mrs. Atkinson, open up. This is the Mercy Enforcement Police."

CHAPTER 17

The lost city of Aeternum, basking in an orange glow, rose from the hologram portal in high-definition. Dex would've bet everything he owned on the sunken city being nothing more than a myth.

Amelia stood across from him, mouth agape as Noah and Maybin looked on.

Maybin ran to the doorway of the small cabin and looked up the short stairwell. "Jack, get your rear end down here. You gotta see this."

The four of them crammed around the small cabin, watching as the J-Cous 5000 delivered striking 3-D images with rotational views. Jack was simply too big to fit into the small cabin with the rest of the team, but he towered over the group, making his view of the hologram and monitor reasonably unobstructed.

"Maybin, it's an astounding discovery," proclaimed Dex. "We need to record this and capture samples of everything to identify the source of the orange substance."

"The J-Cous 5000 records automatically. I have two MS devices ready to deploy for detailed exploration and sample capture."

Amelia looked confused. "What's an MS device?"

Noah laughed at her and said, almost mockingly, "The MS stands for mini-sturgeon."

Amelia recalled the explanation provided in their failed attempt to find Aeternum. Dex and Maybin described how the J-Cous 5000, designed like a sturgeon, contained two miniature versions of itself to explore small spaces, record, dig, and capture samples. "Got it," she said. "It would be great if the MS devices could see through a silt disturbance."

"Actually, they can. We didn't find out till after the last expedition, but the MS units have rotating laser scanners that attempt to do just that," Noah interjected.

"Do they work?" Amelia inquired.

Noah just laughed. "Depends on the day."

Dex refocused their attention on the hologram. "For something that sank thousands of years ago, the preservation of this community is incredible."

Maybin nodded. "Legend has it that Aeternum was an island community, more of a village really, that had been sinking in unnoticeable amounts for hundreds of years. Then one day, a typhoon swallowed it."

Dex kneeled to get an eye-level view of the detailed hologram. "It's clearly suffered some decay, understandably, but my God, you can see the remains of stone housing and other structures, as well as the remnants of either footpaths or a primitive road system."

"I am blown away," declared Maybin. "The most peculiar thing is that the city is enveloped in orange. What in hell is causing that?"

"Maybe it's what you were sent here for in the first place," Dex stated.

"Come again?"

"You told me you came to Australia three years ago to discover whether this area held the key to solving the world's food supply issues."

"I did. Are you suggesting that humans will feast on the orange substance?"

Dex laughed. "Not exactly. But what if the orange substance was the key to the healing power locals claim the Aeternum people had? If that's true, then Nexterus Marine would play a huge part in extending life expectancy."

Maybin's expression changed to one of bewilderment, as if he hadn't considered the possibility. Finally, he replied. "And to think, just a few days ago, we spoke of Aeternum as the longest of long shots. What you are suggesting would be too good to be true."

"Whatever the substance is, there is a lot down there. It covered our dead sea turtle, but she didn't die from it. So, we know that whatever it is, it's not lethal, at least not to turtles." Dex considered aloud.

"We obviously need more data," Amelia said.

Jack was eager to contribute. "I have the remote for the J-Cous. I can deploy the two MS units. We just need to let them know where to go and what to look for."

Dex sensed Amelia's curiosity. Before she could ask, he offered, "The advanced AI in these deployable MS devices is the best in the world. Really, all we need is to offer a few keywords."

Amelia smiled and Dex scored points, answering her question before it could be asked.

Jack picked up the remote, pressed the MS1 and MS2 buttons, and said, "North and South entrances, orange substance, collect samples." He then depressed a green button, and the monitor on the cabin wall showed the two miniature sturgeon leaving their hulls and racing toward opposite ends of the sunken village.

"That's unbelievable," Amelia said incredulously. "Those few voice commands are all you needed?"

Dex smiled, "Advanced AI. Best in the world. Keep watching—it gets better."

Maybin reset the cabin monitor to display dual feeds so they could simultaneously watch both MS units work.

Dex glued his eyes to the screen, watching each unit efficiently make its way to opposite sides of the village remains. Dex estimated the remnants stretched out across two kilometers, so the second unit would need time to find its point of entry. While he waited, he glanced over at Amelia. Her concentration on the MS units was intense. He admired her thirst for knowledge. He knew she was interested, but what kind of life could he offer when he was always planning the next expedition? He remained married to his work. Besides, dating a woman who lived in Australia was the ultimate case study in someone considered "geographically undesirable." Dex snapped back into reality as an unusual scent permeated the small cabin.

To no one in particular, he said, "Do you smell that?"

Maybin was the first to reply. "It smells like an air freshener."

Amelia chirped in, "Like fresh flowers in a meadow."

Noah smirked. "Yeah, like the spray my girlfriend is always using after I leave the dunny."

"Dunny? What language are you speaking?"

Amelia giggled. "Dex, it's Aussie for toilet."

"Now I do feel like a drongo." Dex replied, remembering the word meaning *idiot.*

Noah broke in again. "Know a little Aussie, mate?"

Dex looked over at Amelia and said, "I have an excellent teacher."

Maybin laughed. "It took me quite a while to pick up what they call English here."

Reverting to a serious tone, Jack pointed to the hologram and said, "Look at that."

The hologram began portraying fields of orange flowers all inside the village floor. These plants were alive, and there were millions of them. Dex studied countless numbers of sea floor algae but had never seen a flower like this one. Its bright orange petals were wide, almost floppy looking. On the inside, the black pistil comprised three prongs standing in the center amidst rings of deep red and yellow at the bottom of each petal.

"They're beautiful," proclaimed Amelia.

"The MS units must be inside. These images are being transmitted from close range. Jack, make sure we collect as many samples of these flowers as we can," commanded Dex.

"You got it."

Now, Dex was even more intrigued by the legend of Aeternum. The flowers had something to do with the orange particles. Of this, he was sure. Now that Aeternum was a reality and not just legend, it was time to learn what, if anything, there was to the healing powers these people once claimed to have. Once the team collected samples, they could figure out how it all tied together.

"Maybin, can you help me find a local who has knowledge of Aeternum?"

"Certainly. I know just the guy. He's a superb storyteller, and he loves to talk. I just never took him that seriously."

"It may be time to start."

"I'll set up a meeting with the old-timer. His name is Toby."

"Where do we find him?"

"Don't exactly know. I found him one day sitting on a remote part of Scrimshaw Beach all by himself in a tattered shirt and trousers rolled up to the knees. He was just one with the sand and the sea, lost in concentration."

"Will we be able to find him?"

"I think so. There's a fishing village nearby. They don't use modern-day communication devices, so we'll just have to go there and ask around. I don't think it will be difficult."

Dex wasn't so sure. He also had his doubts about how much they would learn from old Toby the fisherman, but coupled with the data they were collecting, it was a building block in his hopes of helping the world off its perilous path.

CHAPTER 18

Peering out the window of the private plane afforded to the Earth leader, deBaak found it difficult to ignore the idea proffered by the US president, Morton Sofer. He was perhaps the most influential member of the Ruling Council and one whose nation never lost its seat because of a failing economy. Even in downturns, the US economy remained among the strongest in the world. No, deBaak could not afford to lose Sofer as an ally, but what did he really know about the world-famous marine biologist Dex Holzman? *Could Holzman be manipulated? Stupid thought. Of course he could. Everyone had a button to push.*

The plane was comfortable. It contained a private office and a press briefing room, as well as a bar and dining room, a traditional bedroom, and rows of double-wide, overstuffed airline chairs that fully reclined for longer trips. His travel party included staff members and his new security team.

Once in the private office, deBaak closed the door behind him and made sure it was locked. Sitting behind the polished cherry desk in the plane's executive office space, deBaak reverted to the computer screen and the search results on Dex Holzman. A well-known world traveler and explorer, he had literally been all over the globe. Holzman led expeditions on the seven seas and was the recipient of many awards, including the Nobel Peace Prize. Sofer had a point. Holzman was accomplished, respected, and still in his thirties, which meant he likely held a strong sense of ambition for whatever came next.

deBaak recalled Jonah's earlier instructions on how to make a call on the circular console. He liked Currituck, but deBaak wasn't sure he could trust him with anything confidential. deBaak activated the communication device with his thumbprint, placed his face in front of the recognition security screen, and then spoke the name of the person he needed.

In mere seconds, his screen filled with the image of the Crematie COO Hennie Van de Berg. Crow's feet formed around Van de Berg's blue eyes. Her short-cropped blonde hair was graying. After nearly a week in New York, her wide-eyed, toothy smile was a welcome sign.

"Hennie, we are on a secure line. I am calling from ninety-two hundred meters in the private office on my new plane."

He observed how she beamed with each word he spoke. Her normally placid complexion was blushing.

"Erik, you are amazing. The new leader of Earth? I had no idea that's why you were going to New York."

Even though she was his right hand at Crematie, he didn't fully trust anyone and wasn't ready to show his cards. "It's strange how things work out. My aim was simply to persuade Leader Gathee to step down and dedicate herself to Earth Reborn. Her sudden death took us all by surprise."

"But you? You as the new Earth Leader. I can hardly believe it." She paused, laughed out loud, and said somewhat seductively, "And to think, I am the lover of the most powerful man on earth."

deBaak ignored the overture. He didn't do romance and struggled with emotion. "I need your help."

"Anything. Just name it."

"I have a large staff at my disposal, but these resources are meant for the business of Earth. The new Earth Reborn organization is separate, and placing its first leader is a task I cannot ask my new team in New York to perform."

"I understand. Tell me what you need."

"President Sofer has recommended that I consider a marine biologist, Dex Holzman, for the top position. I need you to get a hold of OI and transmit everything they can find on Dr. Holzman."

"I'm on it, Erik. Will you be free tonight?"

"No, Hennie. I am tired and must rest. My new role will have me working nearly round the clock, seven days a week."

She looked crushed, but he wanted to fend off her next advance. He ended the transmission and turned his thoughts back to Holzman.

deBaak had a longstanding relationship with Chang, the owner of Omniscient Investigations, otherwise known as OI. They kept running files on nearly all well-known people. If there was dirt to be found, OI would uncover it. He would get a preliminary report within the hour and the dirt in a day or two.

deBaak engulfed himself in orientation documents from his New York staff and was becoming bored. He hated paperwork, routine matters, and rules. Others would handle the mundane nonsense. His mind must remain clear to handle strategic matters. A bright green ring illuminated around his combox. The display showed a new dossier arrived and was ready to view. He pushed a transmit button, and the dossier of Dex Holzman filled his screen.

CHAPTER 19

Cam looked at Gracie in horror. She was never free of the Mercy system. It was her clients who were often screwed by the warped population control concept. But now, with the Mercy Enforcement Police pounding on her door late on a Friday night, it was she who was victimized . . . again. The anxiety she experienced with her late husband came racing back. Her normally razor-sharp mind was reduced to jelly as she contemplated her son being taken from her. Cam looked at Gracie and said, "Take Corey to the bathroom and lock the door. Don't make a sound."

Before moving to the front door, she passed a waterfall picture and pulled it gently from its hinge, revealing a safe. Carefully, she punched in the familiar four-digit code and opened the vault. She removed her stun gun from its protective case and tucked it into her waistband. There was no way she was letting her son be taken. The stun gun would incapacitate but wouldn't kill. She straightened her hair, drew in a cleansing breath, forced a smile, and tried her best to act surprised as she greeted the unexpected visitors. "Good evening officers," Cam offered confidently with her best courtroom demeanor.

Two MEP officers stood on her porch. Each wore the standard oxygenated filtration mask. One was a tall Caucasian male with a neatly trimmed mustache and a narrow, angular face. His partner was Cam's height, an African American woman with piercing brown eyes. Although her partner was yelling through the door, the lady was the senior officer. She looked at Cam with a dead stare. "Camille Atkinson?"

"Yes."

"We have a report of a sensor going off on your son, Corey. We will need to take custody and transport him back to the Mercy Evaluation Center."

Cam peered over the shoulders of the officers invading her porch. The transport unit was in her driveway. Its flashing red lights were alerting all her neighbors to some sort of problem. She hated the transport units. The sick person rode in a rear isolation compartment to keep the officers safe from illness. There was no medical staff to help the sick person. What was the point? They designed the Mercy system to terminate the ill. They were deemed a burden to society's limited resources.

Cam evaluated her options and saw no good choices. As a civil rights attorney, she knew the MEP officers were well within their legal boundaries to do exactly what they were doing. Ordinarily, she would advise her own clients to let the process play out and allow her time to get the patient released. At that moment, she struggled to take her own advice. "I can't let you take him."

The stern officer stared her down and said, "Ma'am, you don't have a choice. Your son's sensor is indicating a diagnostic code for a mutated strain of virus that can be lethal."

The blood drained from her face. "Mutated virus?" She knew the law. The MEP officers had to give her the details of her son's illness.

The female officer looked down at her portable combox. "It says here, Reuben Syndrome Virus, mutated."

Not good news. Cam lost very few cases, but one of her more prolific defeats was from a nineteen-year-old girl with the mutated Reuben Syndrome virus—or RSV as they called it. They referred her client for immediate disposition. Cam found her temper flaring, as it always did when some sort of social injustice was occurring. This time, the stakes were a million times higher. *They were here to take her son away.*

Cam was trapped. The Mercy rules were changing rapidly. Who knows what surprise would be in store once Corey was inside the MEC? No, she simply couldn't take the chance he would go back to that horrible place and never leave.

"Corey was asleep. Come in. Let me talk to him and make sure he understands."

The dispassionate officer looked put off. "Fine, just make it quick."

Cam took a few steps away from them as if she were heading to Corey's bedroom. She pulled the stun gun from her waistband, turned, and with the element of surprise on her side, disabled both MEP officers.

Having heard the crackling static noise made by the stun gun, Gracie emerged with Corey from their hiding place. Cam wrapped her arms around her son. The sensor on his arm was still blinking brightly. She never wanted her life to be like this, and she certainly regretted her son witnessed her disabling two MEP officers. Cam gathered her resolve and let her logical side take over. "These officers will be down for an hour. Take Corey to your house. I'll be in touch."

Gracie nodded her assent and took Corey by the hand, leading him past the fallen officers and out the front door. Cam's brave exterior wilted as she observed the frightened look on her son's face. Cam watched Gracie help Corey into her car. She had to do something about all the flashing lights, the ones coming from the transport vehicle and the one attached to her son's arm.

Once Gracie's car was out of sight. Cam returned to the house. She went to the transport vehicle and turned off the flashers. No sense continuing to alarm the handful of neighbors who were already peering out their windows. Cam went back into her house, closed the door, and undressed the female officer.

Posing as the MEP officer, with key fob in hand, she got into the transport vehicle and drove it to the nearby Mercy Evaluation Center where she had just been with Corey. She was careful to park the vehicle a block away from the security guards. The objective was to get the vehicle off her street. The neighbors must be led to believe that nothing was amiss at her house and the transport vehicle left empty-handed. It was nearing midnight, and the incapacitated officers would soon regain consciousness. Time was running out.

Cam hopped out of the transport vehicle and pulled the portable combox from her back pocket. Walking away from the vehicle toward the woods where her call would not be overheard, Cam removed the filtration mask and dialed the number of her law partner.

He picked up on the third ring.

In a catatonic state, she uttered words in a voice she herself did not recognize. "Thurm, I've got a problem."

CHAPTER 20

Old Toby the fisherman wasn't hard to find. Locals in the fishing village pointed the trio of Dex, Maybin, and Amelia to a ragged housing structure with a small wooden pier overlooking an offshoot of the Coral Sea. When they approached, Toby was sitting on the pier's edge, fishing line in the water with a wide-brim straw hat propped loosely on his head.

Maybin, having previously encountered Toby on the beach, made the first approach. "Excuse me, Toby, it's Maybin. We met some time ago. Might we have a few moments?"

The old man slowly turned around and attempted to stand. He placed one hand on the pier to balance himself and then gradually stood up. He was a man of average height and had to be around eighty. His dark, leathery skin revealed a life led under the sun's powerful rays. The thing that took Dex by surprise was the old man's eyes. Some sort of growth, an almost opaque film, covered his brilliant green eyes. From the way the man moved, it was obvious he was blind.

Dex slid in behind Maybin to shake the old man's hand that was offered instinctively.

Toby possessed a powerful grip regardless of his advancing years. As Dex moved in closer, two round dots on the tip of Toby's wide nose caught his attention. It looked to Dex as if the old guy had the remnants of a snake bite. As the old man held Dex's hand firmly in his own, he said in a scratchy voice, "You're staring at my nose, aren't you?"

Taken aback, wondering how the blind man caught him in the act, Dex replied, "Uh, I apologize, sir. I guess I was. Unusual markings. Snake bite?"

The old man laughed, "Fishhook."

Before Dex could ask, Toby volunteered the story. "Half a century ago—I lose track of time—I was sitting on this very pier, teaching my grandson to fish. He couldn't have been over five or six. My wife called us in for lunch and with my back turned, the youngster tried to cast the line into the water, but it flew back at me like a boomerang. Just as I turned toward him, the hook lodged in my nose. Took the village shaman a full hour to extract it. The boy felt awful, but I always told him it was like a tattoo. Something no one else had that reminded me of my love for him."

Amelia teared up at the heartfelt recollection.

Dex simply said, "That's really touching Mr. . . . I'm sorry. I don't know your last name."

"Just Toby. It's the only name I ever really needed."

"Would you mind if we asked you some questions about Aeternum?"

The old man grinned. "Aeternum? One of my favorite stories to tell. Generations have handed down those tales."

"Tales?" Amelia asked.

Toby turned his head in her direction. "Some folks think so, but not me. I know it's true."

"How do you know?" inquired Maybin. "What makes you so sure?"

Toby reached into the pocket of his trousers and pulled out a shriveled orange object. "Because of this."

To Dex, it resembled a fragment of parchment in a museum.

Old Toby raised the object to his mouth, took a bite, chewed, and swallowed. He continued, "It's a dried Aeternium petal."

Amelia's curiosity went on high alert. "You mean a flower petal?"

The old man nodded, "Yup. Did you notice that the people in the local village are all old like me?"

Maybin nodded and said, "Yes, although there is nothing peculiar about that."

Toby grinned again and said, "You probably wouldn't believe me if I told you, but I just turned one hundred and five."

Amelia gasped. The old man looked good for eighty. But one hundred and five? He was still pretty active.

"To you, I'm an old man, but in this village, there are many of us over one hundred. We all eat Aeternium petals. If we are sick, the petals cure us. If we are well, they keep us healthy."

It amazed Dex. "How do you know about these flowers?"

"We didn't at first. Plague came and wiped out most of the village about a quarter century ago. It took my wife and most of my family. Somehow, I survived. The village shaman was the one who put two and two together. His family knew more about the Aeternum civilization than anyone. He started handing out these dried petals and advising those of us who survived to eat them."

"We saw endless fields of these flowers at the bottom of the sea. How does your village harvest them?"

Toby laughed. "The bottom of the sea? You can find them most anywhere around here. He led them to the end of the pier and told them to look to their right. Fields of the same orange flower with the three-pronged pistil and the red and yellow stripes danced before them in the gentle breeze.

"They're beautiful," Amelia declared. "And the scent. It's the same as what we smelled on the water."

Dex was beaming. The brief time he spent in Australia was proving to be nothing short of magical. He looked at Toby and asked, "Do you think your shaman would speak with us?"

"You missed by a week."

"Oh," replied Dex. "Is he traveling? When will he be back?"

“He’s dead. His heart just gave out. Old guy was one hundred and nine.”
Amelia jumped in. “Wasn’t he also eating the Aeternium petals?”
Toby just laughed. “Nobody lives forever.”

CHAPTER 21

"I am sorry Erik, but your father is dead."

The words from Uma Nordgren, the Arnhem Center administrator, rang through deBaak's brain like the horrifying screech of a prehistoric bird. The guilt overwhelmed him. Back in Rotterdam for two days, he had yet to visit his parents or sister. The institution housing them was the best in the world. He should know. He founded the treatment center to care for victims of Purple Dust in the aftermath of World War IV. His father was once the CEO of a prominent bank, and his mother an anthropology professor. His sister was in medical school. The deBaaks were an influential family in the province of South Holland. Now, his only living family members had the intellectual capacity of infants. It broke his heart. He was just like Gathee, stashing relatives away where they couldn't be touched by the population control he himself created.

A sharp pain lit up the back of his head. Reaching into his pocket, he extracted one of those useless pills. He swallowed the medicine with a glass of water and closed his eyes while inhaling deeply. The pain would subside, but feeling like a hypocrite would not.

deBaak boarded the AirStadt and waited for his pilot to transport him the short distance to the treatment center in Arnhem. Strapped in, he pondered throwing in the towel on Earth Reborn. While he dreamed of restoring the planet, the original notion was simply to get Gathee out of the way and clear a path for his ascension to Earth Leader.

But something was stopping him. This Holzman fellow intrigued him. As Earth Leader, wouldn't it be politically expedient for him to start a global nonprofit to help the planet's restoration? He shook his head and concluded he was on the right course. deBaak's review of the OI file revealed precious little outside the normal accomplishments and accolades. *If no dirt existed on Holzman, I could create some scandal when and if the time arrived.*

As the pod graced the Dutch skies, deBaak's heart turned heavy as he thought about the day ahead. The Arnhem Center was in a densely wooded area overlooking a serene lake. There were so few places like this left. Even though his parents and sister could no longer process people, situations, or even basic conversation, he wanted them to live out the rest of their lives in serenity. Nothing was more important.

He drew in a deep breath and stepped down from the AirStadt. The scene was familiar. Rolling hills and adults, many elderly like his parents, playing outside with the toys of small children. Physically, the Purple Dust victims were in good shape. They lost the ability to speak and could no longer take part in society. There were no medications or therapies. The aim was merely to care for them like a parent would for a newborn.

As he walked from the landing pad to the beautiful cobblestone building, Uma Nordgren, the facility administrator, met deBaak. She had been with the Arnhem Center since its inception.

"Erik, I am so sorry about your father. Our physician said he merely died of old age."

Taking her hand, he replied, "Thank you, Uma. I take a measure of solace knowing that Papa didn't understand his demise and likely suffered no anxiety about growing old or dying."

"We have the body prepared for transport. I assume you will take him to Crematie in Rotterdam?"

"Yes, my pilot will assist the orderlies in moving the body to the AirStadt."

"Will there be a memorial service? I'd like to attend."

His father deserved better, but he had no family left. Friends and relatives from before World War IV were dead or victimized by the dragon's breath they called Purple Dust.

"I appreciate your support, but the service will be private."

"I understand. Come, Erik. I will take you to your mother and sister."

deBaak sighed. Although he pictured exactly what was to come, he was never truly prepared. They walked in silence toward the main building. deBaak tried to draw strength from the natural beauty of the land. The sun glistened on the lake, and a light breeze rustled through the leaves of the tall downy birch. This tiny haven was a peaceful respite from what the rest of the planet had become.

deBaak ambled, enjoying the intermission from reality. He was in no hurry. As they approached the building, he saw them. His mother and sister were sitting in the grass on top of a pink fleece blanket and gleefully rolling a large rubber ball back and forth to one another. A tear formed in his eye. His stomach filled with turmoil as he meandered toward his remaining family, knowing full well they would have absolutely no idea who he was.

Instinctively, he called out, "Mama, Mama, it's Erik."

The older woman looked up at him and giggled like a baby in a playpen. She turned her head away and rolled the ball back to her younger playmate, his sister, Yara. Try as he might, deBaak couldn't hold back the tears. He told himself he lost his father twenty-four years ago when the lowlife scum from the Southern Hemisphere dropped the Purple Dust on Rotterdam. He never imagined this day to be as tough as it was.

Anyone else would have the comforting embrace of a family member to help ease the despair. For deBaak, there was no one. He wiped his eyes with his sleeve, apologized to Uma for his breakdown, and forced a smile and a wave to the infantile adults who were his mother and sister. Then, he turned and walked away, vowing to avenge his family and the millions of other Purple Dust victims.

CHAPTER 22

"Do you still have the stun gun on you?" asked Thurman Baugh.

"Yes," Cam replied through a shaky voice.

"You are going to need to hightail it back to your house and zap them again. I'll meet you there."

"Understood," was all she said. She never knew how underhanded Thurm could be. Over many years, he was a gentle giant of social justice. This man was a kind soul. But, she reasoned, people in crisis are moved to do strange things. Until tonight, she never imagined herself disabling two MEP officers. *People in crisis . . .*

Cam was a recreational jogger. On this night, adrenaline carried her back to her street in record time. She couldn't risk the MEP officers regaining consciousness before she got home. As she approached her house, Thurm's luxury sedan was in the driveway. He was waiting on her front porch.

"Thanks for coming, Thurm. I didn't know who else to call."

He draped his beefy arm around her shoulders and replied, "You did the right thing."

Cam opened her front door and entered first. The male officer was stirring on her floor. She observed his hand feeling along his waistband in search of the gun she pocketed before leaving.

The officer lifted his head off the wooden floor and with a sudden clarity screamed, "Hey, what the—"

Cam fired the stun gun into his forehead, causing him to fall. She moved the gun to the female partner, lying on the floor in her bra and panties, and fired into her chest.

Thurm nodded his approval. "Get dressed in your own clothes but leave her uniform off. We need to move these bodies. Where did you leave the transport vehicle?"

"About three kilometers from here, just outside the MEC security gate."

Thurm turned his back as she removed the MEP uniform and put her own clothes back on. Thurm looked over at her and said, "We need to get these bodies in my car. One in the backseat, one in the trunk."

"Where are we taking them?"

"Back to the transport vehicle."

"What happens after they wake up?"

Thurm took a pre-filled hypodermic needle from his jacket pocket and with a deftness she didn't know he possessed, injected the female officer in the neck.

Shocked at how little she knew of her mentor and friend, she asked, "What are you injecting her with?"

"We used to call this stuff a date rape drug. It will effectively impair her memory."

It confused Cam. "I appreciate your help here, Thurm, but I'm not following the plan."

"You'll see. Help me get this guy into my backseat."

With Thurm lifting by the shoulders, Cam grabbed the feet and struggled under the officer's weight. She barely had his feet off the ground. Her back strained mightily and her calves roared as she helped Thurm shove the body across the backseat of the huge sedan. Thurm popped the trunk, shifted some loose articles around to make room, and said, "The young lady will be a lot lighter."

After depositing the second unconscious officer in the trunk, Thurm said, "Climb in the front. I need you to guide me to the transport vehicle. We have a little more heavy lifting to do."

The three-kilometer drive took five minutes. Most of the homeless retreated from the suburban streets and into the nearby woods where nights were spent. When Cam and Thurm approached the abandoned transport vehicle, they placed both officers along the road, and Thurm laid out the plan.

"Strip them both down."

"Completely?"

"Every last stitch."

"Thurm, what the hell?"

"They are going into the isolation chamber. We are staging a rape."

"What? A rape? Are you crazy?"

He placed his hands firmly on her shoulders. "Cam, you need to get a grip here. Everything's going to be fine. This isn't my first rodeo."

Her legal instincts kicked into high gear. "You injected the woman with the date rape drug. She won't remember anything. But the guy will remember everything. He'll claim he was set up. And . . ." she continued, "the records still show they were coming to my house to pick up Corey."

Thurm just looked down at her with a confident grin and produced a popsicle-shaped probe. "That's why I brought this."

She looked at the man she once thought of as her personal role model and couldn't escape the feeling of disgust. "Is that what I think it is?"

"Gotta show penetration."

"Oh, Thurm. This is insane."

"Gotta do what we gotta do."

"That man will vehemently deny everything."

"That may be. But consider a naked man on top of a naked woman with a date rape drug in her bloodstream. She will claim he penetrated her. The ER docs will corroborate her story. Who's going to believe the guy?"

"I don't know whether to thank you or report you."

"Oh, you should thank me, for sure!"

Then, with a sudden realization, Cam blurted out. "What about Corey? We'll never be free from the long arm of the Mercy Enforcement Police."

"That's right, you won't. Give me till noon today. You and Corey are leaving the country . . . for good."

CHAPTER 23

"The legend of Aeternum is true after all," declared Dex, who always enjoyed the thrill of discovering new things. This was light-years beyond any prior advance. He high-fived with Maybin and turned to Amelia. Without thinking, he picked her up and spun her around like two figure skaters in a dance. When the move concluded, he gazed into her beautiful blue eyes, caught up in the moment but realizing he could not let emotion dictate his actions. He felt foolish as he looked up and apologized to Maybin and Amelia. Old Toby looked on and was smiling. Dex wasn't sure how, but the blind man knew exactly what just went down.

Toby laughed, "Don't apologize for being in love."

Amelia immediately turned crimson. "In love? We barely know one another."

Toby shook his head and said, "Been around a long, long time. You could have fooled me."

Dex admired the old man and his down-to-earth propensity to see people for who they really were. He desperately wanted to change the subject. "The Aeternium flower is the origin of the orange substance, and if Toby is correct, it is also the source of the healing power the people of the village claimed to have had."

"Still have," corrected Maybin.

"It's the most beautiful flower I've ever seen," Amelia said. "And the aroma is unique."

"With all these plants growing on the surface, we won't have to harvest them from the sea bottom," Dex said with relief.

"Harvest?" asked Toby. "I can't see a lick, but my hearing is pretty good."

"Yes, if these flowers have the healing powers we think, it would solve a lot of problems."

"What kinds of problems?" inquired the old man.

Dex paused and considered that Toby likely never left this village. "Toby, have you traveled much in your lifetime?"

The old man suddenly beamed with pride. "You betcha. Been to every village in this part of Australia, and when I was a boy, I visited Brisbane."

Dex looked at Maybin. They both nodded in realization that the ancient fisherman was oblivious to the overpopulated planet and its related miseries.

Amelia beat them both to the punch. "Toby, where we are . . . where you live . . ." she stammered, searching for the right words to help him understand. "This place isn't like the rest of the world."

"What do you mean?" he asked, his face crumpled in confusion.

Maybin jumped in to help. "Toby, the rest of the planet, it's overrun with people. Many have nowhere to live. There's not enough food to eat. People get sick easily—"

Dex cut him off. "And worst of all, the governments of almost every country in the world have adopted a barbaric program they call Mercy. It is intended to reduce the population to save the planet's resources for future generations."

The old man's face relaxed. He understood. Dex was sure of it. "So, you want to harvest the Aeternium flower to heal the sick and keep everyone else healthy?"

Dex smiled, "Yes, exactly." For an old fisherman who spent his life in a remote Australian village, he was pretty sharp.

"Won't that just make things worse?"

"True. A greater number of healthy people will make the planet even more crowded and place resources in higher demand."

"But," Maybin jumped in, "it is the better problem to have."

"And it can hopefully lead to the end of that awful Mercy program," Amelia stated. "All we need to do is harvest the flower and figure out how to replicate its healing qualities in an easy-to-use form."

Toby smiled and held out his hand. "You mean by sun-drying the petals and eating them like we do?"

Dex wanted to be polite. He hesitated and then replied, "Well, yes, that would be one way. Another might be a serum for an injection or a pill or liquid to swallow."

"I see," the old man nodded. He took off his hat, scratched his head and said, "Only one problem."

"What's that?" asked Dex.

"The Aeternium flower can't be harvested."

CHAPTER 24

deBaak's throat was raw from screaming. The pain from the mindwave contraption was frying his brain. He tossed and turned violently in his bed as the sheet tangled up with his sweat-laden body.

"Erik, Erik, wake up. You are having a nightmare."

He awoke gradually, taking a moment to realize where he was and why Hennie Van de Berg was lying next to him. Then he recalled relenting to her constant overtures. He sought a modicum of comfort following the trip back from Arnhem with his father's remains. He looked up at Hennie, who lay next to him propped up on one elbow. He stared into those sleepy blue eyes he admired more than the woman herself. At least she was someone who cared. He wasn't sure who else he could place in that camp.

deBaak wiped the sweat from his brow and stood up. He went to the bathroom sink, cupped both hands together, and doused his face with cold water. When he looked in the mirror, he was aghast at the haggard man looking back. His normally concave cheeks were more pronounced, and his blue eyes appeared dead, receding deep in their sockets.

Retreating slowly from the metal basin, he turned and fell softly into bed. Lying on his back, he stared at the ceiling, watching the blades of the fan above spin endlessly, like the process in which his mind was presently engaged.

"Erik, what's wrong? If you tell me your nightmare, it won't recur."

"If only that were true," he replied cynically. "That nightmare will never be over."

"But why? I don't understand."

Feeling vulnerable in his state of mourning for his father, he looked at Hennie and said, "I've never talked to you about my experience as a POW."

She shook her head from side to side.

"I was flying a recon mission near São Paulo when my plane began having engine trouble. I was able to make an emergency landing on the remnants of what was once the jungle. I hiked about a kilometer from the plane, trying to distance myself, and then fell asleep against a palm tree. I must have been spotted during the landing, because shortly thereafter, I was apprehended by the Southern Hemisphere allied forces."

She looked stunned. "I . . . I never knew. What happened next?"

"They threw me into a windowless stone cell with nothing but a pot to piss in."

"What did they want from you?" she inquired with apparent concern.

"I was a spy for the Northern Hemisphere. My mission was to discover anything I could about the enemy's plans."

"Were you successful?"

"No, they captured me early in the game. The only information of value I possessed was the names and positions of my side."

deBaak gathered himself, knowing what part of the story came next. He wasn't sure he wanted to, or even could, continue. But Hennie's eyes seared through his defenses. Slowly, he told the agonizing story of his imprisonment, how he wasted away to nothing and was treated like an animal.

The tears were forming in Hennie's eyes. After he completed the recitation, she wrapped her long arms around him and held on tightly. When the embrace concluded, Hennie stroked the side of his shaved head and asked, "What happens next?"

For the longest time, deBaak didn't reply. He measured his words carefully, weighing exactly how much he wanted to reveal. "My mother and sister and other local Purple Dust victims will live out their lives in comfort in Arnhem. Millions of others aren't so fortunate. The Southern Hemisphere leaders who made the call on Purple Dust are dead or out of office. The war of the hemispheres was about population control. As part of the victorious Northern Hemisphere Allied Forces, I introduced and escalated Mercy across the globe. As Earth Leader, I can punish those who oppose limitations in my own way."

Hennie looked alarmed. "What are you going to do?"

He grinned and replied confidently, "I will make sure there is no escaping Mercy."

PART II

CHAPTER 25

The sensor on Corey's arm had to disappear so they could do the same. The device could reveal their location anywhere in the world. Cam held onto Corey's arm while Thurm, using a disinfected kitchen knife, gently eased the blade underneath the sensor and pried it off. As soon as the device dropped to the floor, Cam was ready with a washcloth and bandage to clean and dress the wound.

Then, without warning, she became dizzy. Her mind went backward to the prior evening as she recalled the words of the MEP officer: "Reuben Syndrome Virus, mutated." RSV was deadly. There was no known cure. Cam recalled researching scientific advances toward a treatment, but the FDA had approved none. The medicines they were working on were for the original virus strain, not the mutation. Now, she would be on the run to God knows where without a clue how to help her terminally ill ten-year-old. The world was crashing down, and she had nowhere to hide. Staying in the US with its newly ramped up version of Mercy was a death sentence for her son.

"Your flight leaves in four hours," Thurm stated.

"Where are we going?" she asked, hating the panic in her own voice.

"You will fly to Canberra and meet with Prime Minister Willow Martin. From there, you will travel to a town called Lockhart, just north of Brisbane."

"Australia? I don't understand."

"Willow Martin is a known anti-Mercy leader. Governor Samson was able to arrange a meeting, explain the situation, and ask for help."

Cam shook her head in disbelief. "You got the governor of California to intercede on my behalf?"

He looked at her fondly. "You know I'd do anything for you and Corey. You've had much too much pain in your young life. This will be a fresh start."

Still feeling overwhelmed and confused, she replied, "Thurm, I appreciate everything you've done for me, but how will I earn a living? I can't practice law in Australia. And what about Corey and the Mercy program?" The muscles in Cam's neck tightened, and her eyes moistened. A breakdown was coming. It was just too much to process.

Thurm patted her on the arm in a gesture of assurance. "Everything will be okay. Prime Minister Martin will give you and Corey asylum. She has a patient advocate office for the Australian Mercy program, which is like the US level we just left. You will run that office in Lockhart. It's an administrative post, but you will set policy and guide the staff. They will evaluate Corey soon with the best epidemiologist in Brisbane."

"Will the Australian authorities grant Corey a Mercy exemption?"

Thurm paused. "Cam, I'm going to level with you. There's no guarantee, but if you win over the prime minister, I'd say you have an excellent shot."

She exhaled and tried to remain composed. "I can only pray. You know I will make a compelling argument. Maybe there is some sort of experimental drug being developed that the Brisbane epidemiologist knows about."

She gave him a hug and buried her face in his massive chest. "What will you do about our law practice here? We are already short on needed staff."

He stroked her hair in a parental gesture and replied. "Don't you worry. I'll be over at the USC Law School before the end of the week.

The dean owes me a few favors. I'll start with internships and parlay them into full-time positions once they graduate and pass the bar."

"You've thought of everything. How can I ever thank you?"

He smiled warmly. "Make sure your son gets well and you make a difference in this messed up world."

CHAPTER 26

"Others have come before you," offered the ancient fisherman.

"Others?" asked Dex. "What others?"

Toby shrugged his shoulders. "Couldn't tell you who they were, but they had the same idea. The Aeternium flower will save the world."

"Probably big pharma," stated Maybin. "Something like this would mean billions."

Dex was curious. "Did these others attempt to harvest the Aeternium flower?"

"You betcha," Toby replied. "After they uprooted the first batch, the heavens rained down."

"Are you saying that they ran into some bad luck after the harvest?" asked Amelia

"You could say that. Legend has it that the god who guards these plants caused them to wilt and die as soon as they came out of the ground. Made the petals useless," lamented Toby. "Another time, the flowers caught fire."

"So, this guardian spirit allows you and the other villagers to pick and eat the petals, but no one else?" inquired Maybin.

Toby nodded. "That's right. We don't know why, but Byamee views our village favorably."

Amelia lit up. "Byamee was the name of the Aborigine god who created the world. We studied this in grade school."

Toby smiled. "That's right, young lady. The Aborigines once occupied this land, and their god still rules over the people. The villagers never challenge Byamee."

"And you believe this Aborigine god caused the plants to wilt to prevent profiteering?" asked Dex.

The old man again shook his head in the affirmative. "Never been more sure of anything in my entire life."

"So just to be clear," said Maybin, "If we harvest these flowers for healing, this Byamee will inflict some sort of harm on the crop or us?"

"That's right," said Toby. "You can try, but I've heard of Byamee wiping out boats and planes full of people trying to come in here and take these flowers."

Amelia, the lone Aussie in the group, concurred. "You know, it's quite funny, really. Now that Toby is saying this, I have heard of planes and boats just vanishing in the Coral Sea, but no one could ever explain why."

Toby just laughed gently. "Now you know."

Dex thanked Toby for his time, and the three marine biologists began walking toward the beach.

Toby yelled back to them, "Oh, one more thing."

Walking toward Toby, Dex answered politely, "Yes, sir?"

"You might think you don't need to harvest the flowers here. You know, you could just get the seeds and grow your own somewhere else."

Maybin smiled and said, "I actually thought of that."

"Well, forget about it," the old man replied. "Byamee only allows the flowers to grow in this village. Our village has the younger men guarding the fields to prevent poaching."

"Thanks, Toby. We'll take it under advisement," Dex replied as the three marine biologists once again turned to leave.

Maybin looked distressed. "Dex, where do we go from here?"

Dex was a man of science. He dealt in facts and data, not legends handed down from generation to generation by remote Australian villagers. "It's a good question. We need to think everything through."

"Tell me you're not considering walking away from something that could save the world because of an old fisherman's tale."

Dex placed his arm across Maybin's shoulder in a show of assurance. "We have the Aeternium flower samples brought in from the MS units of the J-Cous. Let's run a few tests on the samples to determine if these flowers have the healing power Toby suggests. Then, we can decide what to do."

"You can't ignore how old all the people in that village are," declared Amelia.

Dex was cynical. "Did you check any birth certificates?"

She blushed and looked down at the ground, clearly embarrassed. "No . . . no, I didn't. But why would Toby lie?"

Maybin shrugged. "Maybe it's just a tale they tell to keep unwanted people out of these parts."

Amelia, looking lost, asked, "Dex, what do you think?"

"I think I want to see the diagnostics on the samples we brought up."

CHAPTER 27

Dex's portable combox illuminated and a mini hologram arose from its base. He instantly recognized the image. Who wouldn't? It wasn't every day that the leader of Earth called. And he had missed the call, which had come in while he was visiting with Toby in the remote village. The hologram began speaking to relay the contents of the recorded message.

"Dr. Holzman, it took some time to track you down. My administrative assistant has been leaving messages at your California research facility. They said you were in Australia and provided the link to your portable combox. I have an interesting opportunity for you and hope that we might speak in the next day or two. I am currently in Rotterdam. If you reply to this message with your availability, I will receive an alert and call you back."

Dex replayed the message. Simply stated, it stunned him. He couldn't fathom why Erik deBaak would want to speak with him. The current time was 9:15 p.m. in Lockhart. Rotterdam was eight hours behind. Dex hit reply and let Leader deBaak know he would be available for the next three hours and again the following evening. Still bewildered why he would receive a call from the man overseeing the entire planet, he stripped down and headed to the shower. He stood and let the hot water pour over him, erasing the stress of the day.

With his eyes closed and his mind lost in deep thought over the mysterious Aeternium flower, he was nearly oblivious to the sound of the shower door opening. Amelia's petite frame nestled up to him as she looked up with loving eyes. "I hope you don't mind," she gently proffered.

For Dex, it was like a fantasy came to life. He took her into his arms, leaned down, and kissed her on the mouth. With their tongues entangled in a furious release of passion, she pressed closer to him as the hot water washed over their bodies, joined as one. Dex reached back, turned off the water, and carried Amelia over the threshold to the bedroom. An hour later, exhausted, he kissed her and asked curiously, "Just how did you get into my condo?"

She giggled in the way he loved and replied, "You didn't lock your door, silly." She sat up and pushed her damp hair straight back with both hands. "Really, I was just coming over to talk about today. When I heard the shower running, well . . . I just acted spontaneously."

He smiled and said, "I'm glad you did." He swung his legs over the bed's edge and pulled a fresh pair of boxers from the dresser. "I have some beer in the fridge. You want one?"

Given her history as an Olympic athlete, he figured she drank little, but it surprised him when she said, "I'd love one."

As his hand pulled on the door of the refrigerator, the portable combox lit up and the robotic voice announced, "Leader Erik deBaak calling."

Amelia hurried into the kitchen, obviously having heard the voice. "What could he possibly want?"

As he was getting ready to answer the call, he said, "Not sure. I got a message earlier today indicating he had an opportunity to discuss with me." With that, he hit the green button on the combox to accept the incoming call without video. "This is Dex Holzman," he stated.

"Dr. Holzman, hold for Leader deBaak," replied the benign male voice.

Seconds later, a gravelly Dutch-accented voice commanded the room. "Dex, I hope I may call you by your first name. It is a pleasure to make your acquaintance. Thank you for agreeing to speak with me."

"The pleasure is all mine, Leader deBaak. How can I help you?"

Awaiting the reply, Dex looked at Amelia, who was wide-eyed in disbelief. Still in the dark himself, he was eager to learn what this call was all about. Finally, the answer unfolded with a question from deBaak.

"If you could do one thing to change the course of life on this planet and make it better for generations to come, what would it be?"

Dex considered his reply. It was a challenging question to ponder—one thing to reverse overcrowding, sickness, and famine? *Who could choose just one thing?*

Feeling inadequate and trying to sound confident in his reply, Dex said, "That's a tough question. As a marine biologist, my mind defaults to the seas. I pursued this line of work because I have always believed in the restorative power of the oceans to reverse our perilous course."

Dex could sense deBaak's pleasure in the reply. "Dex, quite wise. Your intuitions are sound. I may have a job for you."

Shocked, and not being able to imagine what kind of job he might perform for Erik deBaak, he said, "I'm happy to listen, sir, but I keep pretty busy."

"Dex, with all due respect, the work you are doing now has extraordinary value, but what I am talking about is a position of power and unlimited financial resources to restore the Earth."

"You've got my attention, sir."

"Have you ever heard of a nonprofit in the formative stages called Earth Reborn?"

Dex paused. It was a benign sort of name. He wasn't sure, so he demurred. "No sir, I'm not certain I know what that is."

deBaak dove in. Dex sensed the enthusiasm in his voice as its tone and pace escalated appreciably. "Earth Reborn is my vision to enable the world to return to a bygone era where a reasonably populated world can enjoy pristine seas, beautiful forests, and rolling waves of amber grain. A world where the natural beauty of the earth is restored, enabling people to enjoy simple things like hiking on a mountain trail, swimming in clear water, and farming their own land."

Dex exhaled. "It sounds amazing and tremendously worthwhile. How will you accomplish such a daunting task?"

"That's where you come in," proclaimed deBaak. "I will hire you as the top man at Earth Reborn. You, in turn, will hire the world's best and brightest minds. You will have a think tank of sorts. Your team will create the 'how' behind the vision."

Feeling moved by deBaak's overture, Dex replied, "It sounds like an amazing opportunity, but why me? Surely, there are more qualified people you can enlist."

"President Sofer personally recommended you."

Dex glanced at Amelia. Her jaw literally dropped at hearing the president of the United States had personally recommended him. He threw her an awkward smile and raised his arms in a gesture indicating, *Who knew*?

"I am flattered that President Sofer would think so highly of me—"

deBaak cut him off. "You are young, experienced, and passionate about the planet. And let us not forget you are a leading global authority in your field."

"But, but . . . my work. I'm currently on the verge of a major discovery that just might change the world. I can't stop now. If I agree, when would you need me to start?"

There was an eerie silence on the other end of the line. Dex held his breath and glanced at Amelia for reassurance. Had he offended the Leader of Earth?

The delay was interminable, but deBaak finally responded. "What sort of major discovery?"

The sudden change in tone in deBaak's voice gave Dex pause. He took a moment to collect his thoughts and offered the bare minimum. "It may actually be nothing. We backed into the discovery of a sunken civilization in the Coral Sea and some local legend surrounding the life expectancy of the inhabitants."

"Local legend, you say? Hmmm. I agree. It's probably nothing. Think about this, Dex. If you are leading Earth Reborn, you could designate a full-time resource to continue that work if you feel it has value."

The response placed Dex's anxiety at ease. He didn't have to do the work himself. He just had to make sure it was properly explored. He detected the surprise in Amelia's face when he asked, "When do you need an answer?"

CHAPTER 28

Cam clutched her son's hand a little too tightly. There was a stale scent in the air as she navigated the masses in the streets of Canberra. Long lines of disheveled people waited at the personal sanitation chamber located one block from Parliament House where she would meet with Prime Minister Willow Martin. They built the current Parliament House in 2115 near its predecessor overlooking Lake Burley Griffin. It was a sprawling U-shaped complex with an engaging stainless steel and green glass pyramid in the center where the red, white, and blue Australian flag gently waved in the slight breeze.

Cam led Corey up the cement steps to the security check-in for Parliament House visitors. Before entering, she observed the bustling street below overrun with people on their way to work, the tourists, and those who were obviously homeless. These were the folks whose clothes were dirty and ragged. They stood out like a sore thumb. Would Lockhart be like this? Could she help those most in need in her new patient advocacy role?

As Cam and Corey stepped up to the main entrance of the architectural marvel representing the seat of Australia's government, a glass door slid open in recognition of their presence. A digital voice greeted them.

"Welcome to Parliament House. You have arrived at the Medical Screening Station. If you have any contagious medical condition, we will deny your entrance. Please proceed through the scanner one at a time when indicated. Thank you for helping to keep Canberra healthy."

The butterflies in Cam's stomach fluttered. It distressed her how much fear took control of her daily life. *Would this scanner detect RSV? Would Corey be taken to some sort of Australian Mercy program before they even met the prime minister?* She tried to appear nonchalant while urging her ten-year-old son to walk into a simple scanner.

Cam could detect the anxiety in the sound of her own voice. "Corey, go ahead. Walk slowly on the moving conveyor belt, and I'll meet you on the other side."

The trusting face tied to the innocence of youth looked back at her. Corey entered the scanner, and the conveyor moved him slowly through the two-meter tunnel. Cam relaxed when her son was nearly to the end with no incident. And then it happened. Red flashing lights and an overbearing, repetitive horn went through her head like a comet cutting across the darkest night.

She watched in horror as medical personnel in full protective gear grabbed Corey and shuffled him to an area she could no longer see from her vantage point. Involuntarily, she cried out, "Wait, my son. You can't take him away."

A uniformed medical security officer took her gently by the arm as she started toward the scanner's tunnel. "Ma'am, please wait until the scanner resets and then you can go through."

"You don't understand. That alarm! That's my son."

"Ma'am, I need you to calm down. Your son is on the other side of the scanner and isn't going anywhere. The medical security officer who is with your son will talk to you as soon as you come out of the scanner."

Cam's instinct to fight subsided. She didn't want to cause an unnecessary scene before her meeting with the prime minister. "Okay, okay," she stammered in frustration. Cam entered the medical scanner and let the device perform while she waited anxiously to reach her son. The scan took only a minute, but to Cam, it was like trying to hold her breath underwater for longer than was humanly possible. Once Cam was cleared, she saw him.

"That's my son," she declared a bit too excitedly as she brushed past the medical security officer stationed at the end of the scanner. She wrapped Corey in the protective cocoon of her loving arms.

The medical security officer spoke to her in the tinny-sounding voice reminiscent of the MEC staff back in Los Angeles. "Ma'am, we have flagged your son for RSV—the Reuben Syndrome Virus. It is not contagious, so it will allow you to proceed, but we have registered his condition with the Australian Mercy program."

Of course they did. They hadn't been in Australia for more than a day, and the promise of a fresh start and treatment for her son was already dashed. There was no point in debating the medical security officer. She would have to appeal to the good graces of the prime minister.

"Thank you, I understand," she replied.

After proceeding through a second scanner looking for weapons, an aide met them.

"G'day to you both! My name is Sally. I work for Prime Minister Martin."

Sally's engaging warmth disarmed Cam. She was young, perhaps early twenties, and her blonde hair was free-flowing past her shoulders. Cam understood why this young lady was sent to greet visitors.

"Can we get you something cold to drink? Do you need to visit the dunny?" asked Sally.

Settling down, Cam replied, "I'm fine, thank you. Corey?"

"Good to go, Mom."

Sally smiled and said, "Right this way then."

They walked down a hallway toward massive windows overlooking the once-majestic lake, now a murky brown color. The lift to the top of the pyramid enabled full views of the lake and nearby hills.

Cam admired the ingenuity of the architect. Better to face the beauty of the lake than the horrific scene on the other side of the building.

She imagined the lake was crystal blue sixty years ago when the building was erected.

The office of Willow Martin was at the top of the pyramid. It was quite spacious, and because three of the four walls were glass, interior lighting was at a bare minimum. Drywall covered the inner steel beams of the pyramid. On the upper end of each of these "walls," pictures hung denoting Australia's proud history. A photo of Prime Minister Martin and the former Earth Leader, Akeyo Gathee, immediately took Cam's eye. On the opposite side of the office, another photo showed the prime minister shaking hands during a US state dinner at the White House with President Sofer. Behind her desk hung a giant oil painting depicting Australian forces proudly in arms with Southern Hemisphere allies after a key win early in World War IV.

The prime minister came from behind her desk with an extended arm to welcome Cam and Corey. "It is so nice to meet you both. I know you've had a long, arduous journey. I took the liberty of having some food brought in."

With that, Cam and Corey joined the prime minister at a large round table on the room's east side. Cam wasn't sure what all the food was. It had a tangy, fishy odor. Corey, being the finicky ten-year-old, was totally disinterested.

"Thank you for having us here, Prime Minister, and of course, for your help." Cam hoped that wasn't too forward since no formal offer of help had yet been tendered. To divert attention from the potential blunder, she blurted out. "The painting behind your desk is an amazing piece of art."

The Prime Minister chewed her food, glanced over her shoulder at the painting with which she was no doubt familiar, and said, "Yes, it is striking. World War IV didn't turn out quite the way we would have liked. We feel we were on the right side of history. The Southern Hemisphere fought for the elimination of barbaric population control. Unfortunately, we lost, and that dreadful Mercy program was cast upon the entire planet."

Willow Martin flicked back her shiny red hair and controlled her facial expressions to emphasize her point. Cam supposed it was her background as an Australian actress that aided her in politics. Willow Martin was in her early fifties but could have easily passed for thirty-five.

"Mercy has haunted me. It took my husband, and now it is presenting additional concerns." Cam remained cryptic to not alarm her young son.

Prime Minister Martin was fully apprised of her situation. "That's why Governor Samson recommended you for the post in Lockhart. No one can fight for patient's rights as one who has been a victim of the system."

Cam's natural sense of curiosity took hold. "Forgive me—I am an attorney but unfamiliar with international law. Can't Australia simply choose to disband Mercy?"

Willow Martin shifted her slender frame in the oversized chair and huffed, "Don't I wish? As part of the peace treaty ending World War IV, all countries must submit to population controls until the Ruling Council deems the Earth sustainable for future generations."

Cam sighed. "And I am sure the treaty has no calculation built in for an objective endpoint to population control?"

"None," proclaimed a defiant Willow Martin. "In fact, the problem will get worse before it gets better."

"Why do you say that?"

With all the drama she could manage, Willow Martin stared at her guests with paralyzing blue eyes and replied, "Because the new Leader of Earth is named Erik deBaak, the founder of Mercy, an ironic choice of names if you ask me." The tone of her comments made her disgust obvious.

"But each country's government has some flexibility on how to run the Mercy program, right?"

The prime minister sighed. "Well, we did. deBaak is requiring everything to be more uniform. Skirting the regulations will become much more difficult if not altogether impossible."

"Governor Samson thought it best that Corey and I come to Australia because it was our best shot to have . . ."—she paused, again not wanting to upset her young son—"that kind of flexibility for our unique situation."

Willow Martin picked right up on her cryptic comment. "Sally, would you take Corey to our kitchen downstairs and show him our soft serve ice cream machine?"

Cam delighted in Corey's smile as Sally led the boy out of the room.

The prime minister continued, "Now that we are alone, I must tell you. We have set Corey up with our top medical expert in Brisbane, the closest major city to Lockhart. I understand there are some real advances on a cure for RSV. There are drugs on the market right now that can contain it."

Cam relaxed. The tension rolled out of her shoulders. "I guess then my role as Lockhart's patient advocate leader will begin with me advocating for my own son."

Willow Martin took Cam's hand and squeezed gently. "First, both you and Corey are being granted immediate Australian citizenship. Documents for each of you are being drawn up as we speak. In your role as the head of the Lockhart office, you will need command of Australian Mercy law. It is very similar to the level that the US recently employed. But I'm warning you, it won't last for long. deBaak will force a new regimen of Mercy down every country's throat. It will be more stringent than anything the world has ever seen. He is aiming for rapid population control in concert with this new initiative he calls Earth Reborn."

"I understand and appreciate all your help. Can't you override Mercy for an individual?"

"Early on, yes. Since deBaak took over, that's now prohibited by international law. Unfortunately, Corey will have to remain registered in the Australian Mercy database as an RSV patient. The best I can do, if the time comes, is help you hide."

The air deflated from Cam's chest, and the vise of Mercy gripped her heart with all it had. Where this morning she had hope, now the future held nothing but fear.

CHAPTER 29

"Jonah, get in here now!" deBaak bellowed from his new Rotterdam office. He had one of those hideous headaches. Sweat was pouring out of him. His right hand, encased in the ever-present black glove, rubbed his forehead as if the mere motion would give him relief. He reached into the desk drawer. *Where are those useless pills?* Then he remembered. He left them on his nightstand at home. No matter, they rarely helped ease the pain. He would have to find a new neurologist. If not in Rotterdam, then somewhere, anywhere in this godforsaken world.

His executive assistant barreled in, nearly running through the doorway. "Yes, Leader deBaak, how may I help you?"

"You found this office and established Earth's new European headquarters. Tell me, when you signed the lease, did air conditioning cost extra?"

Jonah Currituck, embarrassed, replied hesitantly, "No sir, it did not. Are you uncomfortable?"

"Don't ask stupid questions. Look at me. I am sweating like a pig. Get it fixed. NOW!"

He hated losing his composure. The last thing he wanted was for people to be afraid of him. He preferred to charm them, lure them into a web of security and then strike when it was least suspected. Currituck was young. He would get over it. deBaak was still sweating profusely. *It smells like a goddam locker room in here.*

deBaak closed his office door and retreated to his executive restroom. He removed his black gloves, grabbed a towel, and dried his face. This wasn't the normal headache. He was lightheaded and his stomach was queasy. He glanced in the mirror and in the reflection, the new diagnostic medical chamber stared back. *Oh, what the hell.*

He stepped inside the clear tube and closed the door. Sensing his weight on the chamber floor, the diagnostic medical technology went to work. It took a blood sample when deBaak placed his finger in a designated slot. Then, he urinated into the assigned opening of the chamber wall. In mere seconds, the unit's digital display illuminated with basic vitals. Temperature, 37 degrees Celsius, normal. Blood pressure slightly elevated; cholesterol, normal; kidney function, normal; body scan . . . The flashing red code alarmed deBaak—BRAIN ABNORMALITY DETECTED. The words sent a shiver down his spine.

He had a full day. No time for nonsense from malfunctioning machines. He had never trusted these diagnostic medical chambers. *Why start now?* The machines took a beating in the media. They were fraught with errors. This one was supposed to be the best in the world.

As he stood there contemplating his next move, the device's female voice prompted him for an action. "Do you wish to submit these medical diagnostics to your doctor?"

He reluctantly answered, "Yes."

The chamber voice displayed a list of his preregistered doctors, and by stating the doctor's name, he chose the clown who called himself a neurologist.

"Diagnostics sent to your chosen medical provider," the chamber voice confirmed.

deBaak stepped outside the chamber and closed the door. The device, sensing it was empty, dispensed a sanitizing mist to prepare for its next use. deBaak went to the medicine cabinet, found two painkillers, and washed them down with a small bottle of purified water. He placed his hands inside a disinfection unit mounted to the wall, put the black gloves back on, and returned to his desk in the adjacent room.

On the clear display Palette mounted on the ceiling, he called up the report Currituck prepared on every country's progress in implementing the newest phase of Mercy. These program requirements were the most restrictive in history. It simply had to be this way. For Earth Reborn to hold any real promise, the planet must have fewer human inhabitants. There was no other viable option. The report's preface stated what he already knew—a list of medical conditions now added to the Mercy initiative. It covered nearly any medical condition that could not resolve itself within two weeks or that could not be cured with a single medical treatment. The new rules were especially restrictive on contagions. It would grant no special favors to the uninsured, and medical exemptions were nearly outlawed.

The display scrolled slowly to countries that were resisting the new implementation date or were simply running behind schedule. Another section detailed countries requesting funds from Earth to implement the new law. As deBaak read over the voluminous detail on his signature law, his already pounding head throbbed. There was a highlighted paragraph denoting the insolence of one nation that steadfastly refused to take Mercy any further. This country was already two levels behind the rest of the world. Just reading the name of the defiant prime minister sent him into a near rage. Willow Martin, Australia.

God, how he detested that woman. His enforcement powers were absolute. The Earth leader had the power to call up a military unit from neighboring countries to enforce any global law. While this was his first instinct, he did not want to be too heavy-handed. As the new head of Earth, he was mindful that a unanimous vote of the Ruling Council could send his leadership into a challenge status. That could lead to his being removed from power. He couldn't chance that. He had to rule with a firm hand, but he could not be a totalitarian leader. *Still, what to do about that obstinate woman in Australia?*

His head was on the verge of exploding. All these years later, the pain from the mindwave technology blasted through his brain as if it were the day it happened. He pictured the contorted face of the maniacal Colonel Paz and became faint. The vibration of his personal combox diverted his thoughts. He reached into the breast pocket of his charcoal sport coat and felt worse when he saw who the caller was—the neurologist. He answered hesitantly.

"Erik, I have the results from your chamber scan this morning. I think we need to conduct a zMRI of your brain."

deBaak heard of the zMRI. Beyond the traditional scan, the zMRI technology alleviated the need for biopsy as it could read and diagnose tissue on its own. "I have had brain scans before. They reveal nothing. You said the torture I endured in the war created harmless scar tissue."

"Yes, and I still believe that to be true. But today's results are different. I am concerned you may have an inoperable brain tumor."

Now he really was sick. He disconnected from the doctor for whom he had little respect and cupped his face inside the gloved palms of his covered hands. His long, bony fingers massaged his temples as he considered his next move.

Inoperable brain tumors were on the list for the new level of Mercy. The results were automatically logged into the Mercy database once they confirmed a diagnosis. deBaak mandated that there be no VIP treatment for anyone. When he conceived the new law, Erik deBaak never imagined he was signing his death warrant.

CHAPTER 30

"Dex, its John Thomas from Oceanic Labs. This Aeternium flower sample you sent me . . . my God, it's unbelievable."

The excitement in the older man's voice escalated with each spoken word. The enthusiasm helped lift Dex out of the preoccupation in which he felt ensconced. The offer from Erik deBaak caused conflict.

"John, tell me," Dex replied anxiously. "What exactly did you learn?" Over the years, Dex sent the lab's owner countless specimens for analysis. As far as Dex was concerned, Oceanic was the best lab on the planet.

"Quite simply, you have found some sort of natural healing element," exclaimed John Thomas.

"That's what locals here believe. So, you think there's credence to it?" Dex found the lab owner animated in a way he had never seen.

"Dex, these flower petals contain some sort of molecule that acts like the body's autoimmune system but to a factor of ten thousand. Here, let me show you something, but you better sit down. You won't believe your own eyes."

Dex sat down on a high-back bar stool with the combox propped up on the marble countertop before him. John Thomas took a glass lab dish, holding something not immediately discernable.

"This dish contains gangrenous human tissue. Inside this dropper is an extract we created from the Aeternium petals. Watch."

Dex peered into the combox display. His eyes widened as the small orange drops landed on the tissue sample and caused it to glow a bright orange. Seconds later, the effect faded, and the sample appeared normal.

Dex couldn't believe his eyes. "John, it's simply astounding."

"When we analyzed the post extract samples, they all came back perfectly normal."

"Have you tested it on anything other than gangrene?"

"My team is working on that now. In the next day or so, we will have completed testing on a wide range of cancers, infections, heart disease, pulmonary disease, diabetes, cirrhosis, and many well-known neurological disorders."

"That's quite a list, John. Do you think the Aeternium extract will cure the common cold too?" Dex always enjoyed injecting humor into a situation. It was a reliable diffuser when life got too serious.

"Now, now Dex. Let's not get your hopes up too high," the older man replied in an equally playful manner. "It's only 2175. Maybe we can cure the common cold in the twenty-third century."

Stepping back into his analytical mindset, Dex stated the obvious. "If this extract proves out the way we think it will, we can change the world."

"No doubt, my friend. I'll buzz you in a day or so when the next set of labs are in."

Dex thanked John for his excellent work and retreated to the overstuffed sofa in his rented condo. His mind was swimming in turbulent water without a life vest. In his storied career, he discovered myriad organisms in the planet's vast waters. Many of the organisms played pivotal roles in a more effective understanding of how the seas interact with the life on the land. But this . . . this was something off the charts.

He moved his left hand across his right cheek in contemplation. The three days of beard growth reminded him he needed a shave. A light sweat formed on his nose, a familiar occurrence since childhood and a sign he was onto something big. Dex lifted the neckline of the navy blue Nexterus

Marine T-shirt, a gift from Maybin, over his face and dried the perspiration. Then, he let his thoughts roll to Erik deBaak and his out-of-the-blue offer to head up Earth Reborn. With the power and budget that came with that position coupled with the healing qualities of the Aeternium extract, the possibilities became endless. Still, his heart pumped with anticipation of getting an answer to the most important question. If the Aeternium extract was what they hoped, would Erik deBaak reverse his stance on Mercy and let the population grow with prolonged life expectancy?

His stomach rumbled. In his heart, he hoped teaming with deBaak would enable him to change the world and end the dreaded Mercy program. Intellectually, he considered what he could do with the Aeternium extract if he remained independent of deBaak and Earth Reborn. Until John Thomas confirmed the totality of the extract's healing powers, he could delay the problem's resolution. Still, after that decision, the hardest of his life, Dex would need to consider how much credence to put into the local legend of doom to befall anyone who tried to harvest the Aeternium flower. His recent track record of dismissing local legend proved poor.

Dex's mind was in turmoil, but one thing was for sure: he needed to keep the knowledge of the Aeternium flower under wraps. *In the wrong hands, it could bring on World War V.*

CHAPTER 31

Prime Minister Martin arranged for a government lease on a two-bedroom apartment within walking distance of Cam's office and Corey's school. Eventually, Cam would get her Australian driver's license, buy a car, and settle into something a little more permanent. But for now, this would do. Her first morning in Lockhart promised to be a busy one. She took Corey by the hand and made her way down the two flights of stairs to the sidewalk outside the brownstone building. Corey's school was only a few blocks from their new home. The walk took literally no time at all. The quaint sign was perched beside a flower bed filled with pink rock lilies. It read, "Lockhart Primary School."

Corey looked bewildered. "Mom, why does it say primary school?"

Adjusting to Australian culture would take time for them both, "It's fine, sweetheart. That's how they refer to elementary school Down Under."

"Down Under?" he replied, even more confused.

Cam loved her son's sense of curiosity. "It's an old expression to describe how far south we are on the globe. You know, at the bottom of the Southern Hemisphere."

Corey loved his light-up globe. He studied it all the time. For a ten-year-old, he already knew the position of most every country in the world. "Got it, Mom. We are Down Under," he said with a big smile on his face.

As they walked past the lilies, Cam took in their scent, which offered a moment of peace as she considered how much their lives changed in such a short period. Thank God, she had her little boy with the energetic personality and a smile that could light up a room. He was all she lived for.

They approached the school entrance, and Cam reached for the chrome handle on the set of double doors painted maroon. She held the door open for her son. The lobby held the aroma of cedar chips. She was curious, but there was a renovation project underway in the school gymnasium. The office was on the opposite side of the main lobby. Again, Cam reached for a chrome handle and pulled the wooden door open for her son to enter. Cam went to the first desk and said, "Good morning, my name is Cam Atkinson, and I am here to register my son, Corey, for school."

"Oh yes, the Americans. We've been expecting you. It's not every day we get a call from the prime minister's office about a new student."

Cam was so grateful for all the details Willow Martin tended to on her behalf. She was a nobody. Her presence in Australia held absolutely no benefit for the prime minister. It made Cam realize that there truly were people left on this planet who simply wanted to help others in need.

"Right this way, Mrs. Atkinson. The principal is Mrs. Strawbridge."

Cam entered the principal's office with Corey in tow. The office was small but well-appointed, with educational accolades from Mrs. Strawbridge's long career in public education. Many pictures were displayed of the principal with students. Her image reveled in their company. Corey's attention was immediately pulled to the life-sized, stuffed Golden Retriever next to the principal's desk. Cam smiled as her son kneeled to embrace it.

Mrs. Strawbridge was an older woman, likely approaching retirement. She had a kindhearted manner. "Corey, this doggie is our school mascot. His name is Teddy Bear. He honors the memory of the golden retriever my husband and I had for fifteen years. Before he passed, Teddy Bear would come to school with me, and often he sat in on classes."

Corey was beaming. "Mom, can we get a dog?"

Cam smiled and said, "We'll see, honey. First things first. We need to get settled here in Lockhart."

Mrs. Strawbridge resumed the introduction. "Corey's teacher will be Mrs. Shipley. She has been with us for twenty-five years, and all her students love her. She'll be down here in a minute to walk Corey to the classroom. Once they go, you and I can take care of a bit of orientation protocol."

"Of course," Cam replied. "Might I also get a brief tour of the school?"

"Absolutely," Mrs. Strawbridge said enthusiastically. "We wouldn't think of you leaving without having seen our little school, now would we?"

Mrs. Shipley arrived in the office doorway and introduced herself. "Well," she said while looking at Corey next to the stuffed golden retriever, "you must be my new student. Welcome! I'm so glad to meet you."

Corey immediately took to his new teacher, and this placed Cam at ease. Cam loved Mrs. Shipley's purple floral print blouse and how her personality made her appear much younger than she probably was.

The teacher turned to Cam. "I know how difficult it can be relocating to a new school, especially from another country. If there is anything I can help with, don't hesitate to call." With that, Mrs. Shipley handed Cam a laminated card with her contact information. Cam was already feeling at ease.

Mrs. Shipley turned back to Corey and held out her hand. "Come with me, handsome. It's time to meet your classmates. You'll make lots of new friends today."

Once they were alone, the principal directed Cam to a monitor filled with orientation documents. She was nearly done when she came upon the last section, "Health Records." There was no dilemma on whether to disclose Corey's Reuben Syndrome Virus. It was already filled in. The school system's database was clearly connected to the Australian Mercy Program. An abrupt tremor began in Cam's right hand as she operated the data entry board. Her entire life hung in the spiral of helping sick people. Her memory flashed images of her late husband, Tom, and then her clients back in LA, most notably Ken Barker. She failed Tom. She failed Ken Barker. And now, she prayed with all her might, she would not fail her son.

ooooo

Cam's new portable combox sprang to life on her walk from the Lockhart Primary School to the Patient Advocacy office she would be leading. She was stunned, because she had not yet provided the number to anyone except Corey's new school. They couldn't be calling. She left there only five minutes earlier.

"Hello," she said hesitantly. "This is Cam Atkinson."

"Hello, Mrs. Atkinson. I am calling from Dr. Brighton's office about your son's upcoming appointment at our office in Brisbane."

"I'm sorry. I know nothing about this. Forgive me, but who is Dr. Brighton?"

The caller was put off. "Dr. Brighton is the nation's leading epidemiologist. He specializes in rare conditions. The prime minister's office referred your son, Corey, to Dr. Brighton regarding his Reuben Syndrome Virus diagnosis."

Once again, Cam thanked her lucky stars that Willow Martin was on her side. *How would she ever repay the kindness? How would she ever thank Thurm for paving the way?*

"Oh, of course. When is the appointment and how do I get there? I live in Lockhart and don't yet have a car."

The caller gave Cam the address in Brisbane and then offered, "Brisbane, if you've never been here, is too crowded for cars. The streets are filled with people and cannot accommodate them. You can pick up the high-speed maglev train that runs above ground or, if you can afford it, you can use an app on your combox to summon a pod to fly you directly here. We have a landing pad on our roof."

"Thank you, we'll be there."

Cam walked to the front door of her new office and ruminated that the sparsely populated town of Lockhart was a throwback to another time. Brisbane sounded like the overrun City of Los Angeles or what she just experienced in Canberra. *Where would it all end?* She entered the office building and hoped she could somehow make a small difference.

CHAPTER 32

"You are turning down the opportunity of a lifetime," deBaak declared. Not much surprised Earth's Leader but Dex Holzman's declination of his astoundingly generous offer was simply mystifying.

"I am truly humbled that you would even consider me, but as I told you when we last spoke, I am on the verge of an amazing discovery and wish to see it through."

deBaak weighed his next words. "Can you tell me anything about this discovery? Perhaps I can help."

"I appreciate the offer, but we have things in hand."

Undismayed, deBaak pressed on. "Can you give me at least a hint of what you are working on?"

He sensed the hesitation in Holzman's voice. "Too soon to really talk about it. Let's just say that if what we think comes to pass, it could change the trajectory of the world."

Now his curiosity heightened. deBaak could feel his internal temperature rising as the anger stirred his every sense. In his own unique way, deBaak would make Holzman feel uncomfortable. That was his special gift. He used it strategically wherever he could.

"And you don't think the Earth Leader should have knowledge of a potential discovery that could, as you say, change the trajectory of the world?"

"Sir, with all due respect, I'd rather not say right now. If things pan out, I promise I will call you with a full briefing before anyone else gets wind of the news."

"Very well" deBaak replied. "I'd prefer to know now, but I will respect your position."

He thanked Holzman for his time and ended the call. He slammed his balled-up fist onto the top of the black onyx desk and cursed. It was a total lie. He didn't respect Holzman's position. In fact, he was downright pissed. deBaak was damned if he would just sit back and wait. Now that he knew where Holzman and his team were, he would simply send someone down to Lockhart to covertly investigate.

With that, he made his way to the building's roof and climbed into the AirStadt to take him to the neurologist. Once airborne, he looked down on the overcrowded city of Rotterdam. The throngs of people on the streets obliterated any semblance of the city's former majesty. The sight made him physically ill. The scene below was playing itself out across the world on nearly every habitable landmass. The ramped-up Mercy program, as tough as it was, did not yet shrink the population to an acceptable level. Dex Holzman had his secret, and deBaak had his. He would initiate Operation Control with the Southern Hemisphere countries that were his sworn enemy during the war. Those heartless bastards illegally dropped Purple Dust on his beloved Rotterdam and robbed him of his family forever. Once the operation was complete, people from the Northern Hemisphere could then inhabit unpopulated Southern Hemisphere countries. Along with Mercy and the ability to spread out across the Southern Hemisphere, his idea to restore the Earth while avenging his parents and sister might just come to pass.

The thought of being turned down by Dex Holzman for the leadership post at Earth Reborn infuriated him. Like everything else he ever accomplished, Erik deBaak would have to find a time and the energy to just do it himself. It's a good thing sleep was so scarce. Little time was wasted.

The AirStadt, now over the medical building, began its vertical descent, jarring his attention back to the startling result from the diagnostic medical chamber. He wasn't a religious man, but Erik deBaak prayed the machine simply malfunctioned. After the pod's safety restraint automatically released and lifted, deBaak stood up, stretched, and made his way to the building's rooftop entrance.

He was shown into the private office of Dr. Bradley Kornbloom. Various degrees, accolades, and photos of flowers peppered the office walls. Apparently, Dr. Kornbloom had a penchant for photography. The good doctor dressed in black trousers with a baby blue polo shirt. His rotund face was punctuated by an elegant graying mustache and rosy cheeks.

"Erik, I'm afraid the news isn't good."

deBaak smirked and replied, "In my position, doctor, it rarely is."

"Understood, but this is your life we are talking about."

"I am a busy man. Let's cut to the chase."

"Very well. The scan you sent reveals an inoperable tumor deep in the brain. Even if it's benign, it will cause symptoms affecting your ability to function. The headaches we attributed to your war experience are likely being caused by the tumor."

"And if it's malignant?"

"You would be unfortunately classified as terminal and immediately referred into the Dutch Mercy system."

There it was. Confirmation of the ultimate irony. The man who created Mercy to better the earth for future populations was going to be claimed by his own creation.

deBaak steadied his nerves so he could concentrate on the moment at hand. "I see. What is involved in finding out for sure?"

"We will have you undergo a zMRI of the brain. The machine will scan your brain and collect detailed 3D scans of the entire tumor. If cancerous cells are present, we will know in ten minutes."

"Let's do it."

Dr. Kornbloom summoned a nurse, who escorted deBaak to a room down the hallway. He sat in a stuffed chair while a thin dome was lowered over his entire head.

"This test will take about three minutes. You will hear a constant humming noise. That's normal. Please try to sit perfectly still until I raise the dome," instructed the nurse.

deBaak closed his eyes and thanked the Lord for giving him the wisdom to prepare for every contingency.

Ten minutes later, he walked back to Dr. Kornbloom's private office. He sat in the chair facing the old mahogany desk and studied the sectional model of the brain that sat atop its surface. The model came apart so the doctor could show the presence and function of the different sections of the body's master control system. Looking at the model, deBaak accepted his ignorance. To the layperson, it was difficult to distinguish and comprehend the many functions of the brain.

Looking glum, Dr. Kornbloom parked himself behind his desk with a large, portable tablet and brought up a scan of Erik deBaak's brain. "Erik, this is your tumor. The cells you see here are cancerous. As I mentioned before, they are inoperable. In the days before Mercy, we would recommend a course of extended treatments to kill the cancerous cells and reduce the size of the tumor. As you know, under current law, we may not offer these treatment regimens."

"Doctor, need I remind you I am Leader of Earth and one of the wealthiest people on the planet?"

"Erik . . ." the doctor paused, clearly trying to remain professional in his delivery of the grim news. "Your own Mercy programs make it explicitly clear. No VIP exceptions."

deBaak leaned forward in the chair to stare down at the portly neurologist. "Dr. Kornbloom, I am prepared to offer you a small fortune to treat this tumor in whatever way possible to reduce the chance that it or Mercy may kill me."

The doctor, a nervous type, began to sweat. He was way out of his comfort zone. "Erik, even if I wanted to, there are too many obstacles. It wouldn't be just me and you who know about this. My entire staff would have to be in the loop. I would need the medical technicians to administer the tests—and let us not forget, under Mercy law, all the diagnostic equipment automatically sends test results into the Mercy database. I just don't see how it's possible to subvert the system, even if I wanted to."

For a long moment, deBaak said nothing. He despised the weak-minded doctor. "So, you say that they uploaded the diagnostic test results from today to the Mercy database?"

"I am afraid so," the doctor replied meekly.

"You realize the ramifications of your actions?"

"I . . . I don't follow exactly."

"Think about it, Doctor. What will the world think if it forces the Earth Leader into his own Mercy program? Consider the upheaval on affairs of the planet and the morale of the people, especially on the heels of the recent and untimely death of Leader Gathee."

The doctor was now sweating profusely. He took a handkerchief and wiped his forehead. "I know how upsetting all this must be, Erik. But the Mercy considerations are simply out of my hands."

"As a prominent neurologist, you must have certain administrative privileges in the Mercy database. I assume you can log in and alter the medical records for an individual?"

"Well, yes. I have never done so, but it is theoretically possible."

With that declaration, deBaak rose from the chair, sauntered around the desk, and positioned himself behind the doctor's chair. Erik deBaak produced a sharp knife from inside his blazer and placed it at the base of the neurologist's throat. "Now, you will tell me your login credentials to the Mercy database."

After extracting the required information from the useless doctor, deBaak pressed the spike from his cufflink into the side of Dr. Kornbloom's neck.

It contained three times the toxin he used on Akeyo Gathee. Death came instantly. Kornbloom collapsed in his chair. deBaak reached into the pocket of his blazer and produced a small ring-sized box containing C4 explosive and a timer. He set the timer for five minutes and walked out the door.

deBaak went to the roof where his AirStadt pilot was waiting. He boarded the pod and took off. The explosion ripped the top of the building apart in a flash of fiery brilliance. As the AirStadt made its way back to his new Rotterdam office, he took his tablet, logged into the Mercy system as Dr. Bradley Kornbloom, and erased every detail of his medical history.

CHAPTER 33

"Listen to this," Dex exclaimed to the team in the lounge at Nexterus Marine. He scrolled through the story on his laptop, reading aloud. "A lightning storm on the Coral Sea allegedly claimed a boat and its crew of two dozen."

Amelia shook her head. "Allegedly, you say?"

"The boat went missing, but no evidence of a wreck was ever found. It just vanished without a trace."

Noah shrugged. "Not the first time I've heard a story like that."

"The article states that the lightning bolt literally split the ship in two. The crew must have either drowned or burned to death."

"But no evidence?" asked Amelia.

"Apparently not," replied Dex.

"Do you think this has anything to do with the legend from Old Toby?" Amelia asked.

"I, for one, have come to the point of not dismissing any of these local legends. They have a funny way of coming true," Maybin said.

"My grandparents grew up in this region. I've heard the same oddball story my entire childhood. Made me smile, but I never put much stock in them," Noah said.

Jack perked up. "I'm a cynical New Yorker. You gotta show me proof."

Amelia, head down and busy searching her own laptop, gasped out loud. "My lord, you will not believe this." She projected an article from a local news source onto the Palette for all to see.

Coral Sea Sector Declared Off Limits

Local Authorities Cite Numerous Deaths Across Multiple Incidents

Federal authorities have closed a Coral Sea sector indefinitely while they investigate reports of deadly incidents having taken place over a large area designated as Byamee's Brunt off the coast of Queensland. Five separate incidents have reportedly claimed the lives of nearly 100 people. Causes of these incidents have ranged from severe weather to unexplained explosions. They named the designated sector after locals explained the story of the Aborigine god named Byamee, who they claim guards the plants intruders were attempting to harvest. While no evidence exists, a timetable has not been established for the water's reopening.

"So?" exclaimed Noah. "Doesn't tell us anything concrete."

"You weren't there," stated an exasperated Amelia.

"Wasn't where?" Noah asked.

"In the fishing village. When me, Maybin and Dex spoke with Old Toby the fisherman. He told us about Byamee, the god guarding the Aeternium flower."

"Again, so what?" Noah argued.

"The article cites the flowers. There's a connection here. I know it," Amelia claimed.

"Amelia, when was this article put online?" Dex inquired.

She took a moment to scan the entry. "Here it is." She hesitated and then said aloud, "Oh my. This article is seventeen years old."

"Not surprising," offered Dex. "These types of legends often date back hundreds of years. See if you can find out how long the sector of the Coral Sea was closed."

She skimmed her laptop for a few minutes and declared, "It looks like two years. Since then, no reported incidents."

"Maybe the world learned its lesson," stated Maybin.

"In my experience, these types of stories get passed down from generation to generation. You also have people who wander into unknown places, hear of the legends, and take them back home. It's easy to imagine the story spreading of boats and planes mysteriously disappearing without a trace," Dex said.

"So, where do we go from here?" inquired Amelia. "Do you think these missing boats and planes were searching for the lost civilization of Aeternum or just the healing flowers?"

Dex had to stop himself from laughing. "I'm not sure I believe there were ever any boats or planes. I'm inclined to think the whole thing was made up."

"To what end?" asked Maybin.

"I don't know. Some local politician probably made it up to promote tourism. A good idea gone bad. It makes for an intriguing mystery, so people just keep telling the story."

CHAPTER 34

Corey's face lit up like fireworks on the Fourth of July. The AirStadt ride to Brisbane was a thrill for a ten-year-old, especially on a clear day when the view below was unparalleled. This pod contained a glass bottom so kids who weren't large enough to see out the side windows could still get a magnificent view.

Cam reveled in her son's delight in such simple things that she often took for granted. It differed from looking up at the sky and seeing the pods flying about. From the ground they appeared to be so tiny that they were confused for package delivery drones buzzing the skyline.

"Mom, this is so cool. How come we never flew in pods when we were in LA?"

Cam patted him on the head. "There wasn't much need. We had a car, although driving anywhere in the city was a nightmare."

"I love Australia," her son declared.

Cam's own enthusiasm for her new country was not yet as strong. Everything was happening so fast. Moving on a moment's notice to another part of the world was not something she would recommend. Her brain had been on *go* ever since the Mercy Enforcement Police showed up at her door to take her son away. Sleep had been scarce. Once an abundantly confident person, worry now consumed Cam. She fretted over her son's future, her new job, and learning how to live in another country. The thought that she might never again return to the US left her feeling empty.

When the AirStadt landed on the roof of the Brisbane medical building, Cam thanked the pilot and let him know she added a gratuity to his transport charge via the combox app. Ten minutes later, she and Corey were sitting in an exam room waiting for Dr. Theodore Brighton to make an appearance.

Dr. Brighton walked in just as she was fidgeting. "Good morning," he declared in an uplifting tone. "You must be Corey." An enormous man, Dr. Brighton kneeled, extending his arm to shake hands with her son.

Cam's anxiety subsided. Dr. Brighton was very engaging. He was an extremely tall man and elegantly held a tremendous amount of weight. Cam guessed he was around sixty. His wavy graying hair and rimless glasses gave him a distinguished look.

Looking at her, Dr. Brighton proclaimed, "I have a full set of Corey's medical records from the US. Has he been having any symptoms?"

Cam shook her head. "No, in fact, other than the recent fever, he has been perfectly normal."

Dr. Brighton nodded in acknowledgement and kneeled with a device to shine a light directly into each of Corey's eyes.

"No recent episodes of fever, chills, fatigue, headache, nausea?" he asked.

"No, since we have been in Australia, Corey has been perfectly healthy."

Dr. Brighton then went to a Palette where he summoned magnified images of Corey's bloodwork next to another set that read RSV and a third set that read Normal. He directed Cam's attention to the display.

"On the left, you see Corey's red blood cells. On the far right, you can compare it to what they should look like. Ninety-eight percent of all RSV patients display like the cells on the middle screen. Now look back at Corey's cells and you can observe the RSV mutation."

Cam's spirits sank like a stone in a shallow riverbed. "So, you are saying that Corey's mutated version of RSV places him in the smallest percentile of cases? That it's rare for this disease to mutate the way it has?"

Dr. Brighton stiffened his posture. He looked right at her and replied, "Yes, something like that. The good news is that in collaboration with epidemiologists all over the world, we have experimental drugs that can now contain RSV, enabling most patients to live a normal life for an undetermined period of time."

"Is Corey eligible for these drugs?"

"Well . . ." he hesitated, "technically, yes, but—"

The lawyer in Cam instinctively caused her to cut him off. "But the mutation makes the drug's effectiveness questionable."

"Sadly, yes. In fact, the data on patients with RSV mutations is sparse. Each mutation is different, and the results have been mixed."

"So, what are you recommending?"

Looking resigned to taking the longest of long shots, Dr. Brighton responded glumly. "The experimental drug is called L'Chaim. I suggest we try it. We have little to lose, and while Corey is asymptomatic, it'll give us some time to investigate all other options."

Feeling overwhelmed and confused, Cam asked, "Does L'Chaim have side effects?"

"All medications do. Most of the listed side effects have an incidence rate of less than one percent, so I wouldn't concern myself too much if I were you."

"You mentioned something about investigating other options. What did you mean by that?"

"To start, I will share Corey's bloodwork with the other epidemiologists I collaborate with around the world. If one of the other doctors has an RSV mutation like Corey's, they might have some guidance on successful treatment."

Feeling discouraged, Cam asked, "And if no one has seen this particular mutation?"

"Then I am afraid we will have a limited amount of time with which to engage in a trial-and-error regimen."

Cam was sure Dr. Brighton picked up on the anxiety consuming her once more.

"Let's not worry too much about all that now. If you agree, we can start the L'Chaim treatment today. It's available only in injectable doses. Corey will need to come here once a month for a shot."

"Okay, okay," she said, her head hanging down. Once Dr. Brighton left to retrieve the experimental injection that would likely do her son no good, she looked up and saw her normally happy little boy tearing up.

"Am I going to die?" he asked.

At that moment, a well-placed firecracker blew Cam's heart to bits. She drew Corey in and hugged him tightly. "No way, little man. We will make sure of that."

His mood lightened.

Dreading the worst, Cam wished she were as confident as her words implied.

CHAPTER 35

"Erik, this is madness. I can't be a part of it," declared Hennie Van de Berg.

He looked at her, put on his best phony smile, and replied, "You will do whatever I ask, and you will do so willingly. If you refuse. . ." He stopped short of making a threat, knowing it wasn't necessary. She always did whatever he wanted. She was nothing more than a lovestruck fool and loyal foot soldier.

deBaak exhaled to restrain his anger. "Hennie, it is quite simple. You will supervise a new R&D team based here in Rotterdam. Their work will be secret. You will arrange for living quarters and assure me they will interact with no one outside you, me, and their own team members. I want the plan operational in thirty days," he commanded.

"It will take longer than that to assemble a team," she bemoaned.

"I have no time to waste," deBaak replied, uninterested in her latest protestation. He pushed a button in his Crematie office and told his executive assistant to send in the visitor.

He watched with curiosity as his guest entered the room. Hennie was caught off guard. That's what he wanted.

The woman was at least seventy years of age. Her stark white hair was pulled back tightly, exposing a pale complexion and red cheeks. The bulging eyeballs were black in appearance, and her mouth turned downward, causing her resting expression to cast a scowl.

deBaak looked at his chief operating officer. "Meet Sigrid Viklund, a Swedish chemist who will head the project."

Hennie rose from her chair and offered a welcoming hand to her new report. "Sigrid, it is so nice to meet you."

Viklund held up her hand to command the oncoming train that was Hennie Van de Berg to stop. "You may address me as Dr. Viklund. Show me my workspace. The others will arrive shortly."

Hennie was taken aback. "Others?" she inquired.

deBaak broke in. "Yes, Dr. Viklund was a senior consultant to the leaders of the Northern Hemisphere forces during World War IV. She is an expert in chemical and biological warfare. She has a trusted team who will assist her in fulfilling Operation Control."

"And. . ." Hennie stuttered. "What is my role in this Operation Control?"

Before deBaak could answer, Viklund barked, "To get us whatever we need, perhaps even coffee." And she let go an evil laugh.

deBaak never saw Hennie express anger until now. She would have to get over it.

Refocusing on his strategy, he addressed Viklund. "Is thirty days enough time to prepare?"

Again, she laughed and said, "What you ask is child's play. We will be ready."

Operation Control. To Erik deBaak, it was a stroke of genius. Create a Southern Hemisphere crisis so lethal that it would force him to use his powers as Earth Leader to do two things. Force the sick into the Mercy program, and when that wasn't entirely effective, as he knew it would not be, take command of the hemisphere's own military forces to wipe each country of its remaining contaminated population. Then, Earth Reborn would launch a humanitarian effort to clean up the globe's lower half and ready it for repopulation by deserving citizens of Northern Hemisphere countries. He would install leaders of his choosing, and radicals like Willow Martin would be a thing of the past. The plan unfolded across the pages of his mind as vividly as any vision he ever conceived.

With the help of Dr. Sigrid Viklund, he would create a modern-day Purple Dust. The only similarity to what had struck his family would be the color. This weapon would maim and disfigure while tearing through a person's insides. Operation Control would be deBaak's way of avenging his parents and sister and the millions of countrymen devastated by the Southern Hemisphere fanatics. Their day was coming. No one would point a finger in his direction. The world would place the blame squarely on his sacrificial lamb, a terrorist the entire world would soon fear. A man known only as Viper.

CHAPTER 36

Dex and Amelia sat in a secluded booth at Alexandre's, Lockhart's finest dining establishment. The French cuisine was exquisite, and the sommelier's wine pairings were second to none. The lights were dim, and Dex, having had a little too much wine, placed his arm around Amelia's shoulders, drawing her close.

"You really are stunningly beautiful," he said.

Blushing, she took his hand and gave it a light squeeze. "You are flattering the petite athlete who always thought of herself as a tomboy."

Her touch warmed his soul. The wall Dex normally surrounded himself with was being broken down by the wine. "And just look at you now."

Amelia wore a white dress, leaving her tanned shoulders exposed. Her light brown hair had fresh highlights with bangs gracefully sweeping across her forehead. The lipstick was a subtle shade of pink, accentuating her allure, but it was her crystal-blue eyes in which Dex found himself hopelessly lost.

"Is this the first time you've been involved with a co-worker?" she asked.

Dex hesitated, never wanting to reveal too much. His private life was always that . . . private. Still, he couldn't compel himself to be anything less than one hundred percent honest with her. "Um, no, not exactly."

She arched an eyebrow and smiled. "Okay, Dr. Holzman. Do tell."

"Well," he began. "As you might imagine, a young single scientist traveling the world in some pretty remote places doesn't leave a lot of opportunity to meet the girl of his dreams. Stuff just kind of happens . . . you know."

She goaded him some more, clearly enjoying his naturally shy nature and discomfort in disclosing anything about his personal life.

"There were two. The more serious of them was a redhead named Melanie. We met on the Southern Ocean expedition and shared a frosty night or two keeping each other warm on Enderby Beach." A fool's cloud befell his psyche as soon as the words departed his mouth.

Amelia laughed. "Melanie, the redhead on a frosty beach? Sounds like a scene from a terrible film."

Dex did something of a slow burn, his temples each encasing a hot poker. Through the slight inebriation, he kept his cool. "Okay, your turn. There had to be some sort of hookup on one of those worldwide gymnastic competitions."

"Oh, my goodness," she chuckled. "Those competitions all had chaperones and early bed checks."

Still probing, he asked, "So nothing? No midnight trysts after a long day on the balance beam?"

Now Amelia was blushing. Her slight frame was also experiencing the effects of too much wine. "There was this one competition in Oslo. I celebrated my twenty-first birthday on the road, and our witch of a chaperone happened to have her son along on the trip. His name was Oliver. He was twenty-three and . . ."—she stopped to take another sip of her wine—"he knew how to show a girl a good time."

Dex lifted his glass, relieved he wasn't the only one to share a story that left him vulnerable. "Here's to clumsy road romances," he said as he raised his glass.

She held up her glass to acknowledge the toast, took a sip, and then leaned in to kiss him. Surprised, Dex learned quickly that Amelia was not shy. On an expedition, he had no trouble being in charge. He was confident in his abilities. In romance, it was a different story.

"Did you grow up in California?" she asked.

"No, actually. I grew up on the East Coast in a small suburb of Baltimore."

"You didn't want to live your life there?"

He shook his head. "Too crowded, like most everywhere else. After my studies and expeditions took me around the world, I just wanted something more serene."

"Siblings?"

"Two, an older brother and sister. Both still in the area. My brother is a photographer, and my sister has made a nice name for herself as a software developer for the US Space Force."

"And you are the baby of the group?"

"Yup," he replied. "I was the daydreaming explorer, even as a young boy. Teachers thought something was wrong with me because I had trouble focusing on anything unrelated to science. I wanted to see the world, and I pretty much have."

"Marine biology? What made you choose that field?"

"You're going to laugh."

"Try me."

"When I was eight, I used to go to a creek near my house to study crayfish or whatever else I could find. One day, when I got there, the creek was different. Someone or something polluted it. Every organism in that creek was killed. I think I cried for two days."

"Did you ever learn what caused the pollution?"

"No, but to this day, I remember it vividly. It still pisses me off."

"So, it motivated you to save the world?"

He laughed, falling back into a state of alcohol-induced relaxation. "How about you? Did you grow up here? Family?"

"I grew up outside Brisbane. My father was an oil worker. Mum stayed at home and accompanied me to competitions. I was an only child. Just me and a pet rabbit."

"A rabbit? Really?" Dex found it amusing.

She appeared to feign indignation as she replied, "He was always willing to lend me an ear when I was lonely."

They shared a laugh as the server brought the electronic unit, enabling Dex to settle the bill.

The restaurant was a few kilometers from Dex's rented condo. Choosing not to drive, Dex hailed a ride from his portable combox, and they cuddled together in the backseat for the short ride. When they arrived at the condo, Dex thanked the driver, opened the door for Amelia, and helped her out of the car. She stumbled a bit and laughed, but Dex just regarded it as part of her charm. Dex pulled out his swipe card to enter the unit. Then, he flipped on a light and his jaw dropped through the floor.

Someone had ransacked the place.

CHAPTER 37

Cam looked into the screen of her portable combox and saw the familiar face of Australia's leader staring back. "Prime Minister Martin, thank you for taking my call. You have been extraordinarily kind," Cam expressed with sincere gratitude.

"Cam, it's my pleasure. I'm not sure I told you when we met in Canberra, but my mother died from a mutation of Reuben Syndrome Virus. That was thirty years ago. When I heard about Corey, I wanted to help in any way I could."

"We saw Dr. Brighton. He was very nice but offered little hope beyond trial and error."

Willow Martin furrowed her brow. "Oh, I'm sorry to hear that. I thought Dr. Brighton would have something more definitive to offer."

Cam updated the prime minister on the L'Chaim injection and the doctor's lack of faith in its response to a mutated form of RSV. "I know how busy you must be. I'm not even sure why I called. I am just feeling lost and frankly, somewhat desperate."

Willow Martin ran her right hand through her red hair in a nervous gesture and said, "I hesitate to say anything because my information is spotty, and even if what I think I know is true, the chances of it helping Corey are a billion to one."

Cam's heart pounded with anxiety. "Prime Minister, if you know of anything that might help, no matter how long the odds, please tell me," she pleaded.

Willow Martin exhaled, clearly wrestling with some degree of inner conflict. Then she said, "Are you familiar with Dr. Dex Holzman?"

"Sure, the marine biologist? I've streamed his documentaries. Corey loves his films. Why?"

"I know he's here now, in Australia, leading an expedition in the Coral Sea off our northeast coastline."

"I'm sorry. I'm not sure where you're going."

"Apologies, you wouldn't now, would you? I need to tell you the story of a sector of the Coral Sea called Byamee's Brunt. Seventeen years ago, I had just retired from acting and was in my first term as a member of Parliament. I became intrigued by a series of unexplained incidents killing people who tried harvesting a certain type of underwater flower natives believed had healing powers. The natives claim that a god named Byamee guarded the flowers and brought harm to anyone who attempted to harvest them."

"And that's what Dex Holzman is investigating?"

"Yes, according to the report I have. My interior minister got wind of his expedition and let me know, because all those years ago, I was the member of Parliament who sponsored legislation to close Byamee's Brunt."

"And you think that this underwater flower might cure my son?"

"I told you it was a long shot. The natives back in the day claimed these plants cured most anything."

Cam shook her head. She wanted to believe it. *Did miracles really come true?* She wasn't too confident but, at heart, she was a mother bent on doing anything to keep her son from the awful Mercy system. "Have the plants ever been safely harvested and studied?"

"Not to my knowledge. We were successful in closing the sector for several years, but as environmentalists, we elected not to disturb the delicate balance between man and nature. Besides, most of my colleagues in the day didn't put any stock in the local legend about the healing plants."

"But you? You believe in the legend?"

Willow Martin again fidgeted with her hair. She clearly looked like a woman who wanted to say something but couldn't. Finally, she offered, "I signed a nondisclosure pledging secrecy. I can't tell you why, but I encourage you to contact Dr. Holzman."

Cam thanked the prime minister and clicked off the call. With nothing to lose, she resolved to find Dex Holzman to see if he might help save her son's life.

CHAPTER 38

San Diego, California

John Thomas was a widower. An aggressive form of cancer invaded the pancreas of his wife. After forty-three years together, Mercy prematurely stole his beloved. Life had not been the same since her own government murdered Patty. In his learned opinion, they should have given her the chance to fight for her own life. Medical science supported a reasonable chance for survival, yet the government placed the dwindling resources of the planet over the life of his lifetime love.

Not much of a cook, John gobbled down a hamburger from a local eatery and went to the lab. At sixty-seven, with kids and grandchildren preoccupied with their own busy lives, there wasn't much to do but focus on work, especially on a Saturday evening. None of his staff would be present, so he would have the place to himself. A little soft rock music would relax him while he worked.

John founded Oceanic Labs decades earlier and elected to keep it small. He hated bureaucracy and enjoyed being in the thick of new discoveries. His longtime alliance with Dex Holzman provided many of his career highlights. Nothing he ever worked on was more fascinating than the Aeternium flower. John believed the extract, based on his early experiments, would likely have cured Patty's cancer. The thought made his heart ache. Maybe he could help others save their loved ones. There were so many more tests to run.

He approached the double glass doors to the building and went to the alarm pad to punch in the four-digit code. The unarmed system took John by surprise. *That was weird. We set the darn thing to auto-arm at the same time each evening. It never failed before.*

He went through the glass doors and thought he saw a small light dancing around in the lab. Maybe a member of his team came in to get something they forgot. That would explain the alarm system being disabled, but why not flip on the main light?

"Hey," he called out, but there was no reply.

John ambled into his main lab. He turned on the overhead light just as his foot smashed a glass beaker on the floor. As he looked around, countertops were askew, drawers hung wide open, and fallen debris ruined ongoing experiments. John shook his head. *Goddamn kids.* There wasn't anything in the lab the average thief would want to steal. *Why couldn't they pick on someone else?*

As he moved to the rear of the facility, John smelled something burning. As he stepped into the back storage room, he saw a Bunsen burner lit up under an upholstered fabric chair. Flames engulfed the seat. John reached to the left wall and grabbed the fire extinguisher. He immediately got the small fire under control and opened a window to let the smoke out. It wasn't bad enough these kids burglarized his lab, but they have to burn it down?

Sweating from the heat of the chair fire, John pulled his polo shirt up over his face to wipe it down. His eyes, stinging from the smoke, began to tear. His chest was tight, and he coughed as he stumbled into his office only to discover his computer was gone. It upset him. The computer held all his Aeternium research. *Sure, I backed it up to the cloud, but . . . could someone have broken in because of the Aeternium experiments? How could anyone know?*

It was time to call the police. Before he could turn around, a powerful forearm wrapped around his chest while the sharp blade of a knife slit his throat. As he lay on the floor bleeding to death, John Thomas watched as the intruder relit the Bunsen burner on a different chair, entombing him in an inferno that once held the keys to a better world.

CHAPTER 39

"The place has been turned upside down," Dex declared in a state of abject frustration. He stood frozen, rotating his entire body around, trying to take it all in. The room stank of body odor, telling Dex they hadn't missed the intruder by much.

Amelia surveyed the site. "What do you suppose they were looking for?"

Dex had a sick feeling in the pit of his stomach as he reached for the dangling power cord. "At a minimum, my laptop." He turned to investigate the bedroom when a horrible thought befell him. "Amelia, who besides us knows about the Aeternium flower?"

She crinkled her forehead, illustrating her brain hard at work. "Well, beyond the two of us, Maybin, Noah, Jack, and of course, Old Toby."

"I hate to ask, but how trustworthy are Maybin, Noah, and Jack?"

"I've only worked with them a short while, but I'd find it unimaginable that any of them could be involved with anything covert."

"And I don't think Toby was selling us out." He retreated into contemplation. "Who does that leave?"

Silence consumed them as they considered the less obvious possibilities. "What about the fellow who owns the lab in California?" she inquired.

"John Thomas?" Dex shook his head. "No way. I've been working with him forever. He would never sell us out."

"Can you think of anyone else?"

"Not offhand," he replied as his portable combox sprang to life. "It's Maybin."

Dex pressed the button to receive the video transmission. "What's up?"

"I'm at the office. There's been a break-in. The place is a wreck."

"Let me guess. The only things missing are computers?"

Maybin, clearly surprised, replied, "How could you possibly know that?"

"Because I just walked into my condo with Amelia, and the same thing happened here."

Maybin wiped his right hand across his forehead in a show of frustration.

"You haven't told anyone about our discovery, have you?" Dex asked.

"My God, no. How could you think such a thing?"

Undismayed in his impromptu interrogation, Dex continued. "Noah and Jack? Can we trust they kept our research confidential?"

Maybin was emphatic. "I'd stake my life on it."

Dex took his right hand through his thick hair. "Where does that leave us?"

Maybin just shook his head.

Amelia catapulted into the conversation. "Here's what makes no sense to me. If all someone wanted was our research, they didn't need to break in and wreck Dex's condo or our lab. We store everything in the cloud. Why not just hack in?"

With each passing day, Dex was more impressed with his new love. She had a keen sense of intuition. Her poignant question cleared his head, and he provided the answer. "Someone is obviously trying to send us a message."

No sooner had the words left his mouth than Maybin delivered the death blow in the evening's shocking events. "Dex, you aren't going to believe this."

"What now?"

"I just got a news flash over my combox—a marine biology research lab in San Diego burned to the ground. Someone was trapped inside."

Now Dex really was sick. This was no coincidence. Someone was engaging in a coordinated effort to steal his research. Before Maybin confirmed what he already knew, he felt horrible about the possibility of it being John Thomas. He sympathized with the man's family and the world's potential loss of a profoundly gifted researcher.

"Oceanic?" Dex asked reticently.

"Afraid so," answered Maybin.

"And the body? Was it John?"

"The article didn't say, but I think we might presume the worst."

Dex clicked off with Maybin and immediately entered the code to reach John Thomas. It disheartened him when all he heard was John's normal after-hours recording. Dex left a message and threw himself down on a part of the sofa that was free of debris.

Amelia was deep in thought. Finally, she blurted it out. "I know it sounds crazy, but do you think Leader deBaak has anything to do with this?"

In the heat of the moment, the thought hadn't occurred to Dex. "I can't imagine. I mean . . . I didn't tell him anything about our discovery."

"No, but you told him there was a discovery."

"I did. You're right. But do you think that alone is enough that he would engage in something this monstrous?"

"Stranger things have happened," she stated. "He gives me the creeps."

"I don't know. Given his position, doesn't he deserve the benefit of the doubt?"

Amelia folded her arms across her chest and declared, "Not from me. I don't trust him one bit."

Dex replayed the last conversation with Leader deBaak in his head. He was sure he disclosed nothing of significance. Yet, being shut out put off deBaak. *Is it possible? Maybe,* he concluded. *Probable? Not really.*

Reluctantly, Dex stated, "I guess we can't rule it out. How would we even investigate the possibility?"

"That's a tough one," she said.

Dismissing the thought, he said, "Give me a hand getting this place back in order."

As they began putting the condo back together, Dex cleared his mind of such an outlandish idea. How in the world could the leader of Earth be personally involved in breaking and entering, theft, or even the murder of John Thomas or one of his team? It was lunacy to even think it might involve Leader deBaak.

Seconds later, as he placed the throw pillows back on his rented sofa, his combox alerted him to breaking news. It was the story about the fire at Oceanic Labs in San Diego. Only this version confirmed his worst fear. The owner, John Thomas, was the one trapped inside.

CHAPTER 40

It terrified Erik deBaak. Even as Earth Leader, there was no escaping the simple fact that nearly anyone, including the government of any country, could find person-specific search results . . . no matter how secure a network claimed to be. Still, he needed more information about his brain tumor. How could he learn what he needed to know without alerting anyone to his condition? And just like that, the idea came to him. Back at his Earth office in Rotterdam, deBaak logged into the Mercy database as Dr. Bradley Kornbloom. The Mercy database contained the world's most extensive library on medical conditions.

deBaak found the page showing malignant brain tumors. His was a newer type—"newer" in the sense that it rocketed onto the scene in the last fifty years as a derivative of glioblastoma. Forgetting the Mercy program that he was technically required to enter, his research told him a small percentage of patients with his condition could expect to live just eight or nine months. That wasn't much time. He kept reading. Within ninety days of diagnosis, the patient can expect to experience rapidly deteriorating cognitive skills, memory loss, and the ability to speak. Dementia was also a primary concern. *How rich. Without a cure, my choices are being euthanized in the Mercy system I created or turning into a vegetable like my parents and sister.*

The mere thought of it all made his head hurt. Beads of sweat formed on his forehead. His mouth was dry. He got up, crossed the room, and opened a small refrigerator where he extracted a bottle of purified water. After gulping half the bottle, Erik deBaak considered that he was engaged in a chess game and out of moves. Then the distinctive tone from his combox alerted him to some type of incoming data feed: NEXTERUS MARINE–DATA FILE RECEIVED.

A pleasant diversion from his own medical woes, he considered. *Let's see what Dex Holzman thought might change the trajectory of the world.* deBaak began reading and became instantly amused over the purported healing power of a flower found in and around the Coral Sea off Australia's northeast coast. He read about local legend from Holzman's notes on a fishing village where residents lived well over one hundred years of age. Holzman had commentary and research on failed attempts to harvest the flower and the death and disaster that followed each effort. If only they knew the truth.

Moments later, another message appeared on the combox screen: OCEANIC LABS–DATA FILE RECEIVED. Oceanic was news to him. Chang, the investigator to whom he had given carte blanche, handled things proactively. As deBaak opened the file, his spirits brightened. This was the lab where Holzman sent the Aeternium flower samples for analysis. Oceanic's preliminary findings were both fascinating and scary at the same time. From his personal viewpoint, the promise of a cure for his brain tumor, no matter how farfetched, was a measure of hope. deBaak wished he had recalled this news from prior escapades. On the other hand, an Aeternium extract curing any and all medical conditions would make Mercy futile and cause the planet's already depleted resources to vanish. If life expectancy for the average person suddenly increased from eighty-five to one hundred ten, the earth would simply run out of space to hold the added population. This discovery would also alter his plans for Operation Control.

He exhaled forcefully, trying to relieve his body from the stress of it all. This dreaded file only confirmed what he learned many years ago.

deBaak leaned back in his chair, raised his long arms upward, and stretched his tired frame. While the odds were long and the stakes high, there was really only one move left.

CHAPTER 41

Golden Vines was well-known to Cam. Before Corey was born, she and Tom traveled there several times to enjoy wine country, great food, and the natural beauty of Northern California. It was one of the less populated places in the state. That, she recalled, meant it was only moderately flooded with people. The recording at the offices of Dr. Holzman indicated he was away on an expedition with no specific return date. Callers were invited to leave a message. Cam stood her combox on a table and filmed a short holographic video for the man she hoped held the key to saving her son's life.

Hello, Dr. Holzman,
You don't know me. My name is Camille Atkinson. I am from Los Angeles but currently live in Lockhart on Australia's east coast. I am a single mother with a ten-year-old son named Corey. My son has been diagnosed with a mutated form of the Reuben Syndrome Virus. With the help of Prime Minister Martin, Corey gained access to the best epidemiologist in the country. Still, there is little that can be done. I understand your current work has you in Australia exploring the possibility of an underwater flower with healing properties. I know this sounds desperate, because frankly, it is. I lost my husband a few years ago to cancer. They forced him into Mercy. I can't lose my son. Please help me.

Cam left her contact information, inserted a pop-up image of Corey, and hit "Send." A tear ran down her cheek. *Was she doing the right thing?*

CHAPTER 42

After straightening the condo, Dex and Amelia drove to the office to help Maybin assess the damage and put everything back in order. As they were hard at it, the vibration in Dex's pocket told him a new holographic message arrived. He went into a room down the hallway for privacy. Setting the device on a semi-cleared tabletop, Dex hit the button on the combox to view the message.

The glow from the formation of the holographic message rose from the top of the combox like smoke from a genie's bottle. In mere seconds, an image appeared of a woman who looked to be about his age. She was attractive with long, jet-black hair hanging down around her shoulders. He could sense, however, that this wasn't a social call. The woman's dark brown eyes revealed an obvious tension. Her face bore the weight of a heavy burden.

The holographic message completed in less than a minute. Dex shook his head. How in the world could this woman possibly know about the Aeternium flower? On the heels of the two break-ins, getting this message was too much of a coincidence. Did someone steal their research for the sake of this little boy? It was inconceivable that anyone would go to such lengths.

"Maybin, Amelia, get in here. You've got to see this," Dex bellowed.

They arrived in tandem, both looking quite disheveled from the evening's cleanup activities.

"I just received this hologram from a woman in Lockhart. She knows about the Aeternium flower. Watch this." He replayed the recording for his colleagues.

Maybin's dark complexion appeared sallow. The corners of his mouth turned downward as he stammered out, "But how . . . ?"

Amelia's face crinkled, exposing a mind lost in contemplation. "The woman mentioned Prime Minister Martin. Could she know something?"

Once again, Amelia impressed Dex with her instinct to keep digging for the truth—the mark of an excellent researcher. She was right again. This Atkinson woman mentioned the prime minister. Willow Martin would have knowledge of their Coral Sea expedition from the required permit obtained from the Australian government.

"Isn't that a stretch? I mean, sure, we filed for a permit, but that's a routine matter that the prime minister would have no knowledge of," Dex stated emphatically.

Maybin chimed in. "Besides, we filed the permit under the name 'Nexterus Marine.'"

"But don't you have to list the names of the primary researchers?" Amelia asked.

"Yes," replied Maybin. "But that doesn't explain why Prime Minister Martin would know or even care."

Amelia replied combatively, "She would if the world-famous Dex Holzman was listed as one of the researchers."

Dex was troubled by the evening's events. Two break-ins, the mysterious death of John Thomas in San Diego, and now this hologram from a desperate woman right here in Lockhart. Somehow, it was all related. "Let's finish cleaning up this mess," he stated, referring to the office. "Then, first thing tomorrow, I will contact Camille Atkinson. Maybin, dig into the permit filing and see if you can find anything unusual, and Amelia, if you don't mind, find out whatever else you can about Oceanic Labs. See if the San Diego police will talk to you. Let them know Oceanic was working on research for us and that might have something to do with the crime."

Maybin nodded in agreement.

Amelia pierced his veil of self-confidence. "Are we certain there was a crime at Oceanic? I mean, it is possible that any number of things could have caused a fire. John Thomas could have just passed out from smoke inhalation."

Dex hadn't considered that. He didn't believe in coincidence, and his gut told him the events of the evening were definitely related. "You may be right," he conceded for appearances only, "but we can't leave any stone unturned."

Undismayed, Amelia prodded further. "Just realize, if I contact the San Diego police, knowledge of our research will get out to the world by the end of tomorrow. Is that what you want?"

"No," he now said earnestly. "You're right. Hold off. Let's see what other way we can get the information we need."

Maybin lit up. "Why not hire a private investigator? That person won't be compelled to share anything learned with the local police."

Dex liked that idea. "I don't know any private investigators. Do you?"

Maybin smirked. "No, but it sounded like a good idea."

Dex chucked at Maybin's strategy. He likely got the idea from a movie. *Still, not a bad idea.*

Then, just as quickly, he reconsidered. "Let's work the case on our own—for now, at least."

CHAPTER 43

Erik deBaak was pleased with himself. Had he not commissioned the break-in to Holzman's rented condo and the lab in Australia, all would have been lost. But now, the future was never more certain. His black-gloved hand reached into his office refrigerator and retrieved a can of iced mint tea. He popped the top and threw back the first gulp. A drop of the cold beverage dribbled from the corner of his mouth, and he wiped it away with his shirtsleeve.

Using the portable combox, deBaak dialed a number he had committed to memory. When the call connected, Chang, his investigator from Omniscient Investigations, was on the other line.

"I've completed my review of the files you were able to retrieve."

"Were they satisfactory?"

deBaak hated superfluous questions. "I trust you reviewed the data from Nexterus Marine? That led you to Oceanic Labs in San Diego?"

The scraggly voice on the other end grunted an affirmative acknowledgement.

"Mm-hmm. I thought it prudent to send someone over there. OI leaves no stone unturned."

"Then you know what must happen next?"

"You want everyone who knows about it dealt with."

"Precisely. All of them."

"I am an investigator, not an assassin."

"Based on the way your man took care of Mr. Thomas at Oceanic, I would beg to differ."

"Ten million euros."

deBaak didn't flinch. "Fine. But it must be done quickly. When the job is complete, you will see me in Rotterdam to finalize payment."

deBaak clicked off and got up from behind his desk. He opened the office door and barked to his assistant, "Find Hennie and Dr. Viklund. Tell them both I wish to see them immediately."

Five minutes later, the diminutive frame of Sigrid Viklund entered his office. deBaak marveled to himself how she resembled a mad scientist from an old movie. Just looking at her made him contemplate the possibility of a nightmare. Her resume of wartime terror spoke for itself. It's why he sought her out.

For a woman in her early seventies, her voice was as strong as her character. "We are making excellent progress on Operation Control," she proclaimed.

deBaak just stared at her, not wanting to cede his position of authority. People like Viklund feasted on the weak. "Go on," he stoically commanded.

"We are contemplating two methods of distribution but haven't yet concluded which one is best. Perhaps it will be wise to employ both."

At that moment, Hennie Van de Berg strolled in, coffee in hand with a bright, cheery smile on her face. "Good morning," she almost sang with enthusiasm.

Viklund was totally disgusted. deBaak was idle as Viklund purposefully debased her superior. "I was just updating Leader deBaak on our progress and distribution options," she sneered, her voice dripping cynicism.

Taken aback, Hennie, as always, attempted to maintain her composure. "Distribution? The last we spoke, you were not even sure you could develop the toxin in a compressed formula."

"You are correct. We have made significant progress in a short time. I was going to tell you but didn't want to disrupt your busy schedule."

deBaak felt sorry for Hennie. She was taking it on the chin and was a reluctant player in a strategy her moral compass could not embrace.

"Ladies, this meeting is to get us all on the same page. Let's not fret about who knew what and when. We are all on the side of the planet's preservation."

Hennie smiled, clearly appreciating the attempt to level set a volatile situation.

Viklund just sighed, showing her boredom with the exchange. This became obvious when she monotonically proclaimed, "I'm just here for the money."

While not the sensitive personality that Hennie was, deBaak understood her frustration with Viklund. She was a handful but a necessary piece in his plan to restore the planet while exacting revenge on the entire Southern Hemisphere.

"Back to business," deBaak stated.

Viklund rose and began pacing around the room. She apparently was one of those types that had to walk as she talked. She tapped the Palette in his office and called up the file displaying her research. "Leader deBaak, you told me the Ruling Council has been seeking increased airdrops of Kenya Tabs to stave off pandemics." She coughed and took a drink of water.

deBaak thought the supercharged vitamin tablets costing the world billions were ineffective. A few countries favored them, but most did not. Hence the controversy with no logical end in sight.

Viklund cleared her throat and began once more in her thick Swedish accent. After tapping the Palette with her right index finger, an image of a normally white Kenya Tab appeared, but it was purple.

A nice touch.

"My plan is to have you introduce a new Kenya Tab that will contain antibiotics as well as vitamin components."

Naively, Hennie jumped in and asked, "Antibiotics? Doesn't that seem counterproductive?"

Viklund smirked. "Are you really that stupid?"

Again, deBaak stepped in to calm tensions between the two women. "Hennie, it is merely a ploy to gain the confidence of an unsuspecting public. Let Dr. Viklund continue."

Triumphantly, Viklund returned to the Palette and marched on. "The formula I have created," she said sarcastically "contains a contagion so powerful, just looking at a purple Kenya Tab will cause one to contract the virus."

"But how is that possible?" asked Hennie, incredulously.

Before deBaak could jump in, Viklund looked at him and almost yelled. "Can you get this imbecile out of here so we can get to the work at hand?"

Not wanting to cede authority but knowing she was right, he said, "Hennie, why don't you step out? I will update you myself when my schedule permits."

Hennie retreated from the room, looking over her shoulder at the older woman and doing her best to show contempt. deBaak now understood he would have to exclude Hennie from further planning on Operation Control. Her demeanor was insufficient for such a plan.

Once the door closed, Viklund picked up where she left off. "As I was saying, the purple Kenya Tabs will contain the world's deadliest virus. We will announce that a new partner, a pharma company, has improved the Kenya Tabs and we will deploy them across the Southern Hemisphere countries by airdrop."

deBaak admired her diabolical mind. "Two immediate issues," he proclaimed. He raised the index finger of his black-gloved hand and said, "If there is no known vaccine or antidote, how will we keep the Northern Hemisphere people from getting sick?" He then raised a second finger. "And there are tens of millions who don't consume Kenya Tabs. How will they contract the virus?"

The folds of her fleshy face smoothed as she smiled and said, "Once a person becomes ill from ingesting the purple Kenya Tab, they will become highly contagious. PSCs will aid the rapid spread." She touched a video link on the Palette and the two of them watched the plan's possibilities play out in full living color. Pods dropped the purple Kenya Tabs across the cities, mountains, plains, jungles, and forests while people in more populous areas stepped into personal sanitation chambers seeking a cleansing mist. A toxin they agreed to call Viper would replace the normal sanitizer. The video ended, and Viklund finished answering his initial question.

"Of course, there is both a vaccine and an antidote my team has created. No one will have this knowledge, but Northern Hemisphere residents will get a different Kenya Tab formulation that will contain an ingestible vaccine. We will make this tab available to those who don't normally consume them, emphasizing the benefits of the new formulation. This is the best we can do. There is no way to completely insulate people outside the Southern Hemisphere countries."

deBaak stroked his left cheek in contemplation. He pondered the loss of a small percentage of Northern Hemisphere citizens as a productive casualty exercise, effectively accelerating the effects of an amped-up Mercy protocol. "I see. Walk me through the timing and symptoms of those infected."

Viklund brought up another video file, and deBaak watched in amazement as the simulation showed infected people vomiting blood and losing their bowels. He was grateful he sent Hennie out of the room. She never could have handled the presentation.

"From the time of infection, death will occur in most people within seventy-two hours. The antidote will be effective only for the first twenty-four. You must take the vaccine before deployment, sir."

deBaak nodded in comprehension. This was a heavy burden to bear. What they were contemplating was mass genocide—and yes, there was a component of vengeance involved, but really, he rationalized, he was preserving the Earth for future generations. deBaak had to make the courageous decisions no one else could fathom. By extinguishing his own creation and presenting the humanitarian solution guaranteeing the planet's future, Erik deBaak would be a savior.

CHAPTER 44

Waiting for Dex Holzman to return her call was maddening. For Cam, sleep proved elusive. *Tossing and turning, tossing and turning.* Her mind's endless evening race across the sea of random thoughts left her devoid of energy. Sitting at her desk in the sparse Lockhart office, Cam took a sip of her second coffee. The aroma soothed her nerves. She stood up and walked across the compact space. Tapping the Palette, she commanded it to give her all available information on Willow Martin's actions to close Byamee's Brunt seventeen years earlier.

Before the Palette could begin speaking, Cam closed her office door. She didn't need any of her new staff wandering in uninvited and questioning her research. For most of the last seventeen years, the waters were calm. Before that, her research reported incident after incident, including the last one, the one that really caught her attention.

The video clip was mesmerizing. She stared intently at the Palette as a journalist on a newsreel recounted the discovery. The young woman stood on the edge of the beach with the wind whipping through her long auburn hair as she spoke to the camera. Cam still couldn't believe what was lying on the sand behind the reporter. She listened as the old newsclip recounted the story.

Local authorities remain in the dark this morning as they investigate the cause of death for a man found on this remote part of Scrimshaw Beach on the northeast Australian coastline. The man was discovered earlier today by a teenage boy from Brisbane on a modern-day walkabout in a region once inhabited by the Aborigines.

Standing in front of the Palette, a pain prick occurred in the base of Cam's spine. It gave her a momentary shiver as the camera zoomed in on the body.

Be warned, viewers. The next scene is not for the faint of heart. The view is quite graphic and not intended for youngsters.

A man, perhaps in his early to midforties, was on his back. A spear of some sort was lodged in the center of his chest. His baggy white shirt was blood-soaked, and his mouth hung open from the shocking manner of death. His eyes . . . *Oh my God!* Cam paused the video and held the close-up of the victim on the Palette. In her entire life, she had seen no one with eyes so starkly blue. The brilliant shade reminded Cam of the Blue Grotto on the isle of Capri, the bluest water she ever saw. Even in death, the brilliance of the dead man's eyes was prolific. She held her finger on the man's image and asked the Palette, "Show me any information on this man's cause of death."

Within seconds, a video clip from Brisbane Global News appeared with the information she sought. After watching the short feature, the closing segment intrigued Cam. She replayed it.

The victim's name was Gordon Brown, an oil worker from the refinery off Bulwer Island. From what authorities could learn, Mr. Brown took the job as an expedition leader to earn extra money to support his wife and twelve-year-old daughter. The expedition's mission was apparently to harvest an orange flower. Why? No one knows for sure. Gordon Brown's death is the fifth such incident reported this year. These waters have a secret to hide, and one member of Parliament wants to protect that secret from poachers while saving lives in the process. Former actress and one of the newest members of Parliament, Willow Martin, is sponsoring legislation to shut down the water natives call Byamee's Brunt, named for the Aborigine god whom natives believe was the world's creator.

It took a bit of time to find Gordon Brown's wife and daughter. His twelve-year-old is a talented gymnast competing in the Australian National Championship in Sydney, nearly one thousand kilometers away.

Cam pondered this additional information as she paced back and forth across the small office. Although she had a mountain of files to review on behalf of the Patient Advocacy office, she simply could not turn her attention away from Byamee's Brunt. Intellectually, she understood this research was likely fruitless. Desperation for anything that might save the life of her child dominated her sense of logic. She approached the Palette once more and commanded it to bring up the actual bill sponsored by Willow Martin.

The Coral Sea Protection Act of 2158 was 320 pages long. Cam found an extract from her Palette research and began reading. Not more than five minutes later, the ringing from her portable combox diverted her attention. The display showed the caller was Dex Holzman. A chill ran across Cam's body as she answered the call.

CHAPTER 45

Dex's first impression of Cam Atkinson was one of pity. He sat alone in his condo and watched the emotion pour out of her. Dex had never been a parent or a spouse. Other than John Thomas and the accidental death of a close friend on an expedition, he never really lost anyone in the manner she had. He listened to the details of her story and wished he could empathize with her dismay. When she finished, Dex let her take a breath before responding. This woman needed to unburden herself.

"Oh my God, listen to me. Here I am going on and on about my problems to the world's most famous marine biologist. I can only imagine what you must think."

"It's okay. I'm a good listener. And if you don't mind me saying, you needed to unload to someone."

She fidgeted a bit with her long, jet-black hair. "Actually, you are right. I picked up and left quickly and have lost touch with my friends at home. You know, it's good just to talk to someone else from America . . . and another Californian to boot."

Dex smiled and laughed just a bit. "I'm afraid, like many Californians, I'm a transplant. I actually grew up in a suburb of Baltimore."

"And now you live in Golden Vines?"

Loving his home but feeling guilty about how much space he owned for one person, he simply replied, "Yes, but I'm not there very much. It always seems I'm on an expedition somewhere."

"And you are in Lockhart now?"

He laughed gently and replied, "So it seems. I came here for a few days and discovered something so unique, I'm not sure when I'll be going home."

"As you already know, that's why I reached out. The something 'unique' you refer to. I need to learn whether the orange flower in Byamee's Brunt really has healing powers."

He hesitated to answer. *Where did she get this information?* His team was locked down tightly until the break-ins. He needed to be careful. She seemed innocent enough, but Dex could not rule out the possibility that Cam Atkinson was some sort of plant from the people who stole his research. "Cam, I have to ask. How did you learn about the research of my current team? The orange flowers and Byamee's Brunt are not exactly common knowledge."

She took a minute before replying. He was sure of it! This woman was measuring her words carefully. *Why?* His radar was up. Part of him wanted to conclude the call. Another part of him wanted to find out her source.

Finally, she answered his question. "I don't really remember where I heard about it. I'm thinking maybe it was Dr. Brighton, the epidemiologist in Brisbane."

Now he was sure she was lying. There was no way that any epidemiologist possessed knowledge of their work.

"In your message to me, you mentioned you received help from Prime Minister Martin. Tell me about that."

"In LA, my law partner knew someone in Sacramento who asked Governor Samson to tap her relationship with Prime Minister Martin. Sort of an indirect chain of assistance, but it all came together quickly. The prime minister has been a godsend to me."

Now he had her. "And you're sure it wasn't Willow Martin who gave you information about my research?"

Again, she hesitated.

Dex surmised she was unwilling to betray a confidence. It made sense that Willow Martin would know about his current expedition. Maybin had to file a permit application before they could enter the Coral Sea. Amelia learned of Willow Martin's effort to shut down Byamee's Brunt years earlier. Given her current and past positions, it wasn't too much of a stretch to assume Cam Atkinson got the idea to contact him from Willow Martin.

"You don't have to say anything," he replied. "I think I see what's happening here."

A tear formed in the corner of her right eye. "So, you won't help my son?"

"Cam, the work we are doing is extremely confidential. What you are asking about is nothing more than an old native legend. The Aborigines believed these orange flowers contained healing powers of some sort, but it's never been proven. As much as I would love to help your son, I just don't have the means to cure him."

"I understand," she sullenly replied.

"What type of prognosis have they given Corey?"

She sighed. He could see she was trying to suppress the deep-seated emotion. "He is on a drug called L'Chaim. Results for mutated RSV are mixed. Since he is asymptomatic, there is no exact life expectancy estimate. The mutations affect everyone differently. I've been told everything from six months to ten years. Australia has a more relaxed Mercy system. That's one of the reasons we came here."

Dex really wanted to help. He just didn't know what to offer. The Aeternium flower extract created by John Thomas at Oceanic held early promise, but in reality, they were a world away from the goal line. He resorted to the obvious. "Cam, I can't offer you any solutions to your medical problem, but maybe you and Corey would like to go for a boat ride on the Coral Sea this weekend?"

Her expression brightened, and some life returned to her sad, dark eyes. "Yes, Corey would love that. Thank you for your kindness."

"Cool. Send me your address and I'll swing by with a member of my team around nine in the morning on Saturday."

Dex ended the call and sat back in an old leather recliner. He didn't want to give Cam any false hope. Clearly, she had been through enough. But he couldn't help but wonder what it would take to recreate the extract John Thomas produced. And if he could, what harm would it do to try it on young Corey Atkinson?

CHAPTER 46

Erik deBaak sat alone on a Saturday morning in his newest toy, a luxury exercise chamber wherein, he marveled, all he had to do to was sit on a bench in an oxygenated enclosure while pleasant music played. On the opposite wall, a screen showed the news without volume. deBaak, dressed in a pair of black gym shorts with a tan T-shirt, closed his eyes. From the wall behind him, rollers emerged and massaged his core muscles. Next, a lightweight strap descended from the ceiling and rested itself across his chest. It vibrated to get his heart rate up. Immediately, deBaak began sweating profusely. A sour taste formed in his mouth, and severe panic set in. The machine was working. His heart rate elevated quickly. Being confined in small spaces instantly transported him back to the worst day of his life—being tortured by the maniacal Colonel Paz during the war. Seeing his tormentor's face up close and mocking him, deBaak used his left hand to rip the vibration strap from his body and then jumped off the bench. Opening the chamber door, he grabbed a towel and made for the safety of the larger outer room normally reserved for traditional gym routines.

There was simply no shortcut for exercise. He would have the aide who recommended this infernal machine cast from his employ. Why he even bothered to try it was beyond him. *The things we agree to when we are stressed.*

deBaak walked across the room to the shower. Letting the beads of cool water hit his skin brought him back to a feeling of normalcy. With the shower spray helping him relax, a clear vision of the path forward emerged. When push came to shove, there was only one person he trusted to help with his brain tumor. While Sigrid Viklund was far better qualified to develop the Aeternium flower extract from John Thomas' research files, this job could go only to Hennie Van de Berg, the woman who loved him. Why she loved him was unclear. He treated her like dirt. Mostly, he supposed, but there was the occasional lavish gift, a few nice dinners, and the once-in-a-blue-moon weekend getaway to somewhere that wasn't overflowing with people. Hennie would follow him to the ends of the earth. No matter how far off the deep end his plans went, Hennie was there. Maybe he had some measure of feeling for her.

deBaak toweled off, got dressed, pulled on the black gloves, and placed a call to Hennie. He invited her over, providing instructions on how to enter his home, now guarded 24/7 by the Earth security detail. He called down to the lead man and told him a guest would soon be arriving. An hour later, they sat alone in his kitchen with midmorning lattes.

Hennie dressed in a pair of jeans with a white blouse and floral scarf. Her scarf was an effort to hide the effects of aging around her long neck. Holding her mug with a hand on each side of the cup and her elbows on the table, she leaned in and showed her ever-present expression of worry and concern. "Erik, what is the problem? You look so stressed."

Gathering his thoughts, the muscles in his face tightened. His jaw nearly locked, preventing him from speaking. Finally, he stammered out the words he had yet to say out loud. "I have a brain tumor."

The blood drained from her face. Her mouth fell into an O as her hand with its long, bony fingers reached out to hold his glove-encased hand. "I am so sorry. That's terrible news. What do the doctors say?"

He shook his head, feeling as despondent as he probably appeared. "I have a form of glioblastoma. They give me six to nine months, assuming I don't voluntarily enter the Mercy program."

"Mercy? How could you even consider it? You are the Earth Leader, the most important person on the planet."

His eyes dropped to the table's surface. "It's my law. No, it's *the* law." He straightened up, gathering his resolve. "But not to worry. I have no plans to enter Mercy."

"What will you do?"

"I have to do something quickly. Within ninety days, I will experience rapid deterioration of cognitive skills, failing memory, and the ability to speak. I will be unfit to lead."

Hennie appeared to be holding back the tears. She really did love him. He was making the right choice. "Hennie, I will need your help. It will require discretion and your full attention."

"Anything, just name it."

"I will assume full responsibility for Operation Control and Dr. Viklund. You will need to travel to Australia. My only hope for a cure is in and around the Coral Sea."

"Australia? Erik, I am lost. Tell me what that means."

"I am one of a handful of people possessing knowledge of an orange flower with powerful healing qualities. It grows only underneath the Coral Sea and around a remote fishing village near Scrimshaw Beach. An ancient civilization that sunk to the bottom of the sea discovered the flower. Those citizens of a land called Aeternum believed these flowers could heal almost any human illness. Today, descendants of the Aborigines eat the flower petals and live to be well over one hundred years old."

She shook her head incredulously. "But even if we can find these flowers . . ." She collected her thoughts. "You know I'd do anything for you, but—"

"It seems too far-fetched?"

"Well . . . yes."

"That's because it is. I have come into some confidential information that a group of explorers recently harvested a small quantity of these Aeternium flowers and converted them into an extract that in laboratory experiments showed promising results on a variety of medical conditions."

With a pained expression on her face, she struggled to process the logic of it all. "But wouldn't it take months or years to create the extract?"

"According to my research, only days or weeks. Given my prognosis, there is no time to lose."

"Where did this research come from?"

"As Earth Leader, I am privy to all sorts of classified material. In this case, not even the Ruling Council is aware." The lie flowed with the ease of a waterfall rushing to the river below. "I will arrange everything. You must leave today," he stated firmly. "And Hennie . . ."

"Yes," she looked at him with a curious eyebrow arched like a fading rainbow against a storm-laden sky.

"Outside the team I put together for you, you can tell no one of this mission. Understood?"

"Yes, Erik. I understand," she replied, appearing every bit of the loyal lapdog he envisioned.

CHAPTER 47

Cam was nervous, although she didn't quite understand why. A famous marine biologist was coming to take Corey and her on a boat ride on the Coral Sea. It wasn't like she was going on a date—something she hadn't considered since Tom died. This was likely a pity invite. Dex Holzman felt sorry for her.

All things considered, it would be a nice day for Corey and a way for both of them to get their minds off his illness. Cam had no friends in Lockhart. It was either continue living the life of a stressed-out hermit mom or venture out and enjoy the day. Corey would love being out on the open water, something he had yet to experience in his young life. In the overcrowded City of Los Angeles, that opportunity was reserved for the rich and powerful. In her own life, she had only been on a boat once or twice as a little girl. Her faded memory of it was scant.

"Corey, are you almost ready? Dr. Holzman will be here any minute."

"Coming, Mom," he responded gleefully as he barreled through the hallway. Cam smiled at her son's choice of clothing. He wore a pair of faded jeans with a Superman T-shirt. As only a mother could, she warmed at her boy's adorable innocence and worship of a comic book hero whose story dated back a couple hundred years.

Cam peered out her window. A sizable SUV was pulling up to her apartment building.

Dex Holzman stepped out of the vehicle. He was a little taller than she imagined and more muscular too. He filled out the navy blue T-shirt well. His sun-bleached hair swept lazily across his forehead, serving what she perceived to be a laid-back, easygoing personality.

Although he wasn't here for her, a part of her wished he were. Cam had been so consumed with Corey's health, work, and escaping Los Angeles that she barely had time to consider the possibility of intimacy. *Who knows? Maybe something here will develop.*

That thought crashed when the passenger side of the SUV opened and a petite, athletically built woman in dark sunglasses stepped out. She wasn't stunning by any means, yet she possessed a natural beauty. *Were she and Dex a couple?*

"Corey, they're here. Let's head downstairs."

Cam walked down the outdoor building stairwell, making no attempt to catch up to her eager son, who raced ahead. Before she could say a word, Corey was already in the parking lot greeting Dex Holzman and his colleague.

"You must be Corey," Dex said.

Her son garnered a tight-faced grin, held up both arms in an L-shaped muscle pose, and said, "The name is Superman, mister."

"Superman? Wow! What an honor. I know we'll be safe from trouble today," Dex mused and held out his hand.

"Superman, meet my colleague, Amelia."

Amelia walked over, kneeled to Corey's eye level, and said, "It's my pleasure to meet you, Superman."

Cam relaxed a bit. Corey was in his element, and the day was off to a good start. She walked toward Dex and Amelia and formally introduced herself. Dex held the rear door of the SUV open for her and Corey, climbed in the driver's seat, and looked back at her.

"I have a boat rental up at Scrimshaw Beach. It's about an hour north of here. As you've probably learned, this part of Australia is still relatively barren in terms of people. You can drive around easily. So, it should be a smooth ride."

Cam fidgeted a little in the backseat. "Thank you for doing this. You really didn't have to," she replied.

Dex peered at her in the rearview mirror and grinned, "What? And skip the chance to meet Superman? I wouldn't have missed it for the world."

As they made their way onto the highway leading north, Dex asked about her relocation to Australia. Cam explained, at a high level, Tom's death, the legal practice in LA, and Corey's illness. Never one to focus attention on herself, she switched subjects as quickly as she could.

"How long have you two known each other?"

Amelia turned to face her from the passenger seat. Looking over her right shoulder, she said, "Not long at all. I work for a small research group in Lockhart. My boss called in Dex when we discovered a beached sea turtle near where we're going today."

Dex broke in before she could respond. "That turtle was glowing bright orange from what we later learned was the residue of the Aeternium flower petals."

Cam stayed silent for a moment, recalling the news story she found. Then, with no real forethought, blurted out, "Do you believe in Byamee's Brunt?"

In the blink of an eye, the mood in the car transformed from jovial to solemn. Amelia turned her entire body back toward the windshield, and Dex's posture noticeably stiffened.

Finally, he responded in a cautious tone. "You know, I'm not sure what to make of it. Instinctively, I'd tell you it's malarkey, but there are some alleged events that are pretty interesting."

Cam swiveled her head toward Amelia. "What do you think? You're an Australian."

Amelia didn't answer. To Cam, it was as if the woman had left her body and just checked out.

"Hey," Dex nudged Amelia on the arm with his left hand. "Cam asked you a question." It woke Amelia from her daze.

"Huh? I'm sorry. What was the question?"

Cam repeated her inquiry. "Do you believe the stories about Byamee's Brunt?"

Amelia crunched her shoulders as if shaking off a sudden chill. "Generally, marine biologists are inclined to fall back on the science, not local legends. That's why Dex is apprehensive. I came to marine biology later in life and, as a native of this area, I find the lack of evidence extremely hard to ignore."

Dex just laughed. "I wasn't aware you were so steadfast in your belief."

Amelia appeared a bit agitated. "Maybe you don't know me as well as you think."

Now Cam was certain. Listening to the interchange between them, they were a couple. At least she knew.

Cam sat quietly with Corey in the backseat for the remaining few minutes until the tires traversed the gravelly road leading to the Scrimshaw Beach Marina. On the walk along the dock to the rental, an unusual old man with a wide-brimmed straw hat was sitting on the edge of the dock. He wasn't fishing. He just sat there, looking out over the water as if deep in thought.

A minute later, Dex looked at Amelia and said, "Hey, it's Old Toby. Let's go say hello."

Dex led the group to the end of the dock, but before he could say a word, the old man turned his head back toward them, revealing the see-through gray sheath over both his green eyes. He was blind, yet clearly he sensed their presence.

"The love birds have returned," Old Toby said with a little glee in his voice.

Cam stood, surprised. *Love birds? What did this old fisherman know?*

Dex blushed. "Hello, Toby. It's good to see you again. And by the way, Amelia and I are just friends."

Toby shook his head and let go a laugh. "You can't BS me, son."

Dex elected to disengage from the comment that made him uncomfortable.

Then the old man spoke up again. "Who did you bring with you?"

"This is Cam and her son, Corey," Dex said as he motioned for them to approach. "We are going for a boat ride today."

Corey was taken with the old man. He walked over, and Toby placed the palm of his hand on her son's head and just held it there. Then, he said, "It's great to meet you! I'm guessing ten, maybe eleven years old?"

The perceptive abilities of the old man amazed Cam. "Yes, that's correct. He's ten."

Dex attempted to further the introduction by offering more background. "Toby is part of the village that oversees the Aeternium flower. He tells us he is now one hundred and five years of age."

Cam couldn't control herself. Her legal training and instinct to interrogate a witness took hold. "You have access to the Aeternium petals?"

He just grinned before responding. "That's right."

The blood drained from her face. Cam was being given a gift from God. If only the legend were true. "You must . . . I mean . . . can you . . . ?

Toby appeared sympathetic. "Your boy is sick, isn't he?"

It shocked Cam. "How could you know that?" She looked at Dex and asked, "Did you tell him?"

Dex shook his head.

A stiff wind hit Cam in the face. She glanced up at the sky.

A dark storm cloud appeared out of nowhere. The sun went behind the clouds. The wind picked up considerably and blew the straw hat off Toby's head. Amelia removed her sunglasses and tucked one arm into the neck of her shirt.

For the first time, Amelia's brilliant blue eyes captured her attention. Cam was sure she didn't hide her surprise. She had seen eyes like that only once in her entire life. It was just a few days ago on a long-forgotten newsreel about a dead man in the area in which they now stood. Cam's mouth dropped. Amelia had to be the daughter of Gordon Brown, the last known victim of Byamee's Brunt. Cam would never forget the haunting image of the man's brilliant blue eyes frozen in death following a native spear through the chest.

Cam looked at Amelia and tried to appear casual when asking, "What did you say your last name was?"

"Brown," she replied.

Just as a thread unraveled in the defense of a client, Cam knew she had something here.

Like an attack dog, she kept on coming. "And you mentioned you were late to marine biology. How come?"

Dex answered for her. "She's too shy to tell you, but she's a world-famous Olympic gymnast."

Suspicion confirmed! Gordon Brown's next-of-kin was his wife and daughter. They were a thousand kilometers away at the daughter's gymnastics competition. The timeframes lined up perfectly. Amelia Brown wasn't here by coincidence. She had a secret. Cam would find out what it was.

Gaining confidence, Cam again approached Old Toby and asked, "You are right. Corey has a mutated form of the Reuben Syndrome Virus. There is no cure, and authorities will eventually force him into Mercy. I need to know if the Aeternium flower can heal him. Can you help us?" Amid the gathering storm, Cam stared at the old fisherman in a state of harrowing desperation.

"It is not my choice to make. You must pray to Byamee."

The dagger of deflation pierced Cam's heart. It was the same agony she experienced when they lost the fight to extend Tom's life. Before she could process the rapid turn of events, Dex began waving them all back to the SUV.

"I guess the storm foiled our excursion today," Cam said. But as the words left her mouth, she could see there was something else. Something horrible had happened. Simply viewing the faces and body language of Dex and Amelia confirmed her instincts as an attorney.

In the SUV's safety, she touched Dex on the shoulder and asked, "What just happened?"

Before he could answer, Amelia responded through a cracking voice. "My boss, Maybin, just called. Two of my co-workers, Jack and Noah, were murdered at our research facility."

Amelia broke down in tears.

Dex gripped the steering wheel like his life depended on it and high-tailed it back on the highway.

Lost in a kaleidoscope of emotion, Cam reached across the backseat, pulled her young son toward her, and held on tight as the rain began to fall.

PART III

CHAPTER 48

Murder?

Dex struggled to maintain his normal sense of calm in the face of a crisis. After dropping Cam and Corey back home, he and Amelia made their way to the office to find crime scene technicians combing through the modest research facility. He found Maybin, hunched in a corner of his meager office, sitting on the floor with his head bowed and his arms wrapped across his knees. Amelia bent down and hugged her boss. Tears flowed freely from her crystal blue eyes.

Seeking outward strength he didn't feel, Dex kneeled and put his hand on Maybin's shoulder. "What on earth happened?"

Maybin looked up without answering. The man's face glazed over. Clearly, he was in a state of shock.

At that moment, a crash came from the next room. *Breaking glass.* Funny, the noise was symbolic of their recent days. The adrenaline from the discovery of the sunken city of Aeternum and its healing flower was now being shattered by forces unknown. Dex faced untold dangers on the seven seas, but this was something completely different. No one had ever died to stop his research. Dex was shaken to the core. He refocused and looked back into the despondent face of his distraught colleague.

Amelia handed Maybin a bottle of water.

Maybin took the first sip and cleared his throat, trying to produce some sort of cogent response. "I . . . I came in this morning and found them. Their bodies were riddled with bullets . . . their faces, the blood was everywhere. It was . . ."

Dex waited for Maybin to stop crying.

"When I left last night, they were just finishing the break-in mess. Noah told me to take the rest of the night and relax. He said he and Jack had it covered. I was exhausted, so I took off."

Dex watched sympathetically as Maybin broke down.

"Be right back," Amelia said, looking at Dex. "Got some tissues in my desk."

Collecting himself through bloodshot, tear-laden eyes, Maybin continued. "If I had only stayed. Maybe I could have prevented this."

Dex pulled him in and said, "Maybin, in no way is this your fault. If you stayed last night, you'd be dead too."

"This whole thing makes no sense."

Dex measured his words carefully. He didn't want to alarm a colleague in a state of distress. "The stakes are higher than we might have imagined. The Aeternium flower can change the trajectory of the world. Obviously, someone doesn't want that to happen."

Despite Dex's best efforts to be a calming influence, Maybin became more distraught. "I get that. Steal our fucking research, for God's sake, but why kill two good men like Jack and Noah? They didn't deserve this."

Amelia arrived with the tissues and handed the package to Maybin. He blew his nose and with a second tissue wiped his eyes. Although she was mothering Maybin, Amelia looked frightened.

Admittedly, Dex was scared too. It was clear now that whoever stole their research also murdered John Thomas, Noah Williams, and Jack Brightman. They wouldn't stop until everyone was dead.

Dex rose to his feet and scratched the itchy beard growth on his well-defined jawline. He was out of his depth. In his mind, they were all in danger.

Anyone with knowledge of the Aeternium flower was being pursued. He quickly scanned his memory and determined that he, Maybin, and Amelia would be next on the assassin's hit list. Then another horrible thought struck him. Cam Atkinson knew. She and Corey were also in grave danger.

Dex left Maybin's office and exited the building. He had to think. Who did he know who could help in a hurry? He had an exhaustive list of impresario contacts around the world, mostly people from the scientific community. None of these people would have the power to help. He needed a lifeline, and he needed it fast.

Dex paced around the emergency vehicles that took over the tiny Nexterus Marine parking lot. He leaned against an ambulance. The coolness of the vehicle's steel on the back of his neck eased his mind as he contemplated how he might contact his own country's president for help. President Sofer knew of him but didn't really know him. Could Dex get through quickly?

He now had a pipeline to Leader deBaak, but that might be too much firepower for the situation. Except for the incident at Oceanic in San Diego, the crimes had all taken place right here in Australia. All the people he surmised to be in danger were in Lockhart. Cam had a relationship with Prime Minister Martin, who could offer an immediate protective cloak for all of them while they apprehended the perpetrators. That was it. He had to call Cam.

CHAPTER 49

Grateful he didn't have to fly to New York for a Ruling Council meeting, deBaak entered his new video conference center in Rotterdam. He stood erect in the middle of the floor as the image of each Ruling Council member projected on the enormous wall before him in three rows of three. Along the top row were the leaders of the United States, the United Kingdom, and South Africa. President Sofer wore a necktie displaying the stars and stripes of the US flag. The British prime minister, Winston Nottingham III, puffed on a pipe. deBaak regarded smoking as a filthy, primitive habit. President Karabo Radebe wore a bright orange blouse that highlighted the luster of her dark skin. In the second row, the German Chancellor Gabriele Fischer looked annoyed, as if this meeting were some sort of inconvenience. Next to her on the wall was the Chinese President Zhang Jinhai. His dark, slicked back hair never looked out of place. *How much time did it take him to groom each morning?* The Japanese prime minister, Yuuto Takahashi, looked relaxed and wore an easy smile. On the bottom row of the video feed were the leaders of India, Brazil, and Australia. Selvi Kumar, India's prime minister, sat up arrow-straight as her long, braided hair draped across her chest. Next was Gustavo Souza, Brazil's president. deBaak always thought of Souza as a man who brawled in bars late at night. He was a huge man and still a fighter at heart. And last was the image of the Ruling Council member he despised, Willow

Martin. Her shining red hair and crimson lipstick were a bit much. The former starlet always needed to be the center of attention. deBaak would deal with her arrogance and conceit after Operation Control launched.

deBaak paced left and right, a lifelong trait. "Thank you for joining me today. I have wonderful news that should please all of you."

He took the measure of the faces on the mammoth screen. Everyone was dialed in to what he might say next.

"I have top scientists working on the development of a new Kenya Tab. It has a new formulation of vitamins and a cocktail of highly concentrated antibiotics to keep the population healthy."

Karabo Radebe of South Africa immediately cut him off. "This sounds great, but as we know, the past versions of these tablets are expensive with questionable results."

President Zhang from China broke in. "Suppose it works as planned? Then you will have population explosion beyond our current crushing dilemma."

deBaak shook his head. "Ladies and gentleman, I implore you to consider the needs of the world's people above all else. Population control versus health? I think we should always choose health."

His nemesis, Willow Martin, spoke next. "And that's ironic coming from a man who built the world's largest fortune by euthanizing people in the name of saving the earth."

deBaak did a slow burn but kept his face relaxed. He couldn't give away his true position.

"Prime Minister Martin, your comment about my wealth is accurate. Now, as Earth Leader, I must balance the two issues appropriately. On this subject, I choose health."

She smirked but said nothing else.

The German Chancellor, Gabriele Fischer, fingered the gigantic mole on her right cheek before blurting out, "Who is paying for R&D, production and distribution?"

deBaak expected this question. "No worries, Chancellor. A generous grant from Earth Reborn will cover all costs. All you must do is make your people aware that a new Kenya Tab is coming soon and encourage everyone to take it."

Morton Sofer, the US president, smiled and paved the way. "If all we have to do is create public service announcements stressing the need to take the new Kenya Tab, it sounds like a bargain."

"Yes, I couldn't agree more," offered Winston Nottingham III. "British citizens would welcome this development."

With no real dissent, deBaak pressed forward. "The new Kenya Tabs are being manufactured in facilities around the globe as we speak. Worldwide distribution should begin in two weeks via drones and all other workable modes of transportation."

Willow Martin sneered. "Suppose Australia refuses to take part?"

Before deBaak could answer, the powerful image of Brazil's leader, Gustavo Souza, took over. "Pardon my directness, Prime Minister, but are you insane?"

Martin dug in. "No, I am not, and I don't appreciate the way you are speaking to me. Maybe I just don't trust the new Earth Leader."

deBaak inhaled deeply, reminding himself to stay composed.

Before he could answer, Morton Sofer once again came to the rescue. "Prime Minister Martin, if I may. What has Leader deBaak done since taking over that has engendered these feelings? All his actions have proven to be for the good of the people of our planet. Need I remind you the alignment of words and actions is all any of us can be judged on. Leader deBaak has done nothing to betray our trust."

deBaak couldn't help but grin. He wasn't sure why the US president was such a supporter. He supposed the man was just one of those trusting souls.

Reluctantly, Willow Martin appeared to give in. "Thank you, President Sofer. I will agree at this time."

deBaak once again seized control. "Excellent. This will be in the best interest of the entire planet. Thank you for your help in getting the word out. We will issue suggested verbiage for your public service announcements one week before distribution."

deBaak clicked off and stood alone in the vast conferencing center. His temples throbbed and a mild dizziness befell him. He leaned against a wooden podium to steady himself. *Would the goddamned brain tumor claim his life before Operation Control fully deployed?*

CHAPTER 50

The call from Dex decimated her reality. After hearing the sordid tale of allegedly related assassinations in San Diego and Lockhart, her hand trembled uncontrollably. The combox nearly slipped from her hand. Unbridled terror swept through Cam's brain like a swarm of bats in the clock tower of an ancient structure. With everything she endured, now they were peripherally involved in a plot to kill those who sought control of a rare plant. Cam wanted to help Dex, but her first instinct was to protect Corey. *Where could she run?*

"Cam, are you still there?"

She couldn't bring herself to speak.

"Cam?"

She filled her lungs with the deepest breath possible and exhaled slowly. With her free hand, Cam swept a piece of wayward hair from her eyes and blotted a newly formed tear. "Yes, sorry. I'm here."

"I hate to lay any of this on you, but we are all in danger."

She hesitated, not wanting the cracking sound of her voice to betray the outward strength she possessed. "I understand," she replied stoically.

"Do you own a gun?" he asked.

"No. Should I?"

"It wouldn't hurt. We need to figure out a way to keep you and Corey safe."

"Safe from who?"

"That remains to be seen."

Cam couldn't help the sniffle. She didn't cry often, but when she did, her nose was sure to stuff up. If she were going to protect Corey and help Dex, she needed to get her head in the game. As an attorney, Cam was trained to piece together disparate information to make a case. Now, she was learning about a wide-scale conspiracy that stretched across multiple continents and focused on the quest for a flower that could change the world. The cast of categorized suspects ran through her mind like data streaming from a search engine inquiry. Pharmaceutical companies would make trillions off such a discovery. Government leaders supporting health versus overpopulation would also benefit, and then there was organized crime. Her mind was just considering the myriad possibilities.

"I'm scared. I want to help, but my priority is keeping Corey safe. Tell me what to do."

"I think you need to reach out to Prime Minister Martin. I'm sure she can protect you and Corey. I also think she may be the one person who can tie all the pieces together on the murders and Aeternum."

"I can call her. I know she will help if she can. What about you and your colleagues? How will you stay out of harm's way until they catch the people behind this?"

"Truthfully? I don't really know. I'm hoping Prime Minister Martin can offer all of us a safe house somewhere so the authorities can properly investigate."

Foolishly, she had considered only Corey and herself. Of course they would all need to shelter in safety as a group.

"Dex, I'm sorry. I didn't mean to imply you and your team would be on your own."

"You are a mother with a sick child. Your first instinct is to protect your child. I get that."

She felt better. The last thing Cam wanted was for Dex to think of her as a self-centered wreck of a mother who looked out only for herself. "I want to help. Let me reach out to the prime minister. My legal background makes me an excellent researcher. I can work from behind the scenes to help solve the mystery."

"That's great. I will try to lie low with Maybin and Amelia until we hear from you. In the meantime, don't go to work. Stay inside your apartment with the door locked, and don't open it for anyone."

"Be careful, Dex. Hopefully, with the help of the prime minister, we will all be safe by morning."

CHAPTER 51

In his storied career, Dex had seen plenty of danger. Raging storms on the open sea threatened his life. He once survived an encounter with a few angry sharks after a crew member fell overboard. Then there was the small fire that broke out in his Golden Vines research facility. None of that prepared him for the trouble he now owned. Breaking and entering, conspiracy to commit murder? How could he possibly have fathomed these possibilities when he journeyed to Australia to help with a beached sea turtle?

Amelia stepped outside to get the backpack she left in the SUV. Dex fell back on the secondhand sofa in the Lockhart condo. He didn't drink often, but Dex sorely needed a beer. His thoughts turned to Jack and Noah. *What would Maybin tell each of their family members? How would they possibly comprehend the madness?* He took a swig of the Aussie brew and closed his eyes to think. He was so far out of his element. Dex was a take-charge guy, but in the current mess, he admitted to himself that he was completely helpless.

The vibration of the combox disturbed his thoughts—an incoming call. The ID showed the caller was from Canberra. Dex knew no one in the Australian capital. Probably a junk call. He was going to let it go to voicemail when something compelled him to answer the call.

"Dr. Holzman?"

"Yes."

"Please hold for Prime Minister Martin," said a cheery young female voice.

"Yes, certainly."

Mere seconds of waiting passed like hours as the anxiety escalated. *Would the prime minister really be able to help?*

The familiar voice from her movie star days came on the line. "Dr. Holzman, hello. Cam Atkinson asked me to call. Apparently there is some trouble?"

"That might just be the understatement of the year, Prime Minister."

For the next ten minutes, Dex let every detail of his Australian expedition roll effortlessly off his tongue. He began with his first encounter with Maybin and the dead sea turtle on Scrimshaw Beach and concluded with the murders of Noah Williams and Jack Brightman. It startled him when she didn't immediately reply. For a minute, he thought the line had gone dead.

Finally, she answered. "That is an alarming tale."

"Without a doubt. I am fearful that anyone with knowledge of the Aeternium flower may be on a hit list. That includes Cam and her son, Corey."

"And the team members you mentioned, Jules Maybin and his associate, Amelia."

"I guess I might be on the hit list also," exclaimed Willow Martin.

"You? My God! Why would you think that?"

"Cam hasn't shared her research with you? Do you not know the reason the sector called Byamee's Brunt closed down for so long?"

Dex squirmed on the sofa. He searched his memory but couldn't recall every detail. He punted. "Assume I know nothing," Dex instructed.

"Seventeen years ago, I shut down. those waters to keep pirates and poachers from suicide missions trying to capture the Aeternium flower."

"So, you knew?" Dex was amazed. "Did your government analyze samples to validate the local legend about healing properties?"

"No, we never got the chance. My predecessor scoffed at the notion. The only focus of the government at that time was to stop idiots from attempting to harvest the flowers. The certain death that came to anyone who tried is still a mystery today."

Dex shook his head. He still didn't know what to make of it all. Toby's tales of Byamee were too outlandish for his logical mind. "So, what do you recommend?" he asked.

"I am going to issue an emergency order once again closing Byamee's Brunt. The Australian army will guard the land-based Aeternium flowers. Until we can figure out who's behind this, I am asking you, Cam, Corey, Maybin, and Amelia to come into protective custody."

"I think we can all agree to that. Where and how?"

"Can you get yourself, Maybin, and Amelia to Cam's apartment? I will have a transport pod there waiting to bring you all to Canberra. We have a safe house on the outskirts of town. We can confer there and ensure your safety."

"Yes, we'll all be there."

"Great. Oh, by the way, did Cam tell you about the last victim of Byamee's Brunt? The last man killed before I shut down the waters seventeen years ago?"

Dex again searched his memory and couldn't recall. "No. How is it relevant?"

"The man's name was Gordon Brown. He was an oil worker looking for extra cash to support his family. They found him dead, with his eyes wide open and a native spear through his chest. The police never found the perpetrator. When interviewed, the locals blamed Byamee."

"Byamee? That doesn't sound too likely to me. Why are you telling me this?"

"Because Gordon Brown was the father of your associate, Amelia Brown, our national champion gymnast."

Dex was speechless. Why wouldn't Amelia have told him this? It explained so much about why she was working in marine biology and how she always knew the history of the area. He had to slow his breathing. He needed time to think. "Prime Minister, thank you for your help. I look forward to seeing you soon."

Dex was beside himself. He'd have to think it through later. Right now, the priority was getting everyone to safety in Canberra. "Amelia. We're going to Canberra to stay in a government safe house. We'll swing by your place so you can get a few things, and then we'll pick up Maybin and head to Cam's apartment. The P.M.'s pod will be there to pick us all up in a few hours. I'm not sure how long we'll be away. A few days at least."

No answer. Come to think of it, Amelia never reentered the condo while he was talking to Willow Martin. *Where could she be?*

He walked through the condo calling her name. She wasn't anywhere to be found. When Dex arrived at the front door, it was still slightly ajar. His sense of worry immediately took hold. He swallowed hard and walked toward the lot where the SUV was parked. "Amelia," he called. Still, there was no reply. When he approached the SUV, everything looked normal. Dex walked around to the opposite side of the vehicle, and his heart sank like a stone to the ocean floor.

Amelia Brown lay flat on her back on the hard pavement with a single bullet hole between her eyes.

CHAPTER 52

The lost expression on Hennie's face totally enraged deBaak.

"What do you mean the expedition's been canceled?"

"The Australian military has locked down access to both the Coral Sea sector and the village where the Aeternium flowers can be found."

"By whose order?" he inquired, thinking it was just someone else to assign to Chang.

"The boat captain you hired told me the order came directly from Prime Minister Martin."

deBaak's mind turned rapidly. Taking out a high-profile figure like Willow Martin on short notice would be no simple task. Even Chang wouldn't have the stomach for it. He recalled the months of meticulous planning required to eliminate Akeyo Gathee. Time was a luxury he no longer could afford. His mind, normally a machine for instantaneous solutions to the most troublesome problems, failed him. deBaak's head was full, like he just came out of anesthesia. He couldn't think clearly.

"Dammit Hennie, you know what's at stake!" He was now yelling. His face turned red as an uncontrollable rage took hold. "We must get that flower. The extract is the only chance I have."

Hennie looked back with tears in her eyes. deBaak inherently understood her feelings for him. By the look on her face, she had no idea what to do next and marked the mission as a failure. For all the money he possessed,

Erik deBaak could not buy time. Every day, hour, minute, and second became precious. At this moment, he really didn't give a shit about Hennie Van de Berg's feelings for him. There was only one true motivation, and that was survival. Without a chance of extending his life, his long-awaited vengeance on the Southern Hemisphere countries and desire to restore the planet would perish with him.

Dulled by the now constant headache from the brain tumor, deBaak made a move out of sheer desperation. "You stay put in Australia. I will hire a team of mercenaries to take out the Australian forces and clear the way for your expedition."

Immediately, a look of horror took over Hennie's expression. As the words rolled out of his mouth, he realized he hadn't thought it through. Still, he had Hennie, a loyal foot soldier in position. He had a few weeks before Operation Control launched. There was enough time to take out the Australian military, grab the flowers he needed, and bring Hennie home safely to help steer things from Rotterdam.

Hennie startled him with her response. "Erik, this is madness. Your mercenaries will cause a war. Australia will stop at nothing to figure out who did this and strike back. If they guess incorrectly, they could accuse the wrong country and spark a global conflict."

He ignored her plea for reason. "Just do as I say. It will take a day or so to plan. Stay put and wait for further instruction."

"As Earth Leader, can't you just lift the hold Australia has placed on the areas?" she pleaded.

"No, I have no authority over sovereign lands in peacetime situations." It would be easy enough to create a conflict enabling his authority. *How long would that take?* Every good notion crashed and burned in the face of diminishing time. The mercenaries would be the only plausible solution.

Hennie was now softly crying.

He hated that weakness. People like Sigrid Viklund were deplorable, but he never had to worry about a meltdown when the going got tough.

"Enough!" he commanded. "You are a pitiful human being. I need you in place to coordinate things on the ground for me. There is no time to send someone else. Find your courage."

She nodded gently in agreement.

He didn't have the time to deal with emotion. The clock was ticking, and his life and vision for the planet hung in the balance.

CHAPTER 53

The safe house contained everything they needed. Cam was relieved she and Corey had their own space, including two bedrooms and a bathroom. When they arrived, it amazed Cam that an elaborate three-meter, solid black fence kept the flood of people she saw on her recent trip to Canberra at bay. The perimeter stood like a fortress.

Dex and Maybin were both a wreck. It took all her powers of persuasion to get them both on board the transport pod.

After they dropped their things, Cam and Corey walked the outside grounds, something they were assured was perfectly safe in view of the secure nature of the facility. Cam looked up. Wire mesh netting blocked her view of the sky. It covered the entire property's air space.

"It's protecting against drones."

The prime minister's voice startled Cam. "I'm sorry. I didn't see you there."

Willow Martin smiled at Cam and Corey. "Spy drones are now as small as common houseflies. The protective covering keeps them from entering. The material emits a magnetic wave that disables the drone's ability to spy."

The extraordinary measures one took to be safe. Cam would never have contemplated such dangers. "How do you know one of those little buggers didn't follow us into the complex?"

"Good question." The prime minister pointed up. "You see that pole with the small red box?"

Cam nodded.

"Those red boxes constantly scan for any type of intruding device. If one did cling to your shoulder on the way in, an alarm would sound at our onsite monitoring station. Any such device would be located and instantly destroyed."

"Then I guess we are safe."

"As safe as one can be anywhere in this overcrowded, disease-infested, and crime-ridden world."

"That's a pretty sad commentary on the world." Cam replied.

"I think my time in government has turned me into a cynic."

"How long do you figure we will have to hang out here?"

"It's unpredictable. I have enlisted the minister of intelligence to work with local authorities in Lockhart to figure out who is behind this. They will assume control over the local investigation and have the authority to make inquires in the US and other parts of the world if need be."

Uncharacteristically, the sudden urge to cry overwhelmed Cam. Maybe this was just too much to deal with. She threw her arms around Willow Martin's neck. "I can't ever repay you for all you've done for Corey and me."

Willow Martin ended the brief embrace and stared into Cam's eyes. "Of course. I told you my mother suffered with mutated RSV. I will help you and Corey in any way I can."

A high-pitched beep emanating from the prime minister's combox disturbed their exchange.

Willow Martin glanced down at the display. "Grab Corey. We need to head back to the house. There's some new information."

What new information could have come in so fast? Cam found Corey sitting near a running brook and grabbed his hand. "Come on. We have to get back up to the house."

Cam, with Corey in tow, followed the prime minister, who was clearly familiar with the most expedient path.

When they arrived at the safe house, the trio walked directly to the sunken great room where Dex and Maybin were waiting. Dex looked haggard. Finding Amelia's body took an obvious toll. Jules Maybin looked pallid. The two marine biologists were both in uncharted water.

When Dex noted their presence, he sprung up from his overstuffed chair and feigned normalcy. "Did you guys have an enjoyable walk on the grounds?"

Corey answered before she could. "Dex, I saw a lizard near a rock by the water."

Dex smiled. She could tell it was genuine as she listened to his reply. "That's great, buddy. Did you give him a name?"

Corey placed a finger to one cheek, and his face crunched up in contemplation. "I like Dex."

Dex laughed. "You named the lizard after me?"

Corey smiled the sheepish grin of a carefree ten-year-old and nodded in the affirmative.

Willow Martin spoke up shattering the lighthearted moment. "Sorry to break the mood, but we have new intelligence."

Cam patted Corey on the head. "Why don't you go investigate the basement and let me know what you find." Willow Martin already told her there was a video gaming system down there.

As soon as Corey was out of earshot, Willow Martin took control. "We know that the same gun was used to kill Mr. Williams, Mr. Brightman, and Ms. Brown."

Cam listened without surprise. This wasn't exactly a shocking revelation.

The prime minister continued. "The assassin left behind trace amounts of DNA. Our lab is working on a match across all worldwide databases. We should get a hit somewhere."

"What else have they learned?" Dex asked.

"Not much, I'm afraid. It's been only a few hours, and even with advanced technology at our disposal, it will probably be tomorrow before we hear anything. I have to leave now, but the chef here at the safe house will make you all dinner. I'll be back in the morning to share whatever else we might have learned."

"Thank you, Prime Minister," Cam offered.

Dex and Maybin also expressed their appreciation.

As Willow Martin turned to leave, a member of her protective detail grabbed her arm and said, "Just a minute, ma'am."

Cam stared at the quickly unfolding event. She was not accustomed to being around a head of state.

The aide listened into an earbud and then addressed his boss again. "We are cleared to leave, but we will take you to the residence. There is a disturbance of some sort at Parliament House."

Willow Martin looked agitated as she responded to her aide. "What kind of disturbance?"

"I'm not sure, ma'am. The agent onsite said a distraught Dutch woman was making a scene, demanding an audience with you. She said it was a matter of life or death."

Now Cam was curious. The faces of Dex and Maybin held odd expressions as Willow Martin dismissed the concern. "Probably just a crackpot. This sort of thing happens all the time."

CHAPTER 54

Early the next morning, Dex sat on the wraparound sofa in the great room of the government safe house and just stared at his laptop. He was numb from his inability to focus beyond the image of Amelia Brown lying on the ground. The shock of it all was overwhelming. Maybe he fell in love. He never stopped to really ponder it before now. They were just two colleagues having a good time. But there was more. He was certain Amelia felt the same. Now he would never know.

Dex stared out the picture window overlooking the palatial grounds with its beautiful foliage. The sight of nature always cheered him but not today. A tear formed in the corner of his eye. Dex just couldn't believe everything that was happening.

As he sat lost in grief, the gentle touch of a warm hand settled on his left shoulder. He looked up.

Cam's sympathetic face peered down. She gave his shoulder a gentle squeeze in a display of compassion.

"Hey," was all he could say. Cam just smiled at him. Dex appreciated her empathy.

"Do you want company?" she inquired.

Dex nodded. Being alone right now would not be the best thing for him.

Cam walked around the mammoth L-shaped sofa and sat down next to him, turning her body to make eye contact.

Before she could speak, he started venting. "Why her? Why any of them? Are these flowers really worth killing over?" The more he spoke, the more the grief turned to anger. His skin turned hot as his temper uncharacteristically flared. He prided himself on being mild-mannered and taking things as they come, but this feeling—it was like nothing else he had experienced. If he were to assign a label, it could only be classified as unadulterated rage.

"Sadly, in my line of work, I've learned that people will go to extraordinary lengths to protect secrets," Cam gently replied.

Dex scratched his head. "I suppose," he said. "But wouldn't something that makes the population healthier be a good thing? Even if we can't house everyone, keeping them healthy would be a positive step, wouldn't it?"

Cam nodded in the affirmative. "You are talking to someone who understands. Every single client I had in LA was on Mercy's death row."

"So why keep the Aeternium flower a secret?"

"I don't understand it, but speaking of secrets, Amelia had one."

Dex perked up at the mention of Amelia. "The P.M. told me. Amelia's father was the last known victim of Byamee's Brunt."

Cam again nodded affirmatively. "Amelia never told you?"

Dex stopped to consider her question. "No, but I suppose she would have. I mean, thinking about it. Why is it even significant?"

"Not sure. Maybe it isn't. It just seems awfully coincidental that the daughter of the last victim randomly works on the mystery that killed her father seventeen years earlier."

Despondently, Dex replied, "You may be right. How would we even check it out? The father is dead, Amelia is dead. She was an only child . . ."

"Is the mother still living?"

Dex paused for a moment to think. "You know, she may well be. Amelia said she grew up in Brisbane. The Nexterus Marine human resource file should help. Amelia's mom would be next-of-kin."

"Maybe Maybin would give us the contact information."

Dex liked the idea, if for no other reason than the opportunity to meet Amelia's mother and express his deepest sympathies. "Do you think Maybin knew about Gordon Brown and Byamee's Brunt?"

Cam shrugged. "I can't imagine he knew and wouldn't have said anything."

"True," Dex conceded. "I'll track down Maybin and see if he can access Amelia's employment records from here."

"Great. Let me know how I can help," Cam offered.

"I will and—"

Before Dex could finish his thought, Willow Martin burst into the safe house with her security entourage. "Where is Mr. Maybin?" she demanded without greeting them. "I have a hologram everyone must see."

Dex called for Maybin, and he stumbled in wearing a pair of gym shorts and a T-shirt with two koala bears hugging a tree branch. He was unshaven and extremely disheveled. "What's going on?" he asked.

With that, an aide to Willow Martin set up a projected holographic video device on the enormous coffee table. The light rose from the device and formed the image of two people sitting across from one another in some sort of interrogation room.

"This is in the basement of Parliament House," Willow Martin interjected.

Dex turned his attention back to the display. He spied a tall, thin woman in her midforties with short-cropped blonde hair showing signs of gray. Agitated, she spoke with a Dutch accent.

"The man conducting the interview is my head of security," Willow Martin stated.

The interview unfolded before Dex's eyes. He wasn't sure why this was relevant.

"My name is Hennie Van de Berg. I am the chief operating officer for Crematie in Rotterdam."

Crematie? That was the worldwide conglomerate owned by Leader deBaak. Now Dex's curiosity had been piqued. Cam and Maybin clearly shared the intrigue.

"Keep watching," instructed the prime minister.

They turned their attention back to the hologram.

"Why are you here?" asked the head of security.

"I have come to warn Prime Minister Martin. Something terrible is about to happen."

"What do you mean?"

"I work for Leader deBaak. He was a POW in World War IV. He was tortured and plans to eradicate the entire population of the Southern Hemisphere as revenge."

"That's preposterous."

"He calls it Operation Control. Once the plan has unfolded, the dead will be disposed of in Crematie facilities, and the lands will be repopulated with citizens of Northern Hemisphere countries."

"Assuming such a tale has any truth to it, why are you here in Australia? Why involve our prime minister?"

The blonde woman looked exasperated. She was suffering from some sort of frenetic meltdown. She had a crazed look about her—yet, as bizarre as it sounded, Dex thought there might be a grain of truth to her story. His only encounter with Leader deBaak left him with an uneasy feeling. He listened as the conversation in the hologram continued.

The Van de Berg woman hesitated, as if she didn't want to reveal everything. Then finally, she slowly made a dramatic claim even more outlandish. "Leader deBaak is not well. He sent me here to lead an expedition to find a healing flower in the Coral Sea, but when my team arrived, I learned that the entire area was shut down by order of the prime minister."

With that proclamation, Willow Martin instructed her aide to stop the hologram.

"Is there more?" asked Dex

"A little, but you've seen the important part," replied Willow Martin.

"Did she say what type of illness Leader deBaak has?" inquired Cam.

"No, my security chief didn't ask either. I sure would have. Nothing personal, but I hope the bastard isn't long for this world," stated Willow Martin emphatically.

"Isn't that harsh?" asked Maybin.

The prime minister glared at Maybin and said, "If you'd ever met the man, you'd likely agree with me. He's pure evil."

"So, what do we do with this newfound information? How do we verify its authenticity?" Dex asked.

Willow Martin stared directly into Dex's eyes with a steely determination and replied, "We've got this Van de Berg woman in custody. She isn't going anywhere. Once I get proof, I'll take it to the Ruling Council."

"Assuming this is true, do we have any details about Operation Control and its timing?" asked Dex.

"Van de Berg indicated the threat was imminent. My security chief said she was spent from the session and needed a break before continuing. They are resuming in the next hour."

Aboard a boat on the open sea, Dex was the sure-handed captain, always ready with the next move. In this instance, he was stuck. *What in the world do I do next*?

Cam rescued him with a question he likely should have thought of on his own. "When will we get an update?" Cam asked of the prime minister.

Willow Martin smiled and said, "As soon as it starts. You can watch it live via holographic stream using this device," as she pointed to the projector on the coffee table.

Dex desperately wanted to help. "Prime Minister Martin, since you have Byamee's Brunt and its land-based flower field locked down, would it be possible to have some of the flowers extracted? I think I can access a cloud backup of John Thomas' notes for creating a healing extract. If Cam agrees, I'd like to do that for Corey."

Dex looked over at Cam and thought she might cry. Her cheeks turned rosy, and her dark eyes melted into welcoming passages inside her deepest emotions.

Before Willow Martin could reply, Maybin spoke up. "That won't be necessary."

It confused Dex. "Why not?"

"Because we didn't send Oceanic all the flowers we retrieved with the MS devices."

Cam jumped off the sofa and instinctively screamed for joy. Before Dex knew it, she was planting a wet kiss on his cheek.

Through his blushed expression, he said, "I think you may owe that kiss to Maybin."

Cam walked over to Maybin, wrapped her arms around him, and then gave him a similar expression of gratitude.

"Well, that settles that," proclaimed Willow Martin. "We will reconvene in an hour to watch the second interview with Van de Berg."

Dex was now more in control. With John Thomas' notes in hand and help from Maybin, he was sure they could recreate the healing Aeternium extract. It was Corey's best chance. He also made a mental note to ask Maybin for Amelia's next-of-kin contact and then set his mind to how he could help Willow Martin stop Leader deBaak's plot against the Southern Hemisphere.

CHAPTER 55

The video played repeatedly. deBaak just couldn't bring himself to hit "Send." He regarded his own appearance as sickly, although his normal look was pallid. All that remained was convincing himself that the illness wasn't dominating his perception of the public service announcement. In the end, deBaak had to be the one to send it. It was much better to supply a video from the Earth Leader explaining the new Kenya Tab and the reasons to take it versus each country's leader potentially butchering the recommended verbiage. This way, he gained consistency in the messaging. He leaned back in the rich leather chair and watched one more time.

"Greetings, citizens of the world. I am Leader Erik deBaak. Our planet faces unprecedented challenges with housing, food supplies, and medical treatment capabilities. We at Earth are working on these issues. The building block to all roads forward remains ensuring the good health of people around the world. This includes those with and without shelter. The biggest danger we face is the spread of disease. A global pandemic could prove devastating to the survival of humanity. It is with this concern in mind that I announce the creation of a brand-new Kenya Tab."

deBaak's image paused on the video to hold up the newly designed package, without his ever-present black gloves, careful not to reveal the color of the tablet inside. This was critical, as Southern Hemisphere countries would get the purple tab containing the toxin called Viper while the Northern Hemisphere countries would get a traditional white tab with the vaccine.

"Top scientists around the world have collaborated on this formulation. The new Kenya Tabs contain a mix of antibiotics along with vitamins and a vaccine against known strains of developing viruses."

At this point in his life, deBaak was numb to the lies he told. He simply cast them off as necessary tools to accomplish the job at hand.

"In the coming weeks, the new Kenya Tabs will be distributed throughout the world. They will be free and will deliver right to your homes in sufficient quantities for all your household members. If you are homeless and hearing this over a public address system, you may feel confident that regardless of where you are on the planet, your new Kenya Tabs will be airdropped by drone."

That part sounded sincere. Now for the grand finale.

"It is vital to take the new Kenya Tab as soon as you receive it. Like the old formulation, the tablet is chewable and has a pleasant taste. Some parts of the world will receive a new grape flavored tab while others may receive a coconut flavor. They are the same strength."

He hoped that part came across as genuine. His goal was to appear as the most caring of leaders, although nothing was farther from the truth.

"We are also pleased to announce that some parts of the world will receive an experimental dose of the new formulation delivered in a mist via personal sanitation chambers. If successful, we can expand this method of deployment.

Imagine the liberating power of cleansing yourself while simultaneously being protected from disease."

Nice touch. Getting Sigrid Viklund's Viper toxin to deploy in the personal sanitation chambers across the Southern Hemisphere was a stroke of genius.

"Keeping the earth's population healthy is the first step in our plan to make the world a better place for everyone. This is Leader Erik deBaak urging you to take your new Kenya Tabs as soon as they arrive. Thank you, and be well."

He supposed it was as good as it was going to get. He quickly dictated instructions for all world leaders as to the timing and frequency of the message and then hit "Send." He rose from the chair and retreated to the opposite side of the vast office to consult the list of contacts he maintained in a secure database. Tapping his Palette, he called up the list, categorized by job function, and reviewed the listings under the heading of 'Mercenaries.'

CHAPTER 56

For the first time since she fled Los Angeles, Cam was feeling hopeful. The answer to her prayers was Maybin's declaration announcing some Aeternium flowers had been kept. She now hoped Dex and Maybin could recreate the healing extract developed by John Thomas. *Why couldn't they have Corey simply eat the flower petals the way villagers did at Scrimshaw Beach?* Dex had explained that the outer sheath of the petal offered some benefit, but a chemical process enhanced the effects of Aeternium petals. In a courtroom, Cam was always sure of herself. Where science was concerned, she was lost.

With an hour to kill until the next interrogation of Hennie Van de Berg, Cam vowed to find Amelia's mother. Using information provided by Maybin from Amelia's personnel file, it wasn't difficult. Given locator services available on any basic search engine, anyone could be found fairly quickly—with an address and geospatial code, it was a breeze. With Dex at her side on the sofa in the great room, they sent a video request signal to the last known computer address for Lily Brown in Brisbane.

She answered promptly, and the resemblance between mother and daughter blew Cam away. Lily Brown had to be around fifty years old. Except for her eyes, she was simply an older version of her daughter. The unusual blue eyes came from the father, Gordon Brown.

Cam waded in gently. "Hello, are you Lily Brown, Amelia's mother?"

The woman took on a look of immediate distress. "Yes, yes. Is she okay?"

Dex took over as prearranged. Cam was grateful that Dex would deliver the bad news to Amelia's mother. It was his obligation, Dex explained just prior to the call. "Mrs. Brown, my name is Dex Holzman. I recently met your daughter on a project here in Lockhart. I'm afraid we have some terrible news."

Before Dex could continue, Cam saw the horror wash over the woman's face. Lily Brown was experiencing the sickening feeling that she outlived her child, something no mother ever wanted. Cam's heart ached for the woman on the other end of the transmission. She didn't envy Dex at having to break the paralyzing news.

"I don't know how to tell you this, but Amelia was shot and killed outside my condo where she was visiting," Dex said compassionately.

By now, Lily Brown was sobbing. Cam and Dex gave her a minute to collect herself. Once she came around, Dex explained what they knew.

Through gentle sobs, Lily Brown finally articulated her feelings. "I told her not to go chasing ghosts when she began the marine biology thing."

Cam wanted to be sensitive to this woman's sudden grief. She started out as a parent would. "Mrs. Brown, my name is Cam Atkinson. I am also a mother and can't express how sorry I am for your loss."

Lily Brown nodded, blew her nose, and gave a nonverbal appreciation as a nod.

Cam waited a minute and then resumed her questioning. "What do you mean by chasing ghosts?" Cam asked.

Lily Brown sniffled and wiped her nose with a tissue. "They killed my husband in the same area. He was helping on a paid expedition to harvest some flower from a sunken civilization they claimed could heal anything." She paused and sniffled again. The other woman's agony translated with each falling teardrop. "They never got what they were looking for, but murdered Gordon for trying. The rest of the crew drowned. They ruled the whole thing an accident, but no one could ever explain the native spear that killed my husband."

"I imagine that's what motivated Amelia to work in marine biology in this region. She wanted the chance to learn more or to somehow avenge her father's death?" Dex asked.

"She felt guilty about it," offered Lily Brown. "My husband only took the job for the extra money. Amelia was a child prodigy in gymnastics. Her equipment, training, and travel costs nearly broke us. But it was important to Gordon and me that she got every opportunity to succeed."

"Now it makes sense," stated Dex. "Maybin told me she appeared at his doorstep looking for a job when he had none to offer. She practically agreed to work for free just to get her foot in the door."

Cam was in sync with this woman's pain. She wanted to wrap up the call and let Lily Brown grieve in her own way. "Mrs. Brown, again, we are so sorry for your loss. If you think of anything that might help locate Amelia's killer, please let us know. The investigating officer will likely also reach out to you."

"A fat lot of good they did seventeen years ago when my husband was killed," Lily said, the anger invading her speech.

"Why do you say that?" Cam asked.

"They ignored the most important piece of evidence."

"What was that, Mrs. Brown?" inquired Dex.

"The spear. The one that killed Gordon. The tip looked authentic, but it was made out of a plastic resin."

Cam looked over at Dex, who immediately understood.

"You are saying they staged the whole thing? To make it look like a native attack? Native spears aren't made with plastic resins," Dex concluded.

"That's right," said Lily Brown. "The authorities tried to sell me on the local legend of Byamee's Brunt. I didn't believe that nonsense then, and neither did Amelia."

Cam understood now. There were people that would stop at nothing to procure the Aeternium flower, and from the sound of it, the local authorities in Lockhart were complicit.

CHAPTER 57

Dex still couldn't get over the claims being made by the Van de Berg woman. Even if Leader deBaak had been a POW in World War IV, would that give him motivation to extinguish nearly half of the world's population as revenge? Having spoken to deBaak, Dex just didn't believe he had it in him.

Cam, sitting beside him on the wraparound couch, disagreed. "Call me a cynic," she proclaimed. "But I agree with the prime minister. He seems like pure evil."

"Come on, Cam. You know better than that. You can't judge him by his looks, just his actions. What has he actually said or done to make any of this believable?"

"Nothing that we know of," she replied. "We may find out differently when we watch the second Van de Berg interview in a few minutes."

Dex just shook his head. He really didn't know what to think. He was always programmed to trust people at face value. Cam was right. She really was a cynic. Given her legal background and what she told him of the way she grew up, he guessed it made some sense.

His thoughts were interrupted by the reemergence of Maybin who had showered, shaved, and changed into his normal black trousers with a green Nexterus Marine polo shirt. He was chomping on an apple when he greeted them between bites. "When does the movie start?" he asked, referring to the second Van de Berg interview.

"Any time now," replied Dex. "Just waiting on the PM."

"Did you speak to Amelia's mother?" asked Maybin.

"We did. She was understandably distraught," Dex answered.

"And the father's death? Did you ask what she knew?"

"Oh yeah," replied Cam. "She believes her husband was assassinated to keep the Aeternium flower a secret."

"What makes her think so?"

"Because," Cam reasoned, "the 'native' spear that killed him had a tip made of plastic."

Maybin's face dropped. "Well, that seems like a giveaway, doesn't it?"

Dex jumped in. "I've never seen a native spear with a tip made from plastic."

"Does she have a theory on who might be responsible?" Maybin queried.

"Nothing concrete. She might be one of those government conspiracy theorists," said Dex.

"Nothing conspiratorial about it," said Cam.

Dex could see Cam's cheeks turning crimson. She apparently had very little trust in government officials herself. Yet, she and the PM developed a nice friendship. He pondered this for a moment and remembered that Willow Martin's mother died in Mercy from a mutated Reuben Syndrome Virus. In addition, Willow Martin was clearly not the prototypical government official. Her background as an international movie star painted her an aberration among crooked politicians. Maybe Cam being from southern California and the Hollywood scene made her prone to admire the independence of Willow Martin.

Maybin upended his thought. "I'll call Mrs. Brown and express my condolences. I can also send her Amelia's last pay and personal effects."

"I'm sure she'd appreciate that," offered the softer side of Cam Atkinson.

Maybin plopped down and continued to chomp on his apple.

From behind the couch where they all sat, the familiar voice of Willow Martin permeated the room. “Two minutes till the transmission starts.”

Turning around to look at her, Dex asked, “Do we need to do anything to the device to get it to start?”

“No,” replied Willow Martin. “It will begin automatically.”

Not a second later, a flat-pitched tone came from the projector on the coffee table and light began streaming skyward.

The prime minister took a seat on the couch, and Dex, along with Cam and Maybin, focused on the continuation of the scene that unfolded earlier in the day.

“You said that Leader deBaak was ill. What is the exact nature of the illness?” asked the security chief.

How strained this Van de Berg woman was. She was conflicted. She obviously knew the answer to the question but for some reason did not want to say. She sat there silently, without answering.

The security chief pressed on. “If you wish to gain an audience with our prime minister, you must answer all questions completely and truthfully.”

Dex appreciated that he was firm but not unkind. They still didn’t know for sure whether this woman was for real.

During the silence, Willow Martin spoke up. “We’ve already corroborated her identity and profession. So far, she’s been forthright in her statements.”

They continued watching. The emotional distress on the Dutch woman’s face was so obvious.

Finally, she broke her silence. “It’s . . .” she hesitated. “He has . . .” Van de Berg began softly crying, struggling to get the words out.

“Take your time,” said the security chief, this time more compassionately.

“Erik has an inoperable brain tumor.” With that proclamation, her eyes moistened some more, and she dropped her head into her arms on the metal tabletop.

"Funny how she called him by his first name," said Cam. "It was almost like an intimacy was there."

"Do you think they're involved—romantically, I mean?" asked Maybin.

"It would explain the conflict she is expressing," Cam replied.

Willow Martin winked at Cam. Dex guessed this was some sort of female affirmation that Cam accurately guessed what the PM herself was thinking.

The security chief continued the interview. "I need you to tell me everything you know about Operation Control."

Dex listened as Hennie Van de Berg told the story of Dr. Sigrid Viklund and her past as an engineer of chemical weapons for the Northern Hemisphere in World War IV. She recited details of a plot to create a purple Kenya Tab containing a lethal toxin called Viper. She concluded with the white Kenya Tabs containing the Viper vaccine going to Northern Hemisphere countries. The prospects of something so horrendous mortified Dex. He never experienced such evil. What they were discussing was something limited to novels, movies, and history books. He took a deep breath and, right then and there, resolved to do whatever he could to stop this insanity.

Willow Martin shook her head in disbelief. Cam and Maybin looked as shocked as Dex was.

Cam addressed the prime minister. "Do you believe this?"

Willow Martin exhaled and suddenly looked pale. "It all makes sense now."

"What?" asked Dex.

"The recent Ruling Council meeting. deBaak was uncharacteristically pushing this new Kenya Tab. He was supporting health over Mercy. It was such an abrupt about-face. My instincts told me at the time he was lying, but I had no proof. Then, this morning, we received his recorded public service announcement. He wants it played across the world."

The prime minister, who always appeared to be in complete control, was wounded.

Dex wanted to help, but he had to learn what she knew. "Prime Minister, can you show us the public service announcement?"

"Sure, sure I can." Collecting herself, she said, "Let's see the end of the interview first."

They refocused on the projected hologram.

The security chief stared down Hennie Van de Berg and asked, "Is there anything else we should know."

"Yes, Erik's father just died. His mother and sister are still alive in Arnhem."

"And why is this significant?"

"They were all victims of Purple Dust attacks levied by the Southern Hemisphere on Rotterdam during the war, when Erik was in a São Paulo prison camp."

"And Arnhem? What is there?"

She sighed. "That is the facility Erik created for Purple Dust victims."

"You are suggesting that Leader deBaak has fueled this Operation Control to seek retribution on the Southern Hemisphere countries who kept him prisoner and victimized his family and countrymen with Purple Dust?"

What happened next surprised them all, most notably Dex, who always saw the best in people.

Hennie Van de Berg pounded her fist on the table, became wide-eyed, and screamed at the man across the table. "No, you idiot! I'm not suggesting anything. I am telling you that Erik deBaak is a madman and is on the verge of starting World War V. I need to see the prime minister to stop him. Can you not understand this?"

Willow Martin signed off on the transmission and looked at the group on the couch, throwing up her hands. "I will grant her asylum. She will be brought here later today. She must not feel like a prisoner. We need her help if we are going to stop deBaak."

Dex nodded in agreement.

"In the meantime, I can access the Mercy database and learn the exact nature of the brain tumor. International law would require any doctor diagnosing deBaak to enter the test results and diagnosis," Willow Martin said.

"That sounds like a plan. Can you show us that PSA now?" Dex asked.

Willow Martin summoned the video on her personal combox and streamed it to the projector. A caring Earth leader lied through his teeth about the new Kenya Tab and its benefits. deBaak also mentioned PSCs. If the Viper toxin was deployed in personal sanitation chambers, they had a whole other dimension to consider.

Dex sat quietly, trying to put all the pieces together. He did a mental check on what he knew so far. Erik deBaak was not who he appeared to be. A poisoned Kenya Tab was being deployed to all Southern Hemisphere countries. A version of the same toxin would spray people entering personal sanitation chambers. deBaak would likely dispose of all the dead in Crematie facilities, making billions more that he would funnel through Earth Reborn to relocate Northern Hemisphere citizens to available Southern Hemisphere countries. And, amid all this scheming, deBaak discovered he had a terminal condition and needed the long-shot prospect of healing himself with the Aeternium extract.

As he considered everything he learned, Dex questioned how the death of Amelia Brown's father seventeen years ago had anything to do with deBaak's scheme and who was trying to kill them all now. He sat back on the couch, ran both hands through his thick head of hair, and exhaled, trying to let the stress melt away. He glanced at the prime minister and said, "What can we do to help?"

The PM was back in the driver's seat, in full control. "I've got my top people working the murders of your three colleagues. The next step is to get Van de Berg here and see what actual proof she can get me so I can call an emergency Ruling Council meeting . . . without Erik deBaak."

"Okay, in the meantime, Maybin and I will need to go to the Nexterus Marine office in Lockhart to recreate the Aeternium extract for Corey."

"It's too dangerous. Let me have the samples brought here."

"The safe house does not have a lab. We must return to Lockhart," stated Maybin firmly.

"Okay, but you will travel in my pod with my armed security detail, who will remain with you 24/7 until we can bring you back to Canberra," stated Willow Martin.

"I want to go with them," Cam pleaded.

"Absolutely not," said Willow Martin. "You and Corey will be safe here. I simply can't risk it."

Cam reluctantly agreed. "I'll do what I can from here."

Dex addressed Willow Martin. "Can we leave immediately?"

"Yes, I'll make all the arrangements. Cam, since you'll be remaining behind, maybe you can befriend Hennie Van de Berg and see what else she might offer."

Cam nodded her agreement.

Dex stood up, addressing Maybin, and said, "Let's go."

In the company of four armed men, Dex and Maybin took the short walk to the back of the safe house grounds where Willow Martin's private pod awaited just outside the secure area.

"It'll be good to get back to Lockhart," Maybin said as he swatted a fly from the back of his sweaty neck.

CHAPTER 58

There were some days where nothing went the right way. Erik deBaak was experiencing one such day. Sitting in the Rotterdam Earth office, he contemplated his current situation. The follow-up call with Chang revealed three of the targets remained alive and in the protective cocoon of the Australian prime minister. *God, how he hated that woman.* Hennie had turned into a loose cannon. He was no longer sure he could trust her, but really, what choice did he have?

His feelers to known mercenary groups so far yielded nothing. The one substantive conversation was with a New Zealand group who didn't exactly relish taking on the Australian military.

At least Operation Control was going well. The Viper-laced Kenya Tabs were being produced and airlifted to distribution points across the Southern Hemisphere. The liquid version of Viper already shipped to the public works facilities that would load it into personal sanitation chambers. Public service announcements were now airing on all media and being broadcast on PA systems for those living in the open. Within mere days, Operation Control would be fully operational. If only Chang could complete his mission and Hennie would get her act together. He needed that extract more than anything. If Hennie failed, at least he would cleanse the planet's southern half. Then, future leaders could take advantage of the open land he created. *His parting gift to mankind.*

deBaak ran his fingers across his sunken cheeks. The black gloves were cool against his face. He was leery of recording any of his plans for fear of being found out by hackers. He committed almost everything to memory. Given his advancing condition, his memory could no longer be relied on. Many times during the day, he had to stop what he was doing to try to remember what his prior thought was or what he planned to do next. The headaches increased in frequency and ferocity.

The combox sound pierced his brain like a siren in the dead of night. It was Chang, probably calling to report another roadblock. In no mood for more bad news, he answered abruptly. "Yeah," he growled into the speaker.

"It's Chang. I have news."

"Well, what is it? I haven't got all day."

"Holzman and Maybin left the Canberra safe house and went to the Nexterus Marine office in Lockhart. That will create an opportunity."

"You think you can get them?"

"It won't be easy. They are accompanied by the prime minister's security detail. Let me see what I can do."

"What about the woman?"

"Atkinson? She is still in the safe house with her son. There is no way to get to them."

"So, what's the next move?"

"When Holzman and Maybin left the safe house, I deployed a fly, the nanotech drone, and had it land in Maybin's backpack. That gives me eyes and ears on the group and its plans. Once I know more, I can pinpoint the best time to take them out."

"Chang, don't fuck this up. I want Holzman, Maybin, and Atkinson out of the way quickly."

"Understood."

"If Willow Martin gets in the way, consider her collateral damage." He sensed Chang's hesitation and added, "If Martin goes down, I'll double your take."

Chang appreciated the extra ten million. "One more thing," he added.

"What?" deBaak said in a surly tone. He was in no mood for a give-and-take negotiation.

"The prime minister brought another woman into the safe house today. The woman in the photo I am sending you resembles your COO."

Seconds later, the photo appeared on his screen. It was Hennie being accompanied by Willow Martin's security detail into the Canberra safe house. deBaak couldn't believe his own eyes. The one reason he sent Hennie to Australia was because of her loyalty. Now it was clear she betrayed him in the worst possible way. *That bitch!* The stress exacerbated the horrendous pain in the side of his head. He reached into his desk drawer for the pills. He swallowed two with a chug of water and paused for a moment. He was so mad, it was like fire shot out of his eyes.

He disconnected with Chang, leaned back in the chair, and tried to remember every detail of what Hennie might communicate to Willow Martin and what the prime minister might do about it. Thank God he had gotten Hennie out of the room when Sigrid Viklund was detailing the entirety of Operation Control. That, he assured himself, would mitigate the damage.

CHAPTER 59

With Dex and Maybin headed back to Lockhart, Cam found herself in limbo between their departure and the pending arrival of Hennie Van de Berg. She was supposed to befriend this woman, to see what else she might reveal in casual conversation. Cam was great at interrogating people, but outside Gracie in Los Angeles, she had no girlfriends. Corey delighted in the latest video game in the safe house basement while she hopped on an elliptical trainer to get her blood pumping. She thought it might help clear her head. How could she take what she and Dex learned from Lily Brown and translate it into some sort of productive result? According to Lily Brown, the Lockhart detectives who investigated her husband's death were part of a cover-up. *But who was covering up what?* As she exerted herself more and more, a light sweat built and the old courtroom adrenaline returned. She simply had to return to the Palette to research the death of Gordon Brown. She now recalled that the lead detective was interviewed for the story she read. If she could track him down, he might hold some clue corroborating Lily Brown's claim. She slowed the machine to a safe point of disengagement, grabbed a nearby towel, and told Corey she would be back soon.

Cam accessed the story from her section of saved articles and commenced reading. Third paragraph down, there it was—the quote from Lockhart Detective Stephen Fallon. The detective was quoted as saying, "Like prior incidents of similar nature, all evidence substantiates the native legend of Byamee's Brunt." The article said that, according to Detective Fallon, the legend accounted for both the drowning of the small crew and the spear that killed Gordon Brown. No other physical evidence was ever found.

Cam left the article and accessed the roster for current personnel in the Lockhart Police Department. When she entered the name of Stephen Fallon, a picture came up with a banner across the bottom stating, "RETIRED 2173." That was only two years earlier. That left her a good chance of finding Detective Fallon alive and well.

Assuming that he might still live in Lockhart, Cam used a search tool to find a video link for him. Only one person by that name lived in Lockhart. She clicked on the link and prayed that the Stephen Fallon she was looking for was the one who answered.

After a lengthy delay, it seemed the call would go to video mail, but at the last second, the waiting screen cleared and a man's image formed. Yes, clearly this was the retired detective.

She had thought none of this through. How would she explain who she was or why she was calling?

"Umm . . ." she hesitated. "Detective Stephen Fallon?"

The man had to be at least seventy. He looked older than his police photo, and clearly he was out of shape. "Yes, how can I help you?" he asked pleasantly.

"My name is Cam Ferguson. I'm a reporter for Australian News Network. I'm calling to get your comment on the prime minister's recent closure of the Coral Sea sector known as Byamee's Brunt."

The man's expression changed. His posture became rigid. His eyes took on a steely determination to find out why she was really calling. She had to stay cool.

"I can't help you," he stated firmly.

"But you were the lead detective investigating the last known death involving the area seventeen years ago."

"That was a long time ago."

"Do you think there's a connection between the legend of Byamee's Brunt you cited in 2158 and the recent closure?"

"Everything I have to say about '58 is already on the record." And he clicked off, ending the transmission.

His abrupt behavior only stoked Cam's curiosity. Frustrated, she used her personal combox to connect with Dex. "I tracked down the detective who investigated the death of Gordon Brown."

"I can tell by your tone you didn't get what you wanted."

"The guy totally stonewalled me. He definitely has something to hide."

"Did you think about talking to his supervisor?"

"He's deceased."

Dex furrowed his brow in contemplation. "Hey, didn't you tell me your father was a police officer in LA?"

"Yeah, so?"

"Did he have a partner?"

Of course, Stephen Fallon had a partner. The key was finding and speaking to him.

"Great thought," she said. "I'm on it." Then, before she clicked off, her sense of dread for his safety kicked in. "Dex, be careful out there."

He winked, reassured her he would be fine, and ended the call.

Cam's first instinct was to revert to the news stories she had read earlier. She scoured the main article and came up empty. Then she remembered the police database. There might be something there. Once on the page showing Fallon's retirement, Cam found a link for homicide, the department in which Fallon last worked. The link contained a menu choice to view all current homicide personnel. There was only one active homicide detective, Jerome Purdy. Next to Purdy's listing, there was an empty box indicating a vacant detective slot. In a remote town like Lockhart, there was a good chance Purdy was also Fallon's partner all those years ago. She clicked on the contact link for Purdy.

It was all but impossible. Purdy was a young man, maybe midthirties. Seventeen years earlier, he would have still been in school. There was no harm in communicating with him under the guise of the reporter following up on the recent closure of Byamee's Brunt. She clicked on his contact link and waited for him to answer. *Was Purdy investigating the murders of Amelia, Jack, and Noah?* Then she remembered Willow Martin assigned the investigations to the feds. With likely no other homicides to investigate, Cam found Purdy at his desk.

"Detective Purdy, my name is Cam Ferguson. I'm a reporter for Australian News Network. I'm calling to get your comment on the prime minister's recent closure of the Coral Sea sector known as Byamee's Brunt."

Her intrusion on his busy schedule clearly put him off. He scoffed and said, "Why are you calling me about this?"

"Your department investigated the murder of Gordon Brown at the same location in 2158. I just thought you might have a response to the recent news."

"I wasn't aware it was closed down again. Did someone else get killed there? If that were the case, surely I'd know."

Cam wasn't sure how much she wanted to reveal to this man. "No, not that I'm aware. I'm just seeking reaction for the current piece I'm writing."

"Frankly, I can't speak officially for the Lockhart Police, but from my standpoint, if no one got killed, I don't think we give a shit. Speaking off the record, of course."

"Is there anyone still working in your department who also worked the Gordon Brown murder in '58?"

Purdy paused before responding, as if he wasn't sure he wanted to give up any actual information. Finally, he said, "No, but you could call Detective Fallon. He's retired now."

"Yes, I spoke to Detective Fallon. He didn't appear happy to hear from me."

"I'm not surprised." Purdy paused again, measuring his words carefully.

"He was . . . how shall I say? . . . difficult to work with. He had a certain reputation for looking the other way."

"Looking the other way? You mean he broke the law?"

"I have nothing else to say, but if you wanted to learn more, you could reach out to his partner from '58, Detective Maddox. She's also retired, but I guarantee she is one of the good guys and would add some color to your story."

Cam thanked Purdy and looked up Vivian Maddox, who, like Fallon, still lived in the greater Lockhart area. Feeling lucky, she entered the contact information into the combox and hit "Send."

Like her former partner, Stephen Fallon, Vivian Maddox was also in her early seventies. Her heavily wrinkled face appeared below the short, stark white hair. This woman led a stressful life. After once again introducing herself as the reporter and explaining that Detective Purdy provided her contact information, Cam got her standard introductory question out of the way.

More so than Fallon and Purdy, Vivian Maddox spoke in heavily accented Australian. "Purdy, he's a good one. Fallon, not so much. I remember working the Gordon Brown case in '58. We learned the spear tip wasn't authentic, but Fallon, being the senior guy, shut it down lickety-split, and the whole thing was ruled accidental."

"Why would he do that?"

"You're American, right?"

"Yes," Cam smiled. "Just getting started Down Under."

"Well, let me put it to you this way. Fallon was more crooked than the letter Z you Americans like so much, and I told Internal Affairs every detail."

Cam's eyebrow arched. She could feel it. It had always been her instinctive reaction to discovering a piece of startling new information. "Anything come of it?"

"No. The entire episode got buried. Fallon had friends in high places."

"Can you share what you told Internal Affairs?"

Maddox bristled. "Don't see what harm it could do. Just list me in your article as an anonymous source if you don't mind."

Keeping up the ruse, Cam quickly agreed.

Maddox continued. "He was on the take, that Fallon. I saw the squeeze. A whole packet full of bills."

"Do you know who was paying him off?"

"Oh yeah. I dug into it on my own. Almost got me killed when they found out I knew. The money came from New York. A mobster named Vito Cardelli. His goons were down here killing anyone who tried to harvest those damn flowers from the Coral Sea."

"Why would Cardelli care about Aeternium flowers?"

Maddox shrugged. "I couldn't figure it out until I learned he was under contract to a Dutch business magnate whose identity I never learned. Cardelli was also romantically involved with an international movie star."

"Movie star?" Cam asked. "Interesting but relevant how?"

Maddox laughed out loud. "That's the rub. You know . . . how Fallon got away with it all. That movie star is our current PM."

Cam was sure Vivian Maddox could see her jaw drop. *Willow Martin? Complicit in the cover-up of murder?* She just couldn't believe it.

"I can see the shock on your face. I still have all my research. I'll send you a file when we get off this call."

Cam thanked Vivian Maddox and began pacing around the safe house basement, wondering for the first time whether she could really trust Willow Martin.

CHAPTER 60

Willow Martin's security detail accompanied Dex and Maybin to the Nexterus Marine building in Lockhart and conducted a thorough walk-through before they could enter. Once cleared, Dex observed that the facility was in relatively good shape considering the robbery and subsequent murders of Jack and Noah. The police and federal authorities had been through the place with a fine-tooth comb, but thankfully, they left the storage facility's auxiliary refrigerator alone.

"I keep this small unit back here so the others won't steal my food," Maybin remarked. Maybin kneeled and reached into the very back to retrieve a sealed container. He smiled and said, "Here it is."

Dex laughed out loud. "The investigators probably thought it was a moldy sandwich," as he looked at the opaque lid with the orange flowers underneath.

"They still seem fresh," Maybin said after lifting the lid.

"Before he died, John Thomas established a shared drive in the cloud for documents pertinent to this research. With everything that's gone on, I hadn't seen it until this morning" said Dex.

"That's a relief. Did he include the process for creating the extract?"

"It looks like it. Let's get the drive illuminated on the Palette and start poring through it together."

With that, Maybin placed the samples back in the refrigerator.

The two of them retreated to the conference room where they had studied the turtle necropsy results—the room where their adventure first began. Who knew it would lead to the threat of genocide by the leader of Earth?

As they viewed the documents displaying on the Palette, Dex zoomed in on the one appearing to have the formulaic calculations. He shook his head. "Over the years, I've sent John countless samples to examine. He's never sent me notes with this level of detail."

"Do you think John was afraid? Maybe he was sitting on a powder keg and wanted you to have everything just in case?"

"Seems like a logical conclusion."

They studied the formula, its various iterations, previous failures, and how the tests were conducted.

"Here's the first problem," stated Maybin. "If we can recreate this extract, how will we test it? I don't know about you, but I don't want to experiment with the life of a ten-year-old boy before we have something concrete to prove the possibility of a cure."

Dex nodded in agreement. "And I think we need to work fast. Who knows how long we'll be safe here, even with the PM's security detail?"

"Where can we get mutated RSV samples to test against?"

Dex paused to think. After a minute, he replied, "We can't think like marine biologists. We also can't include anyone else for fear of a leak or placing that person in the same danger we're now in. The best thing we can do is to get what we need from Corey."

Maybin's face lit up. "Of course, how foolish of us. We need Corey's blood."

Dex picked up his portable combox and rang Cam to explain what they needed. The safe house had a full-time medic whom Cam would engage to draw the blood. Then, she would ask the PM to have her pod transport it immediately to Lockhart. In the meantime, Dex and Maybin would work on creating the extract. They had to be careful. There was a decent quantity of flowers remaining but not so much that they had any to waste.

○○○○○

Eight hours later, Dex and Maybin produced the first batch of the extract. Corey's blood samples arrived, and they were ready to have a go of it. Maybin prepped two slides with Corey's blood sample. The first would be the control sample. The other would contain the new extract. On the Palette, they posted a high-definition photo of blood from a normal person under a microscope. After Maybin placed the second slide into the microscope, Dex peered in to see whether he could determine any change.

"You will not believe this," he almost yelled in his excitement and then moved aside for Maybin to see.

"Damn, it's changing right before our eyes. It's almost too good to be true."

"Let's give it a little time and then we can match it up to the normal sample."

"Roger that," said Maybin. "I wonder what else this stuff can do."

"According to John's notes, he had early success with a variety of medical conditions."

Maybin flashed a sheepish grin. Dex could tell he had something up his sleeve. "You know, my company sent me down here to explore the seas for anything that might help mankind and make a profit."

Dex sighed. "Tell your bosses in the UK that Nexterus Marine will get a piece of the action. After all, it was their money that funded the J-Cous rental and your team that retrieved the Aeternium flowers."

"Couldn't have done any of that without you," Maybin replied.

Dex laughed. "True enough, but I don't need or want the money. I hope your company will reinvest profits to continue helping the planet."

"I'd insist on nothing less," Maybin replied triumphantly.

After ten minutes passed, Dex populated the Palette with the sample mixed with the extract on a side-by-side comparison with Corey's RSV-tainted blood and that of a normal person.

Maybin spoke first. "Look at the change in Corey's blood. The extract definitely has an effect."

"Compare it to the healthy sample on the right. There are still significant differences."

"I see what you mean. Did we get the formula wrong?"

"Truthfully, I know enough here to be dangerous. What medicine have you ever taken that cured you immediately? I have to believe time is an essential element."

"Normally, I'd concur, but didn't John's research indicate instantaneous results with experiments on gangrene and cancer?"

"To some extent," Dex conceded. "But mutated RSV is different in every patient." He started pacing around the room, trying to get his head in a game where the rules may as well have been written in another language. "I know we didn't want to involve outsiders, but I think we have to."

"Who do you have in mind?" Maybin asked.

"Cam took Corey to see some famous epidemiologist in Brisbane. I'm thinking we get him on a call and share this screen with him."

"Agreed," Maybin said. "Do you know his name, or should I call Cam?"

"Call Cam. She'll want to listen in, I'm sure."

Dex studied the slides again while Maybin called Cam.

Ten minutes later, a video conference link had been established for the four of them.

After Dr. Brighton viewed the slides on Dex's shared screen, he took off his rimless glasses and made a whistling noise before saying, "It's remarkable."

"Perhaps, but its markedly different from the healthy blood sample," Dex argued.

"True, but not by that much," Dr. Brighton replied. "I mean, you might be looking at a slightly stronger dose or maybe a second treatment. The results are extremely encouraging."

Cam, the concerned mother, asked, "Dr. Brighton, two questions. Is it safe to treat Corey with the extract as is? And if so, how would it change his prognosis?"

Dr. Brighton grimaced. "Cam, I want to be completely honest with you. There is just no way to answer those questions. We are in uncharted waters here."

She took on that look of determination that Dex had come to appreciate. Almost defiantly, she asked, "If this were your son, would you have him take the extract?"

The doctor looked genuine in his contemplation of Cam's question. Finally, he said, "You know, I'd think hard about that, but I would probably wait for more data. Corey isn't in imminent danger. You have months, maybe even years. There is the likelihood that a more definitive extract might be created offering a total cure."

Cam sighed. Dex felt for her. The answer to her prayers was here . . . almost.

Dr. Brighton continued. "On the other hand, if Corey took today's formula, it might extend his current life expectancy."

"Or introduce some unknown and irreversible side effect," Dex exclaimed. He was protective of a little boy he barely knew and wasn't sure why.

The famed epidemiologist furrowed his wavy gray eyebrows and responded. Dex was now regretting the brief outburst. "He's right. Anything is possible here. There is going to be a significant risk in any of these options, even if you get a perfect 'cure' match in your experiments. We just can't predict how the extract will affect any individual."

"So, what do you recommend?" asked Dex.

"With your consent, I can call in contacts from renowned pharmaceutical companies and other noted epidemiologists. We can confer as a team and give you direction from some of the world's best minds on the subject."

Dex replied instantly. "It's too dangerous. We risked a great deal calling you. Everyone who has knowledge of the Aeternium flower is in danger.

Someone is out there intent on killing anyone who knows. Three of our team members are already dead."

Cam looked at him pleadingly. From her expression, Dex could tell that she wanted him to take Dr. Brighton's advice, risks be damned. Before she could speak, he directed his next comment to her.

"Under normal circumstances, we'd embrace Dr. Brighton's recommendation in a heartbeat. I promise we'll do everything we can on our own, share the results with you, and allow you to make the most informed choice possible for Corey."

Tears were already forming in the corners of her eyes. Circumstances placed Dex in an impossible situation. The path he chose gave Corey a good shot at recovery while protecting the lives of others who would be kept out of the loop.

Trying to summarize the current situation, Dex stated, "Maybin and I will work round the clock to perfect Corey's blood. Once we have the precise formula that achieves those results, Cam, you will have to make a decision."

CHAPTER 61

Chang navigated the jam-packed streets of Brisbane. As he commonly did, he wore a surgical mask to prevent contracting the myriad diseases accompanying the world's congested cities. The sound of breaking glass suddenly diverted his attention. Not surprisingly, a group of youngsters were looting an electronics store. Chang shook his head. In this overcrowded world, they reduced law enforcement to video containment. That meant crimes were recorded so the cops could conceivably chase down wayward citizens using facial recognition and GPS. The authorities were insane if they really believed the current system would deter crime. People committing nonlethal crimes like looting rarely got caught. The police simply didn't have the resources. Chang laughed to himself. *And Australia was probably one of the more effective law enforcement countries.*

Chang pushed through the throng of people. The long canvas carry case over his right shoulder was being jostled. He held tight to ensure it didn't erroneously drop—or worse yet, get stolen. *Desperate crowds would steal anything these days.* Through the crowd, the building he was seeking came into sight. It was exactly like its internet image showed, one hundred stories high with dark, tinted glass windows and shining metallic black support rails rising vertically from the ground level. He walked into the building unmolested and took the elevator to the top floor. From there, Chang found the stairwell for the roof and landing deck for pod traffic.

Once situated, he went down on one knee and unzipped the canvas tote, revealing a powerful, single stream flamethrower that resembled a modern-day bazooka. The device would shoot a stream of blue flame thirty meters and eviscerate anything in its path.

Chang took aim at the adjacent rooftop. He achieved the perfect vantage point. Now all he had to do was wait.

Chang was grateful he had deployed the fly drone on the neck of Jules Maybin as he was leaving the Canberra safe house with Holzman. He now possessed knowledge of everything they said and did inside the Lockhart facility where he took out their two friends.

He spied the landing deck for pods on the adjacent building. His target emerged and made his way to the pod. Chang took aim and pulled the trigger. A brilliant stream of bright blue flame shot across the rooftops, hitting one of the world's most valued epidemiologists.

Dr. Brighton was reduced to ash in a matter of seconds. His pod pilot, dumbfounded, frantically paraded around the rooftop, screaming for help.

Chang smiled. Another day's work successfully completed.

CHAPTER 62

Try as he might, Erik deBaak simply could not commit every detail of his life to memory. The attempt, however, was made worthwhile because of paranoia about enemies hacking his files. The advancing effects of the brain tumor made this practice more impractical with each passing day. In his Crematie headquarters, there was the secret safe hiding in plain sight. Many years ago, deBaak installed the theft-proof chamber deep in the recesses of the building's museum, behind the wall of the research and development wing where Hennie previously demonstrated the latest cremation technique using the Tanzig ray. To access the safe, deBaak sealed off the room's main entrance, entered the experimental cremation chamber, and retreated to its back wall.

The seams of the safe were barely visible. deBaak went to the upper seam and placed his hand flat against the surface so all five of his ungloved fingers stretched fully across the horizontal aperture. After five seconds, a circular opening appeared on the wall. deBaak pressed his face toward the hole, centering his right eye into the opening. A buzzing sound informed him his private chamber would soon be open.

deBaak stepped away from the wall as it moved back and to the left, revealing an entire room filled with his deepest secrets. Since he was a fanatic for organization, everything was digitally labeled and stored sequentially. The items from the earliest parts of his life appeared first. deBaak walked past the mementos he kept from his time in World War IV, the old military uniform, his pilot's license, and most importantly, the files on every member of the enemy and their Southern Hemisphere countries. He even had the original mindwave machine used to torture him in the São Paulo prison camp. That little item was procured in a dark web auction years after the war ended.

Next, he passed by his files on Purple Dust, its origins and uses in warfare. Past that, his architectural plans and origin documents for Arnhem, the serene village he created for his parents, sister, and other victims. Finally, he found what he was looking for: the decades-old section he established on the lost city of Aeternum and its magical healing flowers. He needed to refresh his memory on some details. It had been too long, and his head hurt too much.

As he thumbed through the files on the Palette, he smiled as he recalled the details. "Byamee's Brunt," he said aloud to no one. "One of my better schemes." His mind might not be what it once was, but the decades-old call from the Crematie director in Brisbane was something he would never forget. When he first heard the story, he dismissed it as mere legend, nothing more than a ridiculous story handed down for generations. *Imagine people, planes, and boats disappearing with no evidence because some god was protecting a flower with healing abilities. How absurd! Where was the evidence of people's remains? Or the boats and planes that fell victim to this powerful god?* He understood only two things to be true. First, the natives believed this rubbish, and second, if this flower was for real, he couldn't let it leave the Coral Sea. A healthy population meant more people flooding the earth. He simply could not let this happen.

The first thing he did, he now laughed to himself, was to have the area destroyed, both the underwater and above-ground flowers. He made several attempts, but the goddamned plants kept regenerating. deBaak paid thugs and locals for decades to perpetrate the ruse of Byamee's Brunt. Every so often, some journalist would try to peel back the onion a few layers.

That's when he finally manufactured hard evidence. This couldn't be like the twentieth-century legend of the Bermuda Triangle, where boats and planes vanished mysteriously without a trace. He hired Gordon Brown and the meager crew to prove the native legend of Byamee's Brunt was real. Leaving Gordon Brown on the beach with the spear through his chest was all part of the plan.

He snickered to himself as he remembered the mob contact in New York who pulled off the assassination of Gordon Brown and influenced his movie star girlfriend and new member of Parliament, Willow Martin, to close off the Coral Sea sector. She would have a fit if she ever discovered why her mobster boyfriend prevailed upon her to close the "dangerous" waters. She never knew he was behind everything. Willow Martin had simply been a pawn in his master plan to isolate the Aeternium flower from the world.

Now, in his current state, he wished he had an easy way to get those flowers and develop its extract to heal himself. True, he had John Thomas' research notes but not the flowers themselves. Hennie betrayed him. She would become another target for Chang. The nanotech drone revealed the small cache of Aeternium flowers stored in Maybin's Lockhart facility. They had only a miniscule quantity they were using to heal the Atkinson boy. By the time he could send someone to steal the flowers, they would likely be gone. *Maybe I could get the extract they were developing.* No, the formulation they were seeking was specific to RSV. He needed fresh Aeternium flowers, and he needed them fast. He just didn't have a simple way to penetrate the Australian Army guarding the area. Just like seventeen years ago, Willow Martin shut down Byamee's Brunt. Only this time, she unknowingly created a barrier he couldn't evade.

CHAPTER 63

Cam meticulously reviewed the files sent over by Vivian Maddox. Fallon's former partner had not lied. She had names, dates, and photos to prove how crooked Fallon was. Cam could also corroborate Maddox's claim that Willow Martin and Vito Cardelli, the famed New York kingpin, were once romantically involved. News stories showed the couple traveling the globe and appearing at every influential social gathering. The gossip pages included speculation about the two getting married. Cam never could have imagined. *You meet someone so willing to help and assume they are a good person.* She shook off the feeling of being duped by Willow Martin. Her work in LA taught her to be careful who she trusted. People were good at pretending to be someone else to get what they wanted. Of that much, Cam was sure.

"What are you working on?" asked the PM, coming up from behind and startling Cam back into reality.

She quickly shut down the Palette screen, hoping not to appear too obvious. "Researching RSV in kids," she lied, unsure whether the tale resonated with the experienced politician. Maybe it was her imagination, but Willow Martin's face looked suspicious. *Stay cool,* she reminded herself.

"Learn anything new?" asked the prime minister.

"No, same old stuff. Sometimes it helps preserve my sanity if I search for recent information."

"Ah," was all Willow Martin said, stoking Cam's fear that she had been caught in a lie. "Before Hennie Van de Berg arrives, I wanted to let you know that her allegation of deBaak's brain tumor appears to be untrue."

It shocked Cam. *Why would Van de Berg lie about such a thing?*

Before she could express her dismay, Martin proceeded. "My chief medical officer checked the international Mercy database and found absolutely nothing. So far as we can tell, deBaak is the portrait of good health."

Cam couldn't believe it. She was torn. Did she believe the incredible tale told by Van de Berg about the Earth Leader or the Australian prime minister with the secret past? Two people whose beliefs were diametrically opposed to one another. With no other card to play, she opted to feign alliance with the PM in order to maintain her trust. The worst possible thing was to have Willow Martin suspicious of her. That would place all of them in danger and Corey back on a clock where every hour was precious. She put on her best courtroom face and looked the PM directly in the eye. "Where do we go from here, and how can I help?"

"Based on the whopper of a lie Van de Berg told us, I'm at a crossroad. I can offer her the refuge of this safe house to see what else she might reveal, which we may not be able to believe, or . . ."

A noise broke the cadence of their conversation. It was Cam's combox. An incoming call from Dex. She pressed the screen's red button to decline and refocused on Willow Martin. "Or what?" Cam asked.

"Or I could keep her in custody in a police facility where she will be interrogated to ensure we get the truth."

Cam didn't like that idea. Her impression of Van de Berg's instincts told Cam that the woman was saying what she believed to be true, regardless of the newest revelation. Cam was confident in her ability to interview someone and get at the truth, and she wouldn't need barbaric methods to get there. Her training as an attorney and years of successful practice reinforced this belief. *How many times*, she recalled, *had a client lied to her to gain help in securing a Mercy exemption for themselves or a loved one?* She could ferret out the truth. "I'd like a crack at it, if you would grant me the opportunity."

"What do you hope to accomplish?"

"Exactly what you originally asked me to do. I will befriend her and determine her level of truthfulness. Given my work in LA, I am well-schooled in detecting a lie." As the words left her mouth, Cam felt a sinking feeling in her gut. It was the same as when she inadvertently misspoke in Judge Jackson's medical court, derailing the thin hopes of the Barker family. She prayed Willow Martin would let it slide.

"Okay," the prime minister said after a momentary delay that felt like ten minutes. "I'll give you the chance."

Relieved, Cam thanked her and confirmed Van de Berg's arrival for later that day.

Once she was sure she was alone, she returned the call from Dex, filling him in on her research, the news from Willow Martin, and her suspicions.

Dex looked troubled. "We'll figure it all out. Don't worry," he reassured her. "The good news is that we are closing in on an extract specific to Corey's strain of mutated RSV."

Cam welled up. She hadn't experienced this much emotion since Tom died. Like that time, it was a struggle to gain control and keep her professional demeanor intact. "Dex, that's unbelievable. An answer to my prayers. I don't know how I can ever thank you."

He flashed a wide-eyed grin she came to admire. "The only repayment I need is seeing Corey regain his health and live a long and happy life."

She wiped a tear from her eye and hoped her makeup wasn't a total wreck. "When will you be back here with the extract?"

"Maybe tomorrow if all goes well with the final round. Dr. Brighton is helping us confirm the extract results against Corey's blood sample. I'm not sure we could have done this without him. Once he blesses the results of the new batch, we should be able to return."

"Be careful, Dex. I'm worried about whoever it is out there trying to kill all of us."

"We are locked down at Nexterus Marine. We have sleeping bags, food, and a shower facility. The PM's security team has the place surrounded 24/7. You be careful too. Until we know who can be trusted, you need to keep your guard up with everyone, including the PM."

Cam nodded and clicked off. She retreated to her digital legal pad, her preferred tool for preparing deposition notes. That's precisely how she was approaching her upcoming meeting with Hennie Van de Berg.

CHAPTER 64

Dex was so sleep-deprived, dense fog invaded his brain. His eyes were burning, and he wasn't sure whether he was seeing correctly. Nevertheless, he called over to the equally tired Maybin to confirm the latest extract results. According to Dex's weary mind, they finally achieved a precise match for one that would return Corey's blood to normal. Now all they needed was for Dr. Brighton to bless the results and make a recommendation on dosing.

"It looks like a winner," proclaimed Maybin. "Maybe we reward ourselves with an hour of sleep."

"Not a chance. Let's get Dr. Brighton on a call. If we have the correct formula, you can nap on the way back to Canberra."

Maybin followed Dex to the main conference area and activated the Palette. They called up the link for Dr. Brighton. After one minute of trying to establish a connection, Dr. Brighton's mail app kicked in. Dex left an urgent message and clicked on the setting that would notify the doctor immediately. "Knowing what we're up against, he should respond to the urgent notification in the next few minutes."

After nearly an hour passed, Dex became concerned. "Why isn't he responding?"

"No clue. He could be sleeping or taking a shower," Maybin said in a conciliatory manner.

"No way. A doctor like Brighton and a case like Corey's . . . he's not going to ignore the urgent notification."

"Let me call his office and see if they can locate him."

Maybin activated the number for the Brisbane office of Dr. Brighton. The Palette displayed a young woman on the other end of the call asking how she might help.

"We are looking for Dr. Brighton on a most urgent matter," Maybin stated.

Dex quickly observed the change in demeanor on the young woman's face. Something was terribly wrong.

Through gripping emotion, the young woman said, "I'm sorry to tell you this, but Dr. Brighton is dead."

Dex interjected himself into the call. "Do you know how he died?"

The young woman struggled to collect herself. "It was horrible. It's all over the news. A stream of flames shot across the rooftops and killed him as he was boarding his pod."

They thanked the young woman, expressed their sympathies, and clicked off.

"Do you think it's a coincidence?" asked Maybin.

"Nope. Don't believe in them." Dex stood up and began pacing around the room to release the nervous energy. "The only question is how someone found out Brighton was working with us."

"His line could have been tapped."

"Possibly, but why? Who knew Cam took Corey to Brighton for a consult?"

Maybin shook his head. He had no response, and neither did Dex.

In a sudden fit of frustration, Dex kicked a folding chair and exclaimed, "How do we validate our extract now? It's not safe to engage anyone else. Dammit!"

"Take a breath. We'll figure it out," Maybin said reassuringly.

Dex rubbed the back of his neck and bent over to pick up the chair. *Not my finest moment, but this was life and death.* He needed to call Cam and break the bad news.

She picked up immediately, and they updated her on the devastating development.

"Bring the extract to Canberra," she said stoically. "It's the best chance we have."

Dex was sure he looked as tired as he felt. "We can do that, but we don't have any idea how much to give him or for how long."

"Dex, I hear you. You guys have pulled off a miracle for Corey. The best we can do now is what we think is best. Then, we keep monitoring his blood and make sure he shows clear."

Maybin clapped Dex on the shoulder and said, "She's right. What we have in hand is still Corey's best chance at beating RSV. We've done all we can for the moment."

Dex, still suspicious about how the assassin discovered Dr. Brighton's involvement, took on a cautious tone. "Okay. I agree. No one say another word. I will work out a plan to get the extract to you today."

Cam understood. She just nodded and clicked off.

Maybin was about to question his motives, but Dex simply held one finger across his lips, instructing Maybin to remain quiet. Next, he used his hand to let Maybin know he wanted him to follow.

The more Dex thought about it, the more he was sure that somehow they bugged the office. Once outside on the back patio, Dex looked over at the security men guarding the rear of the building and said, "Just needed some fresh air."

Then, he pulled out his personal combox and typed a note to Maybin. He handed the device to his colleague, enabling the communication in silence on a single device that needn't traverse a network.

Say nothing. Either the office is bugged or the security detail is compromised.

You will travel back to Canberra today with the security detail. Take a microscope with you and any other diagnostic equipment we need. Denise will carry the extract. Intercept her at the front gate.

Maybin winked. Clearly, he remembered Denise. He typed back his concern.

It's not safe for you to travel alone.

Dex smiled and typed the last words on the matter.

Got it all under control. Tell the security detail I had to return to Golden Vines.

Maybin took the device, read the message, and typed his reply.

Is that where you are really going?

Maybin handed the device back to Dex.

Nope. Heading to Rotterdam.

CHAPTER 65

All deBaak had to do now was wait. The Viper toxin would soon be in play, causing illness to spread like wildfire. There would be no way to stop it. Operation Control was ready for the crescendo: the cleansing of the world's lower half.

A vibration emanated from his personal combox. Looking at the display, he had a secure voice note from Chang. He hit the green arrow to play the message.

"Brighton is dead. RSV extract and the two marine biologists are traveling back to Canberra today. I will tail them and look for an opportunity. Targets are heavily guarded."

Chang's use of the nanotech drone served them well. deBaak would let Chang continue his mission, even though each passing day made it less important. Once Viper deployed, problems from the toxin would preoccupy the world. deBaak would be front and center as Earth Leader, promising to do whatever it took to punish those responsible. *Even if Holzman, Maybin, or Atkinson remained alive and leveled charges at him, who was going to believe them? There was no proof. Except Hennie!* She could still unravel everything. He leaned against the wall of his secret safe and scratched an itch on his cheek. *How much harm could she really do?* As soon as he discovered Hennie's betrayal, he revoked her security privileges and remotely wiped her laptop and combox.

Maybe Chang needed to firebomb the safe house in Canberra or drop an aerial explosive. *That damned Willow Martin!* She had the place well-protected with terrorist detection devices everywhere. The hard truth was that he knew exactly where his enemies were hiding but could do precious little about it.

CHAPTER 66

The bullet whizzed by Maybin's right ear as Cam watched helplessly from inside the gated grounds of the Canberra safe house. Maybin ducked, and the bullet ripped through the head of a statue honoring Australia's first PM of the twenty-second century. Cam instinctively hit the ground and hid behind a cement bench. *Thank God Corey was still in the house.* Wait. Where was Dex? She looked around frantically but from her vantage point could not see him anywhere. *Had he been shot? Oh my God!*

The front gate was now open, and Cam observed Maybin on the ground, slithering like a snake through the opening. As soon as his shoulders breached the entrance, a piercing siren caused Cam to cover her ears.

A male baritone voice called out, "Mr. Maybin, stay right where you are. Do not move."

Maybin replied, "Someone is shooting at me. I'm a sitting duck."

Cam wanted to help but had no idea what to do. All she could manage was to bite her lower lip and silently say a prayer. Before she could blink, a shot rang through the air and a loud thump occurred on the sidewalk across the street. *What just happened? Is it safe to move?* She lifted her head slightly and looked for Maybin.

He was still horizontal on the pavement, being scanned by one of the PM's security forces.

"Mr. Maybin, I am going to need you to remove the backpack and hand it to me," the man demanded.

Maybin rose to his knees, slipped off the backpack, and handed it to the security man.

Was the extract in there? She watched in horror as Maybin's backpack was placed in a metal box, the kind bomb squads used to detonate an incendiary device. A muffled sound came from the box, and she detected a slight burning odor. Then the security man walked back toward Maybin.

"I hope there was nothing of value in there. You were carrying a nano-tech spy device. Our orders are to destroy such devices before anyone enters the grounds."

Maybin stood and brushed himself off. He shook his head back and forth and tried to reconnect with the situation. He addressed the man who just destroyed his backpack. "Who was shooting at us?"

"Apparently, that man across the way. He's dead, thanks to our sharpshooter."

"Any idea who he is?"

"The scan revealed his identity as Daniel Chang, a Swiss citizen, thirty-five years of age. We'll review his combox and let the PM know when we have more."

"Got it. Thanks to you and your team for saving my life."

"Just doing our job, sir."

Cam came from behind the bench and ran toward Maybin with outstretched arms. "Thank God you are all right," as she squeezed him tightly. "Where's Dex? Is he okay?"

Maybin broke from the embrace and looked her in the eye. "I'll explain later. He had to travel back to Golden Vines." There was an awkwardness in the way Maybin winked to communicate that he wasn't telling her the truth.

"Oh, okay. Understood. At least he's okay." Then the realization of what just happened hit her in the face like the cold slap of an open hand. "The extract . . . was it in the backpack?" She tried not to sound hysterical. The thought of losing her son's miracle was frightening. She was near hysteria.

"Cam, relax. It's all under control. The only things in the backpack were diagnostic equipment, which is all easily replaced."

"But . . .but, if you don't have the extract, and Dex is traveling, how is it getting here?"

Maybin smiled. "Denise is bringing it."

"Denise? Who is Denise? I thought you guys said it wasn't safe to bring anyone else into the loop."

"We didn't. Denise is—"

"What?" she inquired eagerly.

Maybin pointed to the sky just over the front gate and said, "There!"

Cam gazed at the mechanical hummingbird carrying a small parcel in its claws. She was now totally bewildered.

"Denise belongs to Dex. She is a diagnostic bot used for necropsy but doubles as a drone."

Cam's facial muscles relaxed. "I see."

"Dex thought it would be safer given that someone is—or was—trying to kill us. Since we suspected we had been bugged and the assassin knew our every move, it looks like he made a brilliant decision."

Maybin reached up and let the small hummingbird land inside his cupped hands. He handed the small box to Cam. "Your son's extract."

Cam hugged him again.

Maybin handed the hummingbird to the security man for a quick scan and then, as he promised Dex, secured Denise for safekeeping until he returned.

"When can Corey take the extract?" she asked eagerly.

"Anytime you want. On the ride back here, I worked out some calculations to estimate the proper dosage given Corey's height and weight in relation to the sample we used in Lockhart. It's all complete guesswork. My recommendation is we try it and watch him closely for twenty-four hours."

"I know I keep saying it, but I don't know how to thank you guys. Corey is all I have."

Maybin just smiled, draped an arm around her shoulders, and in the British accent she so admired, said, "Let's go see if we can make your little boy all better."

Twenty minutes later, inside the rooms Cam shared with her son, Maybin pulled out one of six vials filled with an orange liquid. Cam loved how cheerful Maybin tried to sound as he kneeled beside Corey and patted his mop of blonde hair. "Hey Champ! I've got some new medicine for you."

"Is it orange flavored? I like cherry best, but orange is good too."

Maybin wasn't sure what to do with that. He likely spent little time around children. "Well, it's orange-colored. That's something, isn't it?"

"It's not gonna taste good, is it?"

Cam never failed to smile when her son said something smart and adorable. His teachers always gushed about his intellect. She silently prayed once more that this extract would guarantee Corey's future.

"I want you to drink this entire vial. Once you start, don't stop until the vial is empty," Maybin instructed.

Corey glanced at her for reassurance.

She was familiar with the look. "It's okay, honey."

Corey placed the thin glass vial to his nose and took a whiff. "But Mom, it smells like perfume."

She patted him gently on the back. "That's because it's made from flowers. You know how pretty they smell."

"After I take this medicine, I'm not gonna smell like a girl, am I?"

Maybin broke in. "No, Champ, but after you get past the rotten taste, it will make you feel better."

"Okay," the youngster said reluctantly. "Here goes."

Cam had seen it dozens of times, the look her young son made after swallowing some medicine or food he didn't like. Corey handed the empty vial to Maybin, and Cam wrapped him in the loving embrace that only a mother could administer.

"We'll test his blood tomorrow," Maybin said.

Cam nodded and told Corey to find a game to occupy himself while she did some work. After her son scurried off, she turned to Maybin. "Okay, tell me what's going on? Where did Dex really go?"

Maybin looked around, still uneasy about having been unknowingly bugged, and whispered, "He went to Rotterdam. That's all I know. I think he's going to confront deBaak."

Cam was aghast. "That's crazy! I'm speaking to Van de Berg later today." She hesitated for a moment and spoke in a hushed tone. "Did Dex tell you about the PM's involvement with the mobster and the closure of Byamee's Brunt from '58?"

Maybin nodded in the affirmative.

"What do we do with that?" she asked, trying not to sound frantic.

"We lie low. Do nothing that might jeopardize our safety. If the PM feels threatened by our presence, we're cooked."

Cam stopped to think while stroking her long, dark hair with her right hand. "But now that the assassin is dead, do we even need to stay here?"

"Are we sure he was the only one?"

"Good point. I guess we are sitting still for a while longer."

"You most certainly are," came the stern voice from behind them.

Cam was caught completely off guard. "Prime Minister, I didn't know you were there."

"No need to be coy, Cam. When I saw you last, you just finished on the Palette. You told me you were researching childhood RSV, but I didn't get to where I am without the ability to know when someone is telling me a lie."

Cam's stomach knotted, and she was unsure how to respond. Her mouth was halfway open when Willow Martin started back up.

"I had my techs dump your Palette. All of the research, all of the video calls."

Cam was now aghast, stricken with fear for the safety of her son. "What are you going to do with us?"

The prime minister's demeanor relaxed. "Things are not as they seem."

"I don't understand."

Cam looked at Maybin. He appeared more baffled than she was. She glanced back at Willow Martin and waited for her to enlighten them.

"It's true that my romance with Vito Cardelli caused me to do some political favors with unintended consequences. These are actions I deeply regret."

"You mean the death of Gordon Brown?"

"Yes, among other things."

"What other things?" asked Maybin. Maybin's temper was brewing, a feeling to which she could definitely relate.

"Until Gordon Brown, there were never any deaths in the Coral Sea sector known as Byamee's Brunt. No planes fell out of the sky. No boats disappeared. The whole thing was staged, largely in the press, by Vito's men. I helped get the sector closed under pressure from the man I thought I loved."

Cam didn't reply. She just waited for Willow Martin to continue.

"It seemed so harmless. So what if a sector of the Coral Sea was closed for a while? No harm, no foul. But when Vito actually killed Gordon Brown and his crew to substantiate the ruse, I broke it off with him. All these years, I never knew how to reconcile things. So, I just kept the whole sordid mess to myself. And then, the world-famous Dex Holzman shows up in Australia and files for an exploration permit of Byamee's Brunt. That's how I knew to send you to him on Corey's behalf. I saw it as an opportunity to make everything right."

"But why did the mob go to such lengths?" Maybin asked.

Cam was wondering the same exact thing.

"Vito would never tell me. All I could find out was that it had something to do with a contract with a European business executive. Vito said it was the biggest payday in the history of his organized crime family."

Willow Martin's aide interrupted the conversation. "Prime Minister, I apologize, but security just entered the grounds with the Van de Berg woman."

"Take her to the east wing suite. Let her clean up. I have to return to Parliament House, but Mrs. Atkinson will meet her in the kitchen in one hour."

ooooo

The hour passed slowly as Cam developed a slate of questions for the crazed woman making wild and outlandish claims about the Earth Leader. Cam's mind reverted to that of the attorney preparing for a deposition. *Leave no stone unturned,* she reminded herself. Time was running short, and Dex was already on the way to Rotterdam to confront deBaak. After all he did for Corey, Cam would do anything to help his cause.

Cam's first in-person look at Hennie Van de Berg eased her mind. Apparently, a hot bath and a change of clothes did wonders for the latest safe house guest. Cam's first objective was what Thurm always preached. Get the witness relaxed. To the extent possible, make them like you.

"They have some pretty good Australian tea in this kitchen. Can I get you a cup?"

The tall Dutch woman took a seat at the round table and crossed her legs. "Yes, please. That would be lovely."

Cam brought the two cups of steaming green tea on a tray with various sweeteners and two spoons. "You've had quite an ordeal here in Australia," she stated.

"To say the least," Hennie said as she blew on the hot liquid.

Cam tried to offer a reassuring expression. "Well, you are safe now."

They sat quietly for a few minutes, just enjoying the tea and its naturally relaxing effects.

"Do you have family back in The Netherlands?"

Hennie shook her head. "No, like Erik, I lost my family during the Purple Dust attacks in the last war. I went to work for Crematie straight from university and essentially married my work. Eventually, I became the chief operating officer."

"Which is how you became privy to Leader deBaak's plans?"

Hennie grinned. "We were very close. He was my lover," she exclaimed unabashedly.

The frank admission stunned Cam. She herself was always very private with her sex life. Certain things weren't blurted out to total strangers.

"Oh, I see," was all she could manage. "Tell me about Leader deBaak's inoperable brain tumor. The international Mercy database reveals no such medical condition."

Hennie looked wounded. Cam could see the shock on her face was genuine. "I am sure of what he told me. It is why I was sent to Australia. To retrieve the Aeternium flower. To heal him."

"As Leader of Earth, would Erik deBaak have a Mercy login where he could have manipulated his own medical records?"

Looking confused, Hennie replied, "I don't know. I suppose it's possible."

"What caused you to break ranks with Leader deBaak?"

A tear formed in one eye. "He has changed. Or maybe he was that way all along, and I ignored what I saw because I loved him."

Cam waited for her to continue.

"When I arrived in Australia and found that the healing flowers were not accessible, Erik wanted to hire a team of mercenaries to take out the military here. That's when I knew he had gone totally mad. I could not sit by and watch half the world's population murdered to fulfill some demented plan."

Sensing that Hennie had more to pour out, Cam waited patiently while she completed her thought.

"You must understand, this brain tumor is real. He has a short period of time before he can no longer lead Earth. By his own design, Mercy offers no VIP treatment options. The man is desperate."

Cam listened, and the old feelings of hatred for Mercy and its creator boiled up to the surface. She urged herself to remain calm. "I'm sure he won't voluntarily submit to Mercy?"

"No, in fact, my guess is he will accelerate the launch of Operation Control. Knowing Erik, if he sees his demise as imminent, he will prioritize his crazy vision for the planet."

Cam was sick just trying to imagine the possibilities. What kind of future would Erik deBaak's vision hold for her young son? Then another thought crystalized. They were in Australia, a prime Southern Hemisphere target for Operation Control. Now she understood why Dex's instincts to travel to Rotterdam were spot on.

"How much time do you think we have to stop deBaak?"

"I imagine it is already too late. Operation Control has likely already launched."

CHAPTER 67

Being in any city was enough to make Dex long for the open sea. The view from the AirStadt left him nauseated. Even from high in the sealed aerial vehicle, Dex could smell the effects of the overcrowding and resultant pollution. People who didn't shower or use a PSC. People who urinated and defecated out in the open. Trash was everywhere. The same putrid scene played across the world's cities. When he was younger, he studied a time in history when the problem was largely restricted to urban areas. Now, almost every square meter of open space suffered from the same horrid conditions. The world had truly gone to hell. His parents always taught him to be respectful of those in authority, but in Dex's experience, there was a stark difference between being respectful of politicians and having respect for their actions. The state of ground conditions always caused him to return to the sea. It is why he became a marine biologist, to find the solutions to the world's problems through the majesty of the earth's waters.

Hovering above the Rotterdam building that housed the corporate office of Crematie, Dex tried his best to filter the anger after Cam briefed him on Maybin's return to Canberra and the conversation with Hennie Van de Berg. deBaak was truly a madman who had to be stopped.

Upon descending from the AirStadt, two armed security men met Dex. They scanned him for weapons, and he proceeded with the guards from the other side of the machine. "Dr. Holzman, follow us please."

Dex nodded and was led into the private office of Erik deBaak. The office was spacious and very metallic. Apparently, the man had a penchant for shiny objects. The black onyx desk boasted a bright sheen, and the floor-to-ceiling windows created natural light while enabling a far-off view of the Kinderdijk windmills.

deBaak made his way toward him and extended a black-gloved hand.

Dex looked at the outstretched arm and declined. He was never a good liar, and being disingenuous wasn't his style.

"It surprised me to get your message," deBaak said in a scratchy voice. "You've reconsidered my offer to run Earth Reborn?"

Dex had to send the meeting request electronically because of his inability to lie. He was sure his voice would have given away his genuine feelings about this sick son-of-a-bitch.

"Can I offer you a beverage?"

"No, sir. I don't imagine I'll be here that long. We need to discuss Viper and Operation Control."

Despite his expectation, there was absolutely no shock value in dropping the names.

deBaak offered an awkward smile, revealing just a glimpse of the crooked front teeth. "What else has Hennie told you?"

"Everything. The only question that remains is how to stop it."

deBaak let go an evil laugh. "Oh, Dex, I assumed that's why you really wanted this meeting. I had such high hopes for you to lead Earth Reborn. If Hennie told you any truth about me, you would know that my intentions for the planet are pure."

Dex was seething. "You call murdering hundreds of millions of innocent people 'pure'?"

deBaak just shrugged. "It is simply a means to an end. You being of such strong moral fiber, I imagine it would be hard to understand the strategy for the planet's preservation. The world has few choices."

"I may not be the leader of Earth, but I can assure you that no sane person advocates your sick plan."

deBaak laughed again. "It's already too late. I deployed Operation Control this morning. There is no stopping it." With that, deBaak signaled for the two guards who escorted Dex in.

Simultaneously, each guard placed a pistol to one side of Dex's head.

"Now Dr. Holzman, you are going to help me figure out how to harness the Aeternium flower to cure a brain tumor. Just like you helped young Corey Atkinson."

"So, it's true! How did you manipulate the international Mercy database?"

"I didn't. A neurologist named Kornbloom took care of that for me."

"Did you have him murdered just like my colleagues and the epidemiologist, Dr. Brighton?"

"Casualties of war, I'm afraid."

"Your fictional Viper character will cause World War V. You know that, don't you?"

deBaak stepped closer so their noses were almost touching. Dex could smell his foul breath.

"Not a chance. As Earth Leader, I will defuse the entire mess and be viewed as the hero who conquered Viper and saved the world. That is, of course, after you help me with the Aeternium extract."

Dex struggled to break free from the armed guards, but their grips tightened like a vise.

"If you refuse, Operation Control continues, I will work till the tumor renders me unable, and my successor at Earth, whoever that may be, will be forced to clean up the mess in much the same way. Whether I live or die, the plan moves forward."

Instinctively, Dex glanced at the guard on his right and stomped hard on his foot. Without thinking, his left elbow crashed into the jaw of the second guard. The first man regained his composure and hit Dex across the forehead with the butt of his pistol. Dex was propelled backward and landed at the feet of the Earth Leader. He rolled onto his stomach, wrapped his arms around deBaak's ankles, and pulled forward, causing the maniacal Earth leader to crash hard on his back. Dex climbed on top of his chest, clenched his right fist, and was ready to land a descending blow when Erik deBaak bellowed to the two guards, "Kill him."

CHAPTER 68

Willow Martin was nowhere to be found.

Cam was frantic. With the belief that Operation Control already commenced, something had to be done. Cam feared for Dex's life. Who knew what Leader deBaak might try once confronted with the truth? The prime minister left earlier for Parliament House. Her top aide was unaware of her whereabouts or when she might return. Cam left an urgent message and sat on her hands to wait. Thirty painstaking minutes passed and finally, her personal combox chirped.

"Prime Minister, I think we have an emergency. Dex is in Rotterdam. I tried to reach him, and Hennie Van de Berg fears they launched Operation Control early because deBaak sees his life expectancy as uncertain."

"So, she maintains the brain tumor is real?"

"Yes, she was emphatic. I believe her."

"The matter is larger than we thought. Our people tell me that Daniel Chang's combox ties him directly to deBaak."

"Oh my God!" Cam exclaimed. She hurriedly updated the prime minister on every detail of her conversation with Van de Berg.

Willow Martin decisively stated, "I need the Ruling Council to meet on an emergency basis, but I cannot be the one to convene the session."

"Why not?"

"I'm small potatoes in the group. I need the leader with the most clout. Your president, Morton Sofer. We'll call him now. You and me."

"You want me to take part on the call with President Sofer?"

"Yes, yes, of course. You have more intimate knowledge of many of the details. Stand by and I will connect us all by video."

Ten minutes later, Cam's combox chirped again.

In Washington, DC, it was the middle of the night. She imagined the president was used to being awakened and looking somewhat presentable on short notice. He was wearing a long-sleeve polo shirt, and his wavy brown hair was combed over neatly.

Willow Martin began the call by introducing Cam and laying out the details of Erik deBaak's plan.

"And you have proof of this allegation?" asked President Sofer.

"Mr. President, we have a woman here who served as Leader deBaak's COO at Crematie. She was briefly in charge of this Operation Control, and she fears it may have already launched."

The US president sighed. "If it's true, he played us all for suckers. We helped him by blasting his self-serving public service announcement all over the world."

"I was going to recommend an emergency Ruling Council meeting to adjudicate the matter, but if Operation Control has launched, there is no time. Our charter clearly states that if the Earth Leader is incapacitated or cannot otherwise serve, the member of the Council's largest economy shall preside in the interim. That's you, Mr. President," said Willow Martin.

Before President Sofer could respond, Cam interjected. "And, Mr. President, if I may, Dex Holzman is at Crematie's office as we speak."

"What? Dex Holzman is there now? He could be in danger." The president rubbed his eyes. Cam wasn't sure whether it was the lack of sleep or the stress of the moment, but it abated quickly as he took on a look of determination.

"We must make sure Dex is safe. We have to apprehend Leader deBaak and figure out how to dismantle his demented scheme. I will contact the Dutch prime minister. Once we have deBaak in custody, we can convene the emergency Ruling Council meeting and update the group."

"Thank you, Mr. President," replied Willow Martin. "Please let me know if I can help."

CHAPTER 69

deBaak was short of breath. The guards each grabbed one of Dex Holzman's arms and hauled him violently off deBaak's chest. Having the younger man on top of him triggered his worst memory: the body of Colonel Paz crushing his meek frame on the day the São Paulo prison camp was liberated. deBaak was now feeling the same inability to draw breath. His hands were clammy inside the black gloves, and his temper was building. deBaak rose to his feet and approached the apprehended menace.

"This has gone far enough! Why you are still breathing is beyond me. Since you are, I think I will introduce you to our newest technology. The Tanzig ray. With one push of a button, I will reduce you to a pile of disappearing ash."

deBaak took a handkerchief from his pocket and wiped his brow. Parched, he walked back to the black onyx desk for his purified water. After taking a sip, he barked to the guards, "You know what to do. Strap him in. I'll be there shortly."

The marine biologist struggled to break free as the guards dragged him from the office. It reminded deBaak of how two guards had dragged him to the room where the mindwave technology began frying his brain. deBaak started to sweat again. After another sip of water, he sat down behind the desk and accessed the Palette, which would update him on the launch of Operation Control.

A world map illuminated, and one by one, a large green check mark appeared over each Southern Hemisphere country. All the nations successfully distributed the purple Kenya Tabs. When the sequence concluded, gold stars appeared to reveal targeted areas with successfully placed PSCs containing the Viper mist.

deBaak smiled. Everything was going to plan. Now to deal with Holzman. As he went to get up from behind the desk, a sharp pain seared through his brain. *Someone just placed a hot poker behind my right eye.* deBaak involuntarily rested his head on the back of the chair and placed a hand over his eye. The pain was unbearable. Come hell or high water, the agony would soon end. deBaak would either get the damned flowers to create the healing extract, or the tumor would kill him. He was almost ready for anything. Fifteen minutes passed until he was strong enough to walk to the chamber where Holzman was waiting to die.

deBaak rose from the chair and took a step toward the door. His left knee buckled, and he lost his balance, stumbling toward the door. He placed his hand on the doorframe to steady himself and then stopped. His head was full. *Where was I going?*

He stood for a moment, leaning on the doorframe, and tried to collect his thoughts. *I know I was on the way to do something . . . What was it?* Vertigo overtook him, and he gripped the doorframe tightly with his left hand. After a few minutes, he was able to steady himself, and his mind, like the parting of dark storm clouds, gave way to clarity. *Holzman!*

deBaak meandered toward the chamber where Hennie first demonstrated the Tanzig ray. He remembered watching the body turn to dust. He recalled how the chamber removed the ashes instantly and prepared for its next use. In a few minutes, there would be no trace of Dex Holzman.

He went through the chamber's doorway, where the athletically built frame of Dr. Dex Holzman was strapped to the table. deBaak smirked at his foe and planned to tell him how he erred in coming to Rotterdam, how much folly it was that he thought he could stop Operation Control on his own. *What a moron!*

Then the fog in his brain returned. deBaak went to say the words aloud but could not get them out of his mouth. *What's happening? I can't speak the words I am thinking.*

"By now, Prime Minister Martin has told the Ruling Council all about your genocidal scheme," Holzman said.

Martin? That bitch? What could she do? What could any of them do? The plan was infallible, a speeding train unable to stop. He tried to say the words to Holzman, but all that came out were garbled noises.

"Leader deBaak, I think you are having a stroke," Holzman said.

No, you idiot. It's the goddamned brain tumor. It won't stop me from pushing the button that will end your life. He made some sort of loud noise in his effort to speak. Saliva dribbled down the corner of his mouth. Just a few steps to the button on the wall . . .

deBaak's effort to take the short walk was like a drunk stumbling out of a bar. His mouth was dry, and he became nauseated, but his objective was clear. *Almost there . . .*

As deBaak reached a quivering hand to the button on the wall that would rid the world of Dex Holzman, a cadre of strange voices startled him.

"Leader deBaak. This is Dutch Secret Service. Move away from the wall with your hands in the air."

The moment of truth. He tried to tell these intruders to fuck off, but all that left his mouth was an incoherent guttural sound. *Press the button,* he urged himself. He lifted his hand toward the button. Millimeters from its target, a bullet prevented the effort and caused him to fall to the ground, clutching the bloody pulp that was once his right hand.

CHAPTER 70

Sitting on the edge of the table to which they had strapped him, Dex tried describing what he experienced to the Dutch Secret Service agents who rescued him. It proved more difficult than Dex imagined. Mere seconds from death, one had no time to mentally prepare for the end. The image of Erik deBaak's quivering finger a whisker away from the button was one that would never leave. The agents wanted answers. There would be plenty of time later for post-game analysis. For now, Dex could focus on only one thing: how to stop the Kenya Tabs and PSC mist from killing hundreds of millions in the Southern Hemisphere.

He stood up from the table, arched his shoulders backward to relieve tension, and asked to borrow a combox. One agent obliged with the proviso that she be able to take part in the call with Cam and Willow Martin. He quickly agreed, and seconds later, the video call connected.

"Dex, what happened? Are you okay? Where is deBaak?" Cam asked.

"I'm okay. I'll fill you in later. deBaak is in custody. Right now, we need to figure out how to recall the Kenya Tabs and shut down the PSCs."

The Dutch Secret Service agent jumped in. "What do we know about this toxin?" she asked.

"We have deBaak's former COO here," declared Willow Martin. "Let her clue you in."

The image of Hennie Van de Berg filled the screen. He had yet to meet this woman in person, but somehow, the image he viewed now looked far more sane than the woman being interrogated by Willow Martin's security chief.

The Dutch agent pressed forward. "We have little time to lose. What do we know about this toxin?"

Oddly enough, Van de Berg radiated an almost cocky confidence. Then, finally, she spoke. "You do not have to worry. The purple Kenya Tabs are harmless, and the same is true for the PSC mist."

"What are you saying?" asked Willow Martin.

It amazed Dex. Van de Berg flashed one of those toothy smiles, the kind from someone who appeared to have twice as many teeth as an ordinary person.

"In all the questions you grilled me with, no one ever asked what I studied at university."

"And how is that relevant?" asked the Dutch agent.

"I was a top-rated student. A chemical engineering major. I may not have the knowledge of a Sigrid Viklund, but it is why Erik had me supervise Operation Control in the first place."

Dex and the others waited, sensing there was more.

"Before leaving for Australia, I hacked into Viklund's computer and altered her formula."

"And . . ." pleaded Willow Martin.

"The purple Kenya Tabs are placebos, mere sugar pills. Completely harmless," Hennie said proudly.

"And the PSC mist?" inquired the Dutch agent.

"Sugar water. It may make people sticky but certainly won't kill them."

"This is a tremendous relief," Dex stated.

"But wait," said Willow Martin. "You knew this the whole time? Why didn't you tell us before?" The prime minister was angry. Hennie Van de Berg duped her.

"I needed an ace in the hole. Erik had to be stopped regardless, and I wanted asylum and immunity for my help."

"Crisis averted," Cam declared gleefully. "Maybe now, the world can get back to normal."

"I will ask President Sofer to issue a worldwide recall of the new Kenya Tabs and a temporary closure of the Southern Hemisphere PSCs. They need to be cleansed and refilled with the proper solution. We should also test the Kenya Tabs just to be on the safe side," stated Willow Martin. Then, addressing the Dutch agent, "Where are you holding Leader deBaak?"

"We have taken him to a secure facility here in Rotterdam while we await further instructions."

"What will happen to him?" inquired Cam.

The prime minister grimaced. "I have a few choice ideas, but ultimately, it will be up to President Sofer as the interim Earth Leader."

"We will chase down Dr. Viklund and the members of her team," interjected the Dutch agent.

Dex was glad this nightmare was reaching its conclusion. He was struggling with the entire mess. The near-death experience, losing Amelia, Jack, and Noah, and of course, his longtime colleague, John Thomas. Maybe he would retreat to the solitude of Golden Vines or perhaps one of the remote islands in the Pacific. There were a few tiny pockets of paradise left in the world, and he knew all of them. He simply had to choose.

Cam's face suddenly filled his screen. In her image, he noted strength that made her the courageous mother and successful attorney he admired. Fate threw them together, but Dex was better for having met her. For the first time, Dex thought about the future and how Cam might play a part.

"Dex, are you coming back to Australia?" she asked in a tone connoting something deeper than a collegial bond. It warmed his soul, but before Dex could reply, the prime minister cut him off.

"No, he isn't. President Sofer has requested that you take Leader deBaak's private Earth jet and fly to DC immediately."

He glanced back at Cam. Not being especially adept at expressing emotion, he simply said, "I'll be in touch."

CHAPTER 71

The safe house medic readied the needle that would draw the blood of young Corey Atkinson.

Cam was nervous, but her cheerful boy took it in stride.

"Roll up your sleeve," said the medic.

Corey complied and sat quietly while two vials of blood were taken.

The medic sealed each vial and said, "I'll get these right over to Mr. Maybin. I know he is eager to test."

"Thank you," Cam replied. She draped her arm around her son and thanked God Corey escaped Mercy. She silently wallowed in her despair. *What would she have done had Mercy claimed both her husband and son?* In that circumstance, Cam wasn't sure she could have soldiered on.

"Mom, do you smell that?"

Cam took a whiff. "I sure do. Are you hungry?"

"You betcha! Smells like pancakes."

Once again, she lovingly squeezed his shoulder and escorted him toward the inviting aroma. Corey always had an appetite typical of growing boys. Cam hadn't been truly hungry since their little RSV adventure began back in LA. She hadn't weighed herself, but Cam was sure she involuntarily dropped five kilograms. Her clothes were definitely loose. But now, things were changing and for the better. *Those pancakes smelled fantastic.*

When they arrived in the kitchen, it surprised Cam to see Maybin in front of the stove.

"I thought you two would enjoy something distinctively American for breakfast."

"And where, pray tell, did you learn to whip up American flapjacks?"

"I have many talents." He chuckled a bit. "Really, to be honest, I once dated a woman from Maine. She was in London for a job, and we fancied cooking on rainy Sunday mornings. These were her recipe."

"Can't wait to dive in. They smell out-of-this-world good."

Corey poured on the maple syrup, drowning the pancake.

"Easy there, Champ. That's a lot of sugar." She really didn't care. Let him consume the entire bottle. Words of warning expressed a mother's instinctive guidance. Right now, all Cam could see was her son's happiness and bright future.

"So, what's next?" inquired Maybin.

"I still have my job running the Patient Advocacy office in Lockhart. Corey loves it here. I think we'll hang out a while and just see where things go. What about you?"

Maybin shook his head. "I love it Down Under, but truth be told, after they killed my three team members, I'm not sure I have the stomach to start over in Lockhart. There would be too many bad memories every time I walked into the building."

"Do you think you will return to the UK?"

"Too crowded. I've been spoiled by the beautiful Australian coastline. I think I'll have a big payday to make the decision a bit easier."

"The Aeternium flowers! That's right. Dex promised your company a cut. You think they will take care of you?"

He smiled. "Oh yeah. I don't suppose I'll ever want for money again."

"You'll figure it out," she said reassuringly.

Maybin washed down the last of his breakfast with a swig of black coffee. "If you'll excuse me, I have some blood samples to analyze."

"Thanks, Maybin. I'll clean up the kitchen."

"I'll come find you when I have the results of the bloodwork."

Cam loaded the dishes into the dishwasher and wiped the table with a sponge. Her son had spilled a good bit of maple syrup. Cam's mind wandered. She thought of Dex, and a pang of jealousy crept in. He was heading back to America. Questions began flooding her brain. Would she ever see her home country again? What did President Sofer want with Dex? Was it possible he might ask her out one day? *My God, listen to me. I haven't thought about something like that since Tom died.*

Cam long ago resigned herself to being a mother and a provider. Relationships and her sex life were off the table. But Dex stirred something in her that she assumed would be dormant forever. *Dammit!* Having feelings for Dex wasn't cheating on Tom's memory, but it sure felt that way. Gracie encouraged her to date, but Cam always shunned the notion. She just wasn't ready . . . until now.

She had just finished cleaning up when Maybin came barreling around the corner.

"That didn't take long," she said. "You're smiling, so I hope it's good news!"

Maybin returned the warmth of her hopeful expression and nodded in the affirmative. "The RSV mutation is totally gone."

Cam threw her arms around him, and they squeezed each other tightly. She looked around for Corey to convey the good news, but he already bolted for the video games in the basement.

"Now that we are free to consult others, I will see who took over Dr. Brighton's practice in Brisbane. They will have Corey's records, and the new doc can recommend a follow-up regimen."

What a blessing these Aeternium flowers were. Now, with the ruse of Byamee's Brunt exposed, the entire world would benefit. Then, the sobering reality diluted her glee. How could the planet support the expanded population made possible by the Aeternium flower?

CHAPTER 72

Erik deBaak thought he was having a nightmare. This couldn't be real. Being strapped tightly to a table constricted his breathing. The wide leather bands pulled across his chest. A stale scent in the air soured his stomach while his eyes burned from sweat. *Was he back in São Paulo?*

deBaak's vision cleared, and he looked around. He was in his Crematie headquarters, bound to the very table used in the R&D center to test new techniques like the Tanzig ray. The same table he strapped Dex Holzman to.

The headache was intense. The pain in his bandaged right hand rippled up his arm and shoulder. deBaak tried to lift his head enough to get a glimpse of the injured limb. He remembered being shot. His hand was gone. All that remained was a balled-up bandage at the end of his arm. He tried to scream for help, but all that came out was that strange guttural sound.

In his mind, he was calling out for Hennie, the only person who offered comfort when he was lost in the abyss. He screamed her name, *HENNIE!* His mind processed the plea, but his ears revealed nothing but the ugly sound that stole his voice. Now it was clear. This was no nightmare. It was a stark reality. This was not how Erik deBaak envisioned the end. He was Earth Leader and one of the world's most successful business executives. They should erect statues in his likeness honoring the legacy of the great Erik deBaak.

He closed his eyes. If this were truly the end of his life, deBaak would wear a coat of pride as he exited this world. Had he not created Mercy, the planet would have spiraled further down a deep, dark hole from which there would be no escape. More importantly, Operation Control was a success! That was the one thing that comforted him. They could ridicule him, criticize him, and even kill him, but one day, he was sure, they would honor the life and times of Erik deBaak.

deBaak opened his eyes and again presumed he was engaged in a bad dream. At the foot of the table, a hologram appeared from a room that was familiar. His brain could not process the scene. *Wait! Yes, that was it.* The magnificent glass table in the room called the Sphere of Humanity! Holzman was sitting in the green leather chair reserved for the Earth Leader. Around the glass table, deBaak could now see the holographic images of each Ruling Council member. The face of Willow Martin sneered at him. *What was happening? Holzman was speaking.*

"Erik deBaak. I have declared you an international terrorist. We have found you guilty of crimes against humanity and the murders of Gordon Brown, John Thomas, Noah Williams, Jack Brightman, Amelia Brown, and Drs. Brighton and Kornbloom. While your Operation Control did not claim a single life, the Ruling Council condemns your actions in the strongest possible terms. In accordance with your crimes and current medical condition, it has been determined you shall be the last person put to death in your depraved Mercy system. We are told that your condition has left you unable to speak. Your sentence will be carried out now."

deBaak wanted to rub his eyes, but they restrained his arms. *This couldn't be true. Holzman? The Earth Leader? Didn't claim a single life? How could Operation Control have failed?* The Viper-laden tabs and mist deployed. And then it hit him. Hennie! Her chemical engineering background! Somehow, she altered Viklund's formula before they sent it to the manufacturers. He had failed.

deBaak scanned the grim faces of the Ruling Council. The transmission went silent as deBaak looked over to the wall where the button resided. A Dutch Secret Service agent stood by. deBaak observed Holzman give the agent a nod, and she depressed the button. deBaak watched as the lights on the ceiling illuminated brightly, activating the Tanzig ray that would remove any trace of him from the planet.

CHAPTER 73

Dex Holzman, or as they now called him, Leader Holzman . . . Earth Leader Holzman. No matter how he said it or how many times, it was still unbelievable. Dex marveled at how an innocent request to help investigate a beached green sea turtle led him to the most powerful position in the world. In his lavish New York office, he stood at the picture window and took in the view from high atop the city. If he looked straight across into the distance, the view was magnificent. Looking down at the throngs of people on the street, however, turned his stomach. *I'll fix that soon enough.* In the whirlwind of events that brought him from Australia to DC and then New York to assume his new position, this was his first moment of solitude.

Satisfying his natural sense of curiosity about his predecessor was the immediate task at hand. President Sofer gave him the rundown before he accepted the position, but he wanted to read it for himself. Dex approached the jumbo Palette and commanded it to give him the biography of Leader Akeyo Gathee. As President Sofer said, Dex and the beloved Leader Gathee had much in common. Gathee ascended to Earth Leader as a young person, same as Dex. Prior to that, she worked in humanitarian efforts to improve life on the planet. Her work with biosphere communities in the African plain put her on the map. Gathee had no involvement in—and according to the historical record, no interest in—politics. Generally speaking, the same was true for Dex. President Sofer and Prime Minister Martin had been his strongest advocates with the Ruling Council. Dex was told his work to save the planet through exploration of the sea and his penchant for placing human life above all else had made him an excellent candidate. The Ruling Council approved of him unanimously. Like Leader Gathee, they forecast a three-decade run with Dex at the helm.

He involuntarily ran his right hand through his thick mane as he contemplated the work ahead.

"Leader Holzman, I have two men here with the photos you wanted hung."

"Thank you, Rebecca," he said to his new executive assistant. When she had asked him what he wanted on his office walls, the answer was simple. Enormous floor-to-ceiling photos of underwater marine life. Dex loved the picture of the approaching great white shark. The marine life in the coral reef always made him smile, but the one that remained most special was the green sea turtle. That's the one he would have mounted behind his desk. Dex wanted the constant reminder of how this adventure began. On the wall opposite his desk, Dex had blown up a photo taken by the J-Cous 5000. Discovering the lost city of Aeternum on the bottom of the Coral Sea would forever alter the course of mankind. He wanted that image front and center.

"The contractor you wanted called and said they would be here later this afternoon to install the aquarium," Rebecca said.

Dex smiled. It was one of the first touches he considered pertinent if he were to spend days on end cooped up in an office tower in New York. The mammoth tank would hold nearly thirty-eight hundred liters of water and closely resemble the one at his Golden Vines office. Through his travels over the next few weeks, Dex would consider types and quantities of fish with which to populate the tank. He would take his time. This was a work of art and not something to be rushed.

Dex would hang three other photographs in his new office. First, he would restore the portrait of Akeyo Gathee. Her image would be a constant source of inspiration. Second, the latest two shots: him and President Sofer and the current Ruling Council. In a short time, he admired them all and knew, just like commanding a crew at sea, his participatory management style would forge strong bonds of trust with these multifaceted world leaders. Tonight, they would all be returning home. But before they departed, Dex would hold one more in-person session. There were major decisions he wanted to announce and, being new to his role, wanted the support of the Ruling Council.

An hour later, Dex sat in the burnished green leather chair reserved for the Earth Leader in the room known as the Sphere of Humanity. The faces around the table greeted him warmly. It would take some time to not feel like a fish out of water. Dex was nonetheless determined. There was so much to accomplish. Having the authority and financial means to accomplish his objectives was of paramount importance.

He greeted the collection of world leaders but thought his voice was shaky. He urged himself to project authority in the face of these powerful men and women.

"Good Lord, young man. Take a breath. No need to be nervous. You are amongst friends," said the British prime minister, Winston Nottingham III.

"Was it that obvious?" he asked.

Nottingham laughed the laugh of an elder statesmen grooming a young mentee. "I'm afraid so."

Dex swigged some water and ponied up the courage to deliver the remarks outlining his agenda. He never enjoyed speaking in front of groups, unless of course it was addressing a crew on the open sea or staff at his Golden Vines research facility. Discussing marine biology came easy. Solving the world's most ominous problems—well, that was a whole other matter. Dex reminded himself that marine biology would still be the guiding light in much of what he was about to implement. That gave him the confidence to continue.

"The first order of business is to make official what we told Erik deBaak. He was the last person put to death by the Mercy system I intend to immediately disband."

Raucous applause came from most of the group. President Zhang from China and Prime Minister Kumar from India were more reserved in their responses.

"Next, we will begin developing plans for harvesting the Aeternium flower into variants resolving a wide variety of the world's most aggressive medical conditions."

Again, tremendous applause, even from the leaders of China and India.

"We will work with pharmaceutical companies across the globe to create the proper formulations for each medical condition. Mercy facilities will convert to hospitals, and all enforcement officers associated with Mercy will be reassigned to a new humanitarian aid effort to feed and shelter the homeless."

Even more applause.

The larger-than-life presence of Brazil's president, Gustavo Souza, interjected. "Leader Holzman, I support the phenomenal effort to create a healthy population and nurture it, but how do you propose to get these people off the streets?"

Dex rose from the green leather chair and stood. In the center of the magnificent glass table was a holographic projector. Dex would show—not tell—them his plan. The images would be far more powerful.

"The Dutch government has assumed control of Crematie. The prime minister has pledged to convert the company into a nonprofit. All the proceeds will go directly to Earth Reborn. Even without Mercy, the amount of money flowing in from Crematie will be staggering. The Dutch prime minister has also told me that since Erik deBaak had no heirs, the government will assume his massive wealth and donate nearly all of it to

Earth Reborn. With those resources, I give you the answer to President Souza's critically important question."

With that, the projector came to life and the holographic video clip, narrated by Dex himself, filled the airspace over the glass table.

"For centuries, man has been searching for answers to growing population problems. We have looked to faraway lands and even to the stars, but the solution has always been right here on earth. With the leadership of every country in the world and Earth Reborn, we will harness the availability and the rich resources occupying over two-thirds of the planet's surface . . . the sea!"

Dex had been up the entire night before finishing this presentation. He beamed as the video displayed scenes of the majestic waves balanced against a picturesque blue sky. A pair of seagulls swooped down around the water's surface as the sun shone brightly.

"With the aid of Prime Minister Willow Martin, construction will soon begin on the world's first underwater community off the country's northeast coastline."

Dex observed the stunned faces of the world leaders as the model of the first underwater community began taking shape.

"This domed habitat will contain a self-oxygenating system using electrolysis, or the breakdown of hydrogen and oxygen. Supplies of food, goods, and services will be created by employing cargo submersibles that will be privatized as a boon to the world economy. Transportation systems for people within the habitat and to and from land will also be developed by private companies and regulated by Earth Reborn."

The hologram flashed images of people and cargo moving about the habitat as well as to and from a transit station at a nearby dock.

The Ruling Council met the idea with awe. They were buying in. He won them over!

But it was Nottingham, the old British prime minister, who rained on the parade. "Dex, this is a magnificent vision. You have overcome the two barriers to population explosion man has battled forever, space and money. But, I have to ask, have you gone daft? What you are proposing will wreck the environment!"

Dex expected this question and was ready with the answer. "Prime Minister Nottingham, you are absolutely right. This project would be deemed an environmental disaster if it weren't being run by marine biologists who, as stewards of the sea, will do everything humanly possible to pull this off in an environmentally responsible manner."

"You said marine biologists, plural. I think I know what you are up to," said Willow Martin.

"Yes, ma'am. I intend to hire UK marine biologist, Jules Maybin, to oversee the engineering and construction of the first habitat in the Coral Sea."

"An excellent choice," responded Willow Martin.

Dex threw in the reference to Maybin's nationality as a nod to Nottingham. It apparently worked. The man looked content.

Willow Martin suddenly appeared troubled. "Dex, who could you possibly find to oversee the astounding job of running Earth Reborn? It's a tall order, to say the least."

"Not to worry, Prime Minister. I know the perfect person for the job."

CHAPTER 74

For now, Cam and Corey were living in Dex's Golden Vines house. He had insisted. It was more of a complex than a home for one person. It dwarfed the massive Australian safe house they just left. Dex would travel extensively. Even when he was home, they could all live there and literally never collide. One day, Dex promised, Cam and Corey would have their own place on the vast grounds of the property.

The more she thought about it, Cam hoped that promise was one Dex would not keep. Her feelings for him had grown, and she fantasized about them making a life together, the three of them living, loving, laughing, and working toward the betterment of mankind.

Cam owed everything to Dex Holzman. He helped save her son's life, and now, in his sudden ascension to Earth Leader, he enabled her and Corey to return home to California. Now she was the CEO of Earth Reborn. Not a bad accomplishment for a hardworking civil rights attorney who was once homeless.

Besides deBaak's fortune, the original seed money, and Crematie revenue stream, Dex had gotten each member of the Ruling Council to donate one percent of its annual GDP to Earth Reborn. Who ever heard of a startup company with a budget in the hundreds of billions?

She already made one decision. Earth Reborn would adopt a logo depicting the healing power of the Aeternium flower. While she was no artist,

Cam sketched out the image of the beautiful flower from memory. She loved the floppy orange petals with the interior rings of brilliant red and yellow. Once her new corporate office was constructed, she would find a way for the scent of the Aeternium flower to permeate the building.

Cam had no employees yet except for Maybin, who would head up the underwater habitat project. Dex had his staff in the Golden Vines research facility clear out a corner office for Cam. Dex planned to use the rest of the land he owned to build a new corporate campus for Earth Reborn.

The work ahead was daunting. She felt totally unqualified, but then again, Dex expressed the same sentiment to her about his new role. They were both young, he reasoned, and while there would be some on-the-job learning, they could do what few people would ever attempt: restore the earth to its past glory. Cam envisioned a world where her son could go hiking, take a swim in a clear mountain lake, or simply walk freely in one of the planet's grand cities. One day, she surmised, it would all come together.

An incoming video call interrupted Cam's thought when her personal combox sprang to life. The caller ID said, "Aqua Habitat." She didn't know what to make of it. She ignored the call and went back to organizing her new office. The combox went off again. She disregarded it as spam and returned her focus to the myriad boxes spread across the floor. Seconds later, a red flashing light appeared on the combox indicating a video message had been left. Cam clicked on the message and smiled at the sight of her two favorite men, Dex and Maybin, floating on a boat extending warm greetings from the grandeur of the Coral Sea.

CHAPTER 75

"Isn't it a bit soon for you to be on holiday, bobbing about in the water without a care in the world?" asked Maybin.

Dex laughed. He pushed his sunglasses up the bridge of his nose and took another swig of the cold beer. "Dude, this is research we're doing."

"Ah yes, the Leader of Earth and the new—wait . . . what's my title again?"

"Whatever you want it to be," Dex replied, flicking his flip-flops into the air.

In the brilliant sunshine, Dex looked out at the horizon. He was in his element. There was nowhere on the planet he was more at ease than on the sea. He lowered his gaze to the calming water. The outline of a yellow tang swam by. It reminded him to add a pair to his new aquarium in New York.

"What made you become a marine biologist?" Maybin asked.

Dex smiled at the memory. "I was eight years old. I used to play in a creek near my home. One day, I arrived to find it had been polluted beyond repair. There was no way to save the living organisms. I vowed then and there to dedicate my life to the world's waterways."

"Quite ironic if you ask me."

"What do you mean?"

"Thirty years later, you are taking on a polluted planet that had no reasonable chance of saving the living organisms."

"I guess when you put it like that, it is ironic. In a million years, I never could have imagined I'd be where I am today."

"I'll second that," Maybin said as he downed the rest of his beer. "The single best thing that ever happened to me was finding a beached green sea turtle on Scrimshaw Beach."

Dex poked his finger into Maybin's shoulder. "Maybe, but the single best decision you ever made was calling me to come help you."

"Touché," Maybin said. They sat quietly for a moment, just soaking up the serenity of the water.

"Dex, Cam said I should name the underwater community, and despite our joke call to her, I don't think we can go with 'Aqua Habitat.'"

As the water carried the boat gently up and down, Dex became serious and replied, "Let's call it Aeternum. The name signifies eternity and optimism for a brighter future."

ACKNOWLEDGEMENTS

The idea for Escaping Mercy began with a future world and a sunken civilization. I chose the Coral Sea for its known beauty and sense of intrigue. Like you, I am a bookworm who enjoys learning while I read. Writing a novel of this sort requires a fair amount of research, so the construction of the story fed my hunger for knowledge of new places, and different professions.

For this novel, marine biology was an essential element. I was fortunate to enlist the help of several talented people in the field who guided me through the lengthy process of researching, drafting, and rewriting. With apologies, I wish to emphasize that these experts in their field provided me with a ton of technical data, much of which I left out or altered to preserve readability for the layperson. I took extensive creative liberty, and any omission, error, or departure from fact is solely my doing. With that said, I'd like to gratefully acknowledge Dr. Alan Friedlander, the Chief Scientist for National Geographic Pristine Seas. Alan is a leading expert in the marine biology field and, although he is now based in beautiful Hawaii, he and I do hail from the same small suburb of Baltimore. Alan graduated high school with my older brother, Ed, and was the first marine biologist to advise me during the earliest stages of the novel's development. Shortly thereafter, I was introduced to Dr. Matt Kendall, a prominent marine biologist for the National Oceanic and Atmospheric

Administration (NOAA). Matt wholeheartedly embraced his role as a volunteer consultant and offered many great suggestions throughout the writing process. When the idea for using an autonomous underwater vehicle (AUV) arose, Matt introduced me to a colleague at NOAA with expertise on the subject. Dr. Chris Taylor, an ecologist, was instrumental in helping me create the J-Cous 5000 and its many wonders. In talking with Chris, he mentioned that his spouse, Dr. Larisa Avens, was also with NOAA and routinely performed necropsies on sea turtles. Larisa's expertise as a research fisheries biologist was key in crafting an easy-to-digest necropsy scene with a hummingbird named Denise.

Creating the identity for the hummingbird was an easy call. Like the magical device belonging to Dex Holzman, my wife, Denise, possesses an uncanny ability to read situations and offer cogent advice. She is my best friend and is always willing to lend an ear when the next crazy story idea pops into my head. As with prior books, Denise was my first reader and sounding board when I got stuck or wrote myself into a difficult corner. She provided the idea that had Hennie Van de Berg altering the Viper formula before departing Rotterdam. Denise is my rock, my source of strength, and a constant ray of sunshine helping me to be my best.

My son, Ryan, and my daughter, Leah, were as always, supportive throughout the book's development. Both read multiple drafts and offered great advice on everything from plot to marketing. I appreciate your love and support of my writing habit more than you will ever know.

With each book, I rely on an inner circle of early readers I can count on to tell me when I have gone off the rails. The group includes Chuck Ferraro, Greg Harmis, Alexandre Hebert, my father Jay Polakoff, Bruce Savadkin, and Greg Tutino. Thanks to each for the time and candor.

Proofreading is an essential element of publishing. Special thanks go to my mother, Sheila Weinstock, as well as Jeanne Brooks and my aunt, Ellie Mioduski.

Gwyn Flowers of GKS Creative once again gets props for designing an excellent book cover and doing a phenomenal job with the interior book design. Kim Bookless, my copyeditor, brought forth her meticulous eye to ensure this book was professionally produced for maximum enjoyment.

I would also like to thank three of my fellow Nexterians, Scott Reifsnyder, Lisa Flohr, and Peggy Stewart. Unlike me, Scott has actually spent time on Australia's northeast coast. His recollections of the area helped me to shape the fictitious Scrimshaw Beach. Lisa and Peggy, two of our operations leaders, both spent time with me theorizing how a green sea turtle might be transported from a beach to a research facility.

In *Escaping Mercy*, the name Nexterus was lent to Maybin's marine research employer. In reality, Nexterus is a supply chain engineering and technology company (www.nexterus.com) catering to the needs of small and midsized companies. Nexterus was founded by my grandfather, Abraham Allan Polakoff, in 1946 and today is headquartered in New Freedom, Pennsylvania. Its sister company, Nexterus Technologies, also based in New Freedom, provides IT consulting and support to small and midsized companies (www.nexterustech.com).

A writer gets to live and travel vicariously through the characters he creates. Those journeys are always brewing in my mind. I look forward to sharing the next adventure, wherever it may lead.

Sam Polakoff
April 16, 2021

ALSO FROM SAM POLAKOFF

Shaman

See what readers are saying:

"It had that indefinable addictive element that sets some books apart from the crowd."

"Shaman *really pulled me in and after a few chapters wouldn't let me go."*

"Engaged from the get-go."

"Polakoff does it again."

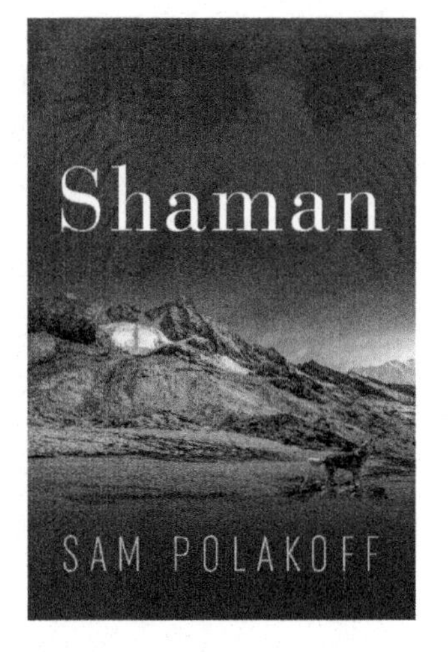

Dan Alston questioned his sanity. A successful businessman and US senator, his entire life had been plagued by strange voices and visions. The episodes were ambiguous and easily ignored. But on his fiftieth birthday, during a climb in the Andes, Dan Alston is involuntarily transported on a spiritual journey and shown something horrifying: an environmental apocalypse.

Dan learns he is experiencing episodes from another lifetime, a lifetime from which he has been reincarnated and once lived as a shaman during the Inca Empire. His chief of staff, Talia Clayton, tries to help him understand the meaning of his experience and to fight his demons, both real and perceived.

While he struggles to make sense of his predicament, Dan and Talia cross paths with ancient forces reborn to hasten the earth's destruction by weaponizing climate change. In a race against time, Dan Alston must summon his innate courage to save the planet from an apocalyptic end.

Shaman is the story of a man who thought he knew what serving his country meant until he discovered his true purpose and the power required to fulfill it.

Shaman may be purchased at www.sampolakoff.com, Amazon, Barnes & Noble, or via your favorite online bookseller.

STAY IN TOUCH

Join our mailing list for updates on future releases.
Visit www.sampolakoff.com/contact

Facebook @sampolakoffauthor

Twitter @spolakoffauthor

Made in the USA
Middletown, DE
23 July 2021